To Kathy
Happy Reading

THE INHERITANCE
of the
Cedar Grove Resort

Deloris Packard

Deloris Packard

 FriesenPress

Suite 300 - 990 Fort St
Victoria, BC, V8V 3K2
Canada

www.friesenpress.com

Copyright © 2021 by Deloris Packard
First Edition — 2021

All rights reserved.

ISBN
978-1-5255-9710-7 (Hardcover)
978-1-5255-9709-1 (Paperback)
978-1-5255-9711-4 (eBook)

1. FICTION, FAMILY LIFE, SIBLINGS

Distributed to the trade by The Ingram Book Company

Acknowledgements

Special thanks to Louise Van Den Hoogen, Darlene Wright, Michelle Scott and Norm Matthews for reading my draft copies. And the utmost thanks to Marlene Heickert for always supporting my big ideas. Special thanks also to Michelle Scott for creating the beautiful art work for my cover. Thanks to Linda Jackson for being my photographer and to family and friends, thank you all for your support and encouragement.

Dedicated

In loving memory to
Joyce Catherine Packard.

Chapter 1

Stunned. That's what she was. Stunned. Debbie sat there, staring blindly out her office window at the sunrise coming up over the frozen lake, her coffee quickly cooling beside her. She was thinking about the phone calls she had to make. She had to call both Janice and Susan, her two sisters. There was just no easy way to tell them that their mother had just passed away. Debbie knew that no matter what words she used, they were going to be just as shocked as she was. She still couldn't believe it herself, couldn't quite wrap her head around the idea that Mom wasn't coming down for her morning coffee this morning, or any other morning ever again.

How could she go on without her mom, her rock, her best friend? It was as if there was this huge hole in the middle of her world, a world they had both cherished. Together they ran the resort like a fine-tuned machine, working side by side day in and day out. Now there would be no one to bounce ideas off, no one to discuss the future with. Now instead, there would need to be changes and major decisions made. But first, she had to call her sisters. Debbie Delanie was concerned that they both would blame her for Mom working too hard, pushing herself too much. All the stress of running a resort this size was just too much for their mom to handle. But the truth was that Mom loved the resort. It was her pride and joy. She loved the day-to-day challenges and adventures as she used to call them. It was her reason for getting out of bed each morning.

Mom was only sixty-three and although she had slowed down, she was still a going concern. Debbie and mom had worked side by side for the past ten years. They knew each other so well that they could finish each other's sentences. They bounced ideas off each other and discussed all things both business and personal. They made a good team.

Both sisters had just been home for the Christmas holidays. Janice and Susan were both older and wiser than Debbie . . . or at least they both thought so.

This Christmas was the first time in five years that they could all be together to celebrate the holiday, even though they did have it two weeks early. It is hard for them to all get time off their jobs to be able to come home at the same time. Mom had been so happy to have all her girls home together all under the same roof. Just two short months ago Mom had been so happy, and now just like that, she was gone.

Debbie decided that she would call Janice first and catch her before she left for work. Debbie was concerned about giving her sister more bad news. Janice was still a little fragile since her divorce.

Debbie noticed her hand was shaking as she listened to the phone ringing. After the third ring, Debbie was deciding to hang up. This is not the kind of message you would leave on an answering machine.

Janice picked up with a cheerful, "Morning sis, you just caught me on the way out the door."

Debbie said, "You better sit down, I have some bad news."

"Oh, what's up? Deb, talk to me."

"I have the most awful news, Janice, Mom passed away last night."

"WHAT? What happened?" she gasped.

"She woke me up this morning at about three o'clock in the morning. She was having chest pains and trouble breathing. She was scared but still talking when she left in the ambulance, but she didn't make it to the hospital. I followed the ambulance into town and by the time I got to the hospital, Mom was already gone."

"Oh Deb, I can't believe it, that's horrible. Tell me what I can do to help." Debbie could hear Janice crying all the way from Ottawa.

"I don't know what to do. I am still in shock, I think. I have just been sitting here since I got home from the hospital and can't seem to think clearly."

"Deb, hang on, I am on my way. I should be there before dinner. Did you call Susan yet?"

"No, I called you first so I would catch you before you left for work."

"Okay sis, I am on my way. See you soon."

After Debbie hung up from talking with Janice, she took a minute to clear her head and then called her big sister Susan.

"Morning sis, didn't I just talk to you yesterday?"

"Yes, but Susan, I have horrible news to tell you."

"What's wrong? You sound upset."

"Are Keith and the kids still there?" Deb was hoping they hadn't left yet. Keith usually dropped the kids off at their schools on his way to his.

"Just getting them hustled out the door. Deb, what's wrong?"

"Susan, Mom passed away last night."

"No, no way. What the hell happened?"

"She woke me up at three o'clock saying she wasn't feeling very well, and was having quite a time trying to breathe. I called the ambulance immediately, but you know it takes them at least a half hour to get all the way out here. She was still giving me orders when they put her in the ambulance, but she didn't make it to the hospital. Susan, I am sorry to have to tell you this over the phone, but I didn't know how else to tell you."

Deb could hear Susan sobbing in the background, and she had to repeat it all for Keith's benefit.

"Oh Deb. I am so sorry. Susan will need a minute. Can she call you right back?" Keith asked.

"Of course." Debbie said and hung up the phone.

There. Her coffee was stone cold, but both dreaded calls had been made. Stunned. She just felt stunned.

Chapter 2

Debbie was on her way to get a fresh coffee from the waitress station in the dining room. As she passed through the kitchen, she heard the back door open. Chef George was just arriving for his breakfast shift.

He did the usual, "morning boss" while he replaced his winter coat with his apron. Time to get breakfast started for the guests. As usual, he was preoccupied with his morning prep routine and so he barely noticed how upset Debbie was. As she helped herself to a fresh coffee, she decided it was best to avoid Chef until her dining room manager Gail arrived. Then she could tell them both together. In the meantime, there were a million things to do in the office to get ready for another day.

Located in the Muskoka's, the heart of cottage country, the Cedar Grove Resort has a dozen cabins, three luxury chalets, and a big boat house. There is a three bedroom house on the edge of the property, just before the trailer park and campground.

When you enter the lodge from the main front doors you will be in the lobby. To your right is the screened in patio. If you turn left you will see the gift shop and office. If you go straight you will enter the main dining room. Looking left you will see a two sets of doors leading into the big commercial kitchen which includes the dish room and the big walk in cooler. To the right you will see the big stone fireplace that goes through the wall into the lounge on the other side. You can enter the lounge from the dining room, or from an outside door. If you walk to the back of the dining room you will enter a hall that leads into two banquet rooms and a door that will take you outside or upstairs to the second floor. Just past the door you will find the washrooms.

Upstairs you will find ten guest rooms and a large central washroom. At the end of the hallway the last two rooms are now two small adjoining apartments for the manager and the owner, Debbie and her mom. Each apartment has its own bedroom and living room and through adjoining doors, they share a small kitchenette and washroom. They used to live in the house but since the big addition, they now live in the lodge year round.

If you turn around and look out the wall of windows behind you, you'll see the beautiful Muskogie Lake. Across the lake you will see cottages, Bunkie's and boat houses dotting the hillside.

Each morning Debbie always paused a moment in front of the large front windows to admire the view. People paid good money to come see this view and because she lived there, she was able to enjoy it year round. For Debbie, it was food for her soul. Her two sisters could only enjoy this view when they came home for holidays.

As she warmed up her cold, black coffee, Debbie looked around the lodge. She couldn't help but think about her mom. It was her mom who suggested they sponsor some local sports teams, and now the team photos and trophies were all on display down the dining room wall to her left, the backside of the kitchen wall. The back wall held pictures and memorabilia from the history of the resort. That was also Mom's idea. To her right, looking at the fireplace, she couldn't help but remember her mom asking the contractors a million questions about the addition and how adamant she was about wanting a two-sided fireplace. Before the renovation the fireplace was on the outside dining room wall and now since the bar was added on, the outside wall was now an inside wall and the fireplace went through the wall and was now accessible from both the dining room side and the bar side.

Debbie was not good at conceiving what an idea would look like on completion, but her mom was a visionary and had it all mapped out in her head. Mom knew exactly what she wanted and did not settle for anything less. Debbie always admired that quality in her mom and now, as she stood looking around the lodge, she couldn't help but see her mom's influence in every nook and cranny. Debbie walked over to the fireplace, stirred the ashes, and put another log on the fire. Mom had loved this fireplace and Debbie was sad thinking Mom wouldn't be stirring the ashes anymore.

The Cedar Grove Resort could be found on Muskogie Lake Road. It was your typical rural country road with lots of twists and turns. When you follow the road going north, up and around a couple of corners, you will see the ski hill. It opened three years ago. With the 400-foot vertical hill providing four different runs, double chair lifts and numerous cross-country ski trails around the bottom, it boasts having over twenty thousand visitors last season. They have a small clubhouse with a small canteen where you can purchase a soup and a sandwich or get a warm drink. Guests who need accommodations or would like a more substantial meal go to the Cedar Grove Resort.

Down the winding road to the south of the resort is a beautiful eighteen-hole golf course. It has a large driving range as well as a putting green. The clubhouse is big enough to hold the office and has a few vending machines for anyone looking for a cold drink. It's perfectly manicured greens surrounded by trees and the panoramic view of the lake makes it the place for golfers to be. They are always holding large tournaments and have had some big-name golfers play there. In last year's season, they had over thirty-two thousand visitors. When the guests are finished golfing, they go to the resort for drinks, meals and accommodations. The ski hill and the golf course both attract tourists to the area and the Cedar Grove Resort purchased a new shuttle van two years ago to transport guests between locations.

This gloomy January morning was cold, which seemed to suit Debbie's mood just fine. On this particular morning there were guests in three of the cabins as well as the three guest rooms full upstairs. So breakfast could be for as many as twenty people. Although winter was the off season, this weekend was going to be busy. There was a local hockey tournament as well as a skidoo rally that the resort was hosting.

One of Debbie's morning duties as the resort manager was to figure out the daily, weekly, and monthly projections to notify her staff of any upcoming events booked that they needed to prepare for. Back in the office, as she glanced at the reservation book, she quickly realized that her heart just wasn't in it this morning. She knew that the show must go on, but perhaps it could just go on without her for a minute or two.

She decided to go upstairs and shower; perhaps that would help clear her head and get her focused on the day and whatever challenges that would bring. The hot water sure felt good, but it could not penetrate the pain in her heart. How much difference a day can make. Yesterday she and her mom were happily planning upcoming events and today she felt lost and alone. Her dad had passed away a few years ago. Now she lost her mom as well. She was now an orphan and she had never ever felt so alone.

Debbie was only thirty-four years old, but standing in front of the mirror she saw a sad old lady. Her eyes looked tired from lack of sleep. She felt like the reflection was someone else, just an empty shell of her former self. She had black wavy hair cut in a short bob around her face. It was usually a happy face with a big warm smile and brown eyes that were always moving, always observing her surroundings. She was always neat and tidy, dressed comfortably and usually only wearing a bit of blush and lipstick. On special occasions she would get all dressed up but that didn't happen very often. At just over five feet tall Debbie is shorter than both her sisters.

Debbie is still single and doesn't even seem to notice. She had her share of boyfriends all through high school and one serious relationship in college but now she is so busy running the Resort that before she knew it, here she is, 34 years old. Both Susan and Janice tease her about being the old maid of the family.

She thought about her sisters who would both be home before the end of the day. Susan, Debbie's oldest sister, is a 40 year old real estate agent who lives with her husband Keith and their two children, thirteen year old Katie and eleven year old Josh. Currently they live about 30 minutes north of Toronto. Five years ago they purchased their first house. It's a bit of a fixer upper but thankfully Keith is a very handy man and has done most of the renovations himself. Between Keith's teacher's salary and Susan's real estate commissions, they have been slowly renovating their house as they could afford to. Most of the renovations are now done except for Katie and Josh's rooms.

Susan has an office at the real estate agency in Toronto but works mainly from her home office. Most of the time she meets her buyers on location at the sellers house so she really only needs to go into the agency for staff meetings. She hates driving in the city rush hour traffic so this is a perfect set up for her.

Debbie's other sister Janice is a 37 year old florist who just recently divorced her now ex-husband Fredrick. They had only been married four years when Janice accidentally found out that Fred was cheating on her. While she was busy getting her new florist shop up and running, Fred was feeling neglected and sought comfort in the arms of other women. Janice sold her house and her flower shop as part of the divorce settlement.

After her marriage imploded the usually bubbly, life of the party gal went into a deep funk. It was several months before she could pull herself out of her depression and start to function normally again. She eventually got a small apartment, got working at a friend's flower shop, and has started rebuilding her life. Janice is just now starting to appreciate her new found independence and is focusing on looking forward to what the future has in store for her.

Both sisters were on their way and Debbie was looking forward to seeing them. In the meantime, she had to go downstairs and get the day started.

Debbie was freshening up her cold coffee at the waitress station in the dining room just as Gail came bouncing through the door. She took one look at Debbie and could see that her boss was visibly upset about something.

"What's wrong?" she asked.

"Morning, Gail. Why don't you get a coffee and we can meet in the kitchen? I have some news to tell you and Chef."

They usually had a morning meeting half an hour before they opened the dining room doors. This gave them all time to get ready for the breakfast rush and when things were ready, they would all meet for coffee and a muffin to discuss the upcoming day.

Gail had worked at the Cedar Grove Resort for the past five years as the dining room manager. She was not only a valued member of the team but a good friend as well. Gail and Deb had gone through school together and had always been friends. But Gail had big dreams that took her away for a few years. She had aspirations of being a singer, but quickly realized that it wouldn't pay the bills. Gail also was not into the drug scene and her experience taught her that a musical career could definitely lead her down that wrong road. So she decided to put that on the back burner and come back to her roots. Now she was back home to stay. She eventually married Peter, her high school sweetheart, and they had three beautiful kids. They bought a house about five minutes from the lodge.

Chef George was also back home to stay. He had traveled and cooked in some fancy restaurants all across Canada and the United States, but he was starting to feel his age. He would be seventy on his next birthday. Although he was over-qualified for the cook position at the lodge, it was enough for him. He didn't want to retire, but didn't want to work as hard as he once had either. The lodge was a perfect fit for him, and he has happily worked here for the past eight years. He had two children, a daughter who was married and living somewhere around Ottawa, and one son who lived in the States. His wife had passed away over ten years ago and now he lived alone. He had become part of the family and he took a lot of pride in taking care of Debbie and her mom.

Debbie joined them at the back kitchen table. In one end of the big commercial kitchen there was a big ten-seater table that was used by the staff for eating as well as food preparations. Only chosen guests were ever invited to the back kitchen table.

"So, what's up with you this morning?" Gail asked. "You look like you didn't get much sleep last night. Shouldn't we wait for Mom?"

"Mom's not here. She passed away last night." Debbie told them both.

"What did you just say?" Gail asked, as if she couldn't believe what her friend had just told her. Mom was just like another mother to her, and to all the staff for that matter. Gail started to cry, and Chef George had to get up and walk over to look out the front windows. He didn't notice the sun rising on the far side of the frozen lake. They both loved and cherished Mom; they were part of her extended family. Working closely with the same people in a small family-run resort, it doesn't take long before everyone is part of the family. They both loved and respected Mom and neither one expected Deb to tell them that.

Debbie let them have a moment and then called them back to the table.

"Mom would want us to carry on. You know her, business as usual, but things are going to be crazy for the next few weeks," she told them both. "I don't know what all is going to have to happen now, but please be patient with me as I get it all figured out."

"Of course, just let us know if there is anything we can do to help." Chef told her.

"Thanks guys. Just give me a little time to sort things out. It will all work out the way it is supposed to, somehow."

Although she expected they both had questions she knew she didn't have any answers. They would both be concerned about the future of the resort and about their jobs. She had no idea about the future of anything. She wasn't even sure if she could make it through today, never mind worry about tomorrow.

They all went back to their usual jobs. Chef George was getting the bacon started, and the meal prep for the breakfast rush. Gail was getting the dining room set up for the breakfast crowd. She was putting the jams and condiments on the tables, making sure the coffee was made and generally getting things ready for the expected hungry guests.

At seven o'clock they met at the back kitchen table again but this time for their usual morning meeting. They discussed their reservations for that day and the next few days as well. Saturday they were hosting a big Ski-Doo rally and would need extra staff. They also had a valentine-themed wedding planned in two weeks which meant there were a lot of last-minute details still to be confirmed.

And in there somewhere they would be holding Mom's celebration of life. That was a day none of them wanted to discuss just yet.

Debbie went back to the office but just could not seem to get focused. She just sat there at her desk trying to think about the tasks at hand but couldn't muster up enough enthusiasm to accomplish anything. The phone was ringing, and the answering machine was blinking. This day was going to go on, with or without her, and she had a business to run. She finally checked her messages. Most of them were inquiries which would be dealt with later in the morning, but there was also a message from Susan. Her message said that they were on the way and would probably be there before Janice.

Obviously, Susan had called Janice as well. The troops were rallying, and Deb had to admit she was relieved to know they were coming. She could sure use their support right now. She turned to her mom's desk to tell Mom the girls were on their way and it finally hit her. She couldn't tell Mom. She wasn't sitting there and would never be sitting there again. The floodgates opened, and the tears poured out.

Chapter 3

Mr. and Mrs. Swanson were the first guests in for breakfast. They were early birds and enjoyed sitting in the dining room having a leisurely breakfast watching the sunrise. The colours in the reflection on the snow covering the lake were usually quite spectacular. Mrs. Swanson was the first to notice the flag was flying half-mast.

"I see the flag is lowered this morning, what's happened?" she asked Gail.

"Mom passed away last night."

"No, what happened?" Mr. Swanson asked, with a shocked expression.

"They are saying it was her heart. We are all a little shocked this morning," Gail told them.

"How's Debbie? I should go check on her." Mrs. Swanson said as she jumped up from the table. Before anyone could stop her, she was out through the dining room door and into the main office, where she found Debbie.

"Debbie, oh my dear, how are you? I just heard about your mom. Is there anything I can do for you? Do you need a hug? What can I do?"

Debbie came out from behind the counter and got a hug from Mrs. Swanson. She and her husband had been coming to the resort for the past twenty eight years. They always joked that they came with the resort. They were guests before Debbie and her family had even bought it. They used to bring their kids and eventually their grandkids for vacations, but his trip was just Mr. & Mrs. Swanson senior. They both enjoyed the downhill skiing and planned to spend a few days at the ski hill. Then they would both participate in the upcoming Ski-Doo poker rally.

"What happened? Gail said it was her heart."

"Yes, she was still talking when then loaded her into the ambulance here at the Resort, but she didn't make it to the hospital."

"Oh gosh, Debbie I wish there was something I could do to ease your pain. I know what it is like to lose someone special to you." Mrs. Swanson told her.

Mr. Swanson came in and immediately hugged Debbie.

"So sorry for your loss, sweetie, if there is anything we can do to help, please don't hesitate to ask. We will obviously be extending our stay until after the funeral service."

"Of course." Debbie gave him a half-hearted smile.

Mom's passing would be felt by many people, but none as much as the staff and friends. As for the guests, the regulars, the ones who returned yearly, and the weekenders who were just passing through, they would all react differently to the news. In a resort like Cedar Grove, every guest would eventually hear the news. But it was the staff that would miss Mom the most. She was always there for a kind word or a piece of advice. Mom had a knack with people, much like Debbie did, and was able to read people and know what they needed.

The blinking answering machine and the constantly ringing phone were proof enough that although it felt like her life was over, it in fact was not. Debbie wanted to crawl into bed and never come out, but she knew that the show must go on and there were things that still needed to be taken care of. She could almost hear Mom's voice in her head telling her to *put on your big girl pants and get the job done.*

As the day continued, Debbie felt like she was on automatic pilot. Fortunately, the resort ran quite smoothly, and winter was usually a quiet time. However, this year they had record snow falls so the local ski hill and snow mobile clubs were all doing quite well. In the tourist areas, if one business was thriving, usually they all were as they all depended on the same clientele. The local retail, grocery stores and gas stations were also doing great this year.

The only possible problem could be the upcoming wedding scheduled for Valentine's Day for a hundred guests. She needed to have room in her walk-in cooler to keep ten large buckets of flowers. And of course, there was the stringing of miles of tulle and twinkle lights from the ceiling that still had to be figured out. To date, the tulle had arrived, but the twinkle lights were still missing in action. Just the usual last-minute wedding stuff.

Henry, her local handyman, had just arrived in his beat up old pickup truck. It always amazed Debbie that his whole life bounced around in the back of his truck, usually inside one tool-box or another. Henry was quite like Chef George. He was semi-retired and still liked to stay busy. He liked to tinker with different things and worked at a very slow steady pace. Today he was giving one of the cabins a face lift.

In the down time, usually the winter, the cabins all got some attention. This was the time to make any minor repairs and painted as needed. This winter they had decided to winterize three of the larger cabins. Debbie and her mom had done cost estimates on the three cabins in question and had budgeted for the renovations. They all would be stripped inside and insulated. While they were at it, they were installing heaters, as well as upgrading the hydro and hot water tanks in each cabin. Next fall they would re-evaluate again to determine what if anything they could afford to upgrade.

Every winter, they undertook some major projects, and improvements were really starting to show. Guests were starting to comment on how nice things were looking. Debbie was quite proud of all their accomplishments.

Henry brought his coffee into the office. "Geez Deb, so sorry to hear about Mom. You okay?"

"Yes, thanks Henry. Still a little shell shocked I think, but my sisters are coming home today and that will help. Speaking of which, would you stop by cabin one and turn the heat up? Susan's gang will be more comfy in a cabin." The heat was kept at a minimum unless the cabin was reserved, then it was turned up for comfort.

"Sure, okay. Did the lights come in for that wedding yet?"

"No, I was just thinking about that. I was thinking that you could install the tulle first and put the lights on later, but I also think it would look much nicer with the lights entwined or at least behind the tulle. What do you think?"

"By tulle you mean that gauzy netting fabric? I think we need to wait for the lights. That's okay, I am going to install the new tile in the bathroom in cabin six, so I have lots to keep me busy. Unless you need me for anything more pressing, I guess I will get to work."

Henry was worth his weight in gold. Debbie trusted him completely. He had been the handyman at the resort for the past few years. Since he lived just a few minutes up the road from the Resort he was always available in a crisis.

As Debbie walked through the kitchen, she remembered to thank Chef George.

"Chef, thank you so much for wading out there and lowering the flag. I hadn't even thought about it. Did you put the snowshoes on or did you wade through the snow to reach the flagpole?" Debbie asked.

"I used the snowshoes. There has to be like three feet of snow on the ground. I haven't been on snowshoes in a long while, so it was quite interesting. Glad no one was taking a video."

"Well thank you from the bottom of my heart. I was going to ask Henry, but you beat us to it. You do take such good care of me, of us all. I just don't know what I would ever do without you."

That was exactly what Debbie liked about the resort so much, everyone pitched in wherever needed. It was not uncommon to see a waitress doing food prep, or staff from the boathouse driving the shuttle van. All the staff was trained and expected to step in where and whenever they were needed. It made the employees more useful and valuable. Whenever she needed something done in a hurry, she could ask any one of her staff to help and it was done. But she never asked anyone to do anything that she wasn't prepared to do herself. The staff all liked and respected her for that reason. It was not uncommon to see Debbie mixing drinks in the bar, or cooking a meal or serving customers in the dining room. On days when there were no expected guests, there was no staff and if an unexpected customer came in for a meal, she cooked and served it as well.

Just before supper Susan burst through the back door, and seeing Debbie, broke instantly into tears. As soon as Debbie saw her, she started crying too. Keith, Josh and Katie brought in the luggage and Debbie told them to take it over to cabin one. If this was the summer busy season, they would have stayed upstairs, but seeing as there was a cabin available, they would have more room and be more comfortable in a cabin. Susan followed Debbie into the office.

"Oh Deb, I am so sorry, are you okay? What can I do to help? You just tell me what you need, and I'll do it," Susan said.

"I'm okay, just numb. The staff are here today so everything is being taken care of. I just don't seem to know what to do with myself. I can't quit crying."

"Well that is okay, you just go ahead and cry. I'm here now."

"Thanks sis, let's get a coffee."

"I don't know about you, but I could sure use something stronger than coffee. I think a stiff shot of tequila might calm my nerves."

"Well then, let's head to the bar."

Keith and the kids came in and joined them. Keith helped himself to a beer and got a pop for both of the kids.

"I am so glad you guys are here," Debbie told them. "I just don't know what at do. How do we say goodbye to the best mom in the whole world?"

"We'll help you through it," Keith said. He noticed Janice was just arriving and went to help her with her luggage, which consisted of at least five suitcases and a couple of big beach tote bags.

"Janice, you do not know the meaning of an overnight bag, do you?" Keith asked her. "Are you moving in?"

"You never know. How's Deb doing? Is she falling apart?" Janice asked.

"Surprisingly no, but I don't think it has fully sunk in yet." Keith took Janice's luggage upstairs and put it in an empty room, beside Debbie's.

Janice joined her family in the bar. She cracked open a beer and poured them all another shot of tequila.

"So now tell us all what exactly happened," Susan said.

"Mom called me on the monitor just before three o'clock in the morning. I went into her room and she was sitting in her recliner chair. She was having a hard time breathing and she was white as a sheet. She said her chest felt heavy and she was having shooting pains. I immediately called the ambulance. I even offered to drive and meet the ambulance but they said they were on their way so we should just wait for them here," Debbie explained.

"You must have been so scared," Susan said.in a consoling voice.

"I went downstairs and turned on the lights and opened the door and then went back up to Mom. She was really struggling to breath. I even opened the window a bit but that didn't seem to help. Mom wanted me to help her get dressed. She didn't want to go to the hospital in her pajamas. I remember telling her not to worry about it, I was sure the paramedics have seen people in their pajamas before."

"Yeah I can see her saying that," Janice said with a nod of her head.

"The paramedics came upstairs and immediately gave her oxygen, checked her vitals and loaded her onto the stretcher. They carried her downstairs and out to the ambulance. I told Mom that I would be right behind the ambulance and she told me to take my time and drive safely. She told me she would be fine and not to worry, she was in good hands now. I told her I loved her and would see her soon. And then they were gone, lights flashing and all that." Debbie told them while the tears ran down her cheeks.

"So what happened when you got to the hospital?" Keith asked.

"Well that was the weird part. I asked the first nurse I saw where Mom was, and she immediately took me into an office and instructed me to wait there for the doctor. I didn't want to wait in no damn office. I wanted to see Mom. After about ten minutes or so the doctor came in and told me that mom was non-responsive when they arrived at the hospital. He said Mom had expired in the ambulance. They tried resuscitation but they were unsuccessful. She was gone."

"Oh honey, I am so sorry you had to go through that all alone." Janice told her as she put her arms around her sister.

Susan came over and sat on the other side of Debbie and wrapped her arms around both sisters. The three of them had a good cry. They all felt a little better now that they were all together. It was amazing the strength they had when they all came together to support one another. Mom used to call it their superpower. The last time they needed their superpower was when Janice split up with her ex-husband. Both sisters had gone to Janice's and helped her cry through the breakup. After all, that's what sisters were for. Now that they lost their mom, they would surely need all their combined superpower to get through this.

Chapter 4

Debbie fell into bed totally exhausted. Physically she ached all over and emotionally she was totally wiped out. Although what she needed was a good night's sleep, it evaded her. Her alarm was usually set for six o'clock, but she was awake long before it went off.

With a heavy heart, she got up and made her first coffee of the day in her little kitchenette. Usually she would make two coffees, but this morning she only needed to make one. She couldn't stop herself from going through the adjoining door to see if maybe Mom would be there, and this had all just been a bad dream. But Mom's room was empty, and the crying started all over again.

A new day always brings with it a new sunrise and new challenges. Resorts like this have a life of their own. There are always guests needing something, be it help checking in, settling in, getting acquainted, or getting pampered, spoiled, and catered to until they checked out. Then there was the cleanup and changeover for the next guest. And each guest was made to feel that they were the most important guest there at resort at that time. Some guests were easygoing and self-sufficient, but some guests required a lot of personal attention. Debbie had learned how to read people and was good at anticipating their needs. She treated the guest from the trailer park just the same as she treated the guest renting an executive chalet.

By the time Debbie showered, dressed, and got downstairs, Janice and Susan were just finishing their breakfast. Keith and the kids were still in bed. Debbie had another coffee and a muffin. Chef had offered to cook her anything she wanted but her stomach was feeling queasy and the muffin was the safest bet.

Besides the usual Friday routine, there were things that needed to be tended to for Mom. The three sisters had an appointment at the local funeral home in Clifford, the next town over and thanks to another snowfall last night it was going to add more time to the half hour drive ahead of them. Debbie drove because she was the only one of them that had a four-wheel drive. The snowplows had the roads plowed and sanded but it was always a slower drive on the snow-covered roads.

Clifford was the closest little town. It had one Main Street and all businesses were there except for the car dealership located on the highway heading south out of town. There was a bank, a drug store, a grocery store, the hardware store, the flower shop, a small diner, a clothing store, and few buildings for the dentist, lawyer, real estate agent, and doctor's offices. Whatever store you needed was within walking distance on the Main Street. Just last summer they had added an appliance store and an ice cream parlor. Debbie was always impressed how they dressed up Main Street for the various holidays and seasons. At present they were still decorated for Christmas, but she noticed the flower shop now had Valentine's Day decorations in the windows.

The first stop they had to make was at the hospital. Because the small hospital was full, they were informed that their mom was already down in the morgue. The morgue was so cold and sterile it gave them all shivers. At least the attendant was very kind and helpful. He left them alone to say their goodbyes. This was by far the hardest thing any one of them had ever had to do. The three girls joined hands and through their pain and tears they tried to sing Mom's favourite hymn, Amazing Grace. It sounded awful, but Mom would have appreciated the effort. Leaving Mom there in that cold place was incredibly hard to do but they found strength in each other. Together they would somehow get through this.

The funeral home was waiting for them when they arrived. They were escorted into the office where the funeral director reviewed mom's final wishes with them. Because mom had everything pre-arranged there wasn't much left that they needed to do. Mom was going to be cremated and the celebration of life would of course be held at the lodge. The undertaker would deliver the ashes to the lodge on Monday morning before the service. They knew she wanted her ashes scattered on the lake in front of resort but they needed to pick out an urn for the service.

When they finished there, they were all needing a break. Each one of the girls just needed time to collect their thoughts and catch their breaths. They went to the local diner for a coffee. Some people had already heard the news about Mom and many of them stopped by the table to express their regrets.

They stopped next at the local flower shop to pick out the flowers for Monday's service. Ann, the owner of the flower shop, came out from the back and gave Debbie a big hug.

"So sorry to hear about your mom. She was a wonderful woman and will be missed by a lot of folks," Ann told her.

"Thanks, we are still processing it all. Ann, these are my sisters, Janice and Susan."

"Nice to meet you both. I have known your mom for many years and always valued her friendship," Ann told them.

"Thanks, you have a beautiful flower shop. I owned a shop quite like this once upon a time in my other life," Janice told her.

"Oh, so you like flowers as much as I do then. You don't own it anymore?" Ann asked her.

"No, I sold my shop and now I work for another florist," Janice said.

"We are here to pick out some flowers for Mom's service on Monday," Debbie injected into their conversation. "Janice will do the arrangements so today we just want to pick out the flowers she will need."

"Of course," said Ann. "Let's go take a look in the walk-in cooler. What kind of flowers did you have in mine? I just got an assorted shipment in this morning but haven't cleaned them yet. Pick out what you want, and I will set them aside for you."

The final stop on their tour was at the lawyer's office. Normally they would wait to do this, but because there was a business involved, they needed to know all the legalities of Mom's will and all it would entail. Susan had said they should wait until after the service, but Janice and Debbie outvoted her. Also, it was very rare that all three of the sisters were together at the same time so they needed to take advantage of that situation. Mr. Sherman, the family lawyer, was ready for them when they arrived, so they got right down to business.

"Come in girls, so sorry to hear about your mom. She was such a special lady and I am sure you are all going to miss her terribly" he sat down in his big leather chair and opened the file in front of him. "Well I guess you want to know what is in the will, so let us get right to it then."

Mom said in her will that the Cedar Grove Resort and all its assets were to be divided evenly between the three girls. The resort was to be valued and each would own one third. If any of the girls wanted to sell their share, it had to be sold to their sisters at the agreed price of the original evaluation. Mom had always held out the hope that the three girls would all live there at resort and work together in the family business. After five years, if none of the girls wanted to keep the resort, it would be sold and be divided among the remaining owners.

"Does anyone have any questions?" Mr. Sherman asked.

"No, I think it is clear. Mom is going to get her wish even if she has to die to do it." Susan said a bit sarcastically as they all stood up to leave.

"Susan, what a thing to say." Janice scolded her.

"Well take care of each other and if I can help in any way, please give me a call." Mr. Sherman opened the door.

On the drive home the three girls discussed the will. Janice thought that perhaps coming home could be a possibility, but that would mean a whole lifestyle change for her. She would have to give it some serious thought. She was just starting to like her life again. She liked her new job, she still got to play with flowers all day but didn't have the business stress that she always felt when she had her own business. And she liked her little apartment and was just getting used to living alone. Janice told them that mom had asked her about moving home when she was here for Christmas but she had told Mom that she was quite happy to stay where she was.

Susan of course would have to talk this all over with Keith and the kids. She had a good real estate business in the city but in reality, she could sell houses anywhere so for her it was possible, but nothing could be decided without Keith. She had mixed feelings about giving up her job. As much as she loved her job, Keith hated his. She told them that Mom had also asked her the same thing when they were there for Christmas, and Susan had told her that they were fine where they were.

They had purchased a fixer-upper kind of house a few years ago and had spent a lot of money renovating it. They had figured they would need to live there for the next ten years to get their initial investment back. Keith was a handy kind of fellow and they had done most of the work themselves so if they ever sold it, they would make a profit but they had planned to live there for a while to be able to make serious money on it.

There were also their kids' school years to think about. They would still be in school for another four months and then off for the summer break. Perhaps they could come to the resort for the summer. They usually spent a couple weeks there each year but maybe this year they could look at making it the whole summer.

As for Debbie, she had spent the past twelve years working alongside Mom in the day to day operation of resort. She had gone away to college for two years to study hospitality management but spent the summers and holidays at resort helping her mom. She knew she was capable of running the resort by herself but did she want to? The successful resorts usually involved families working together. Family labour was the cheapest labour and when you had to pay more qualified staff the profit margins would definitely reflect that. She could do it on her own, but perhaps it was time for a change. She kept those thoughts to herself at least for now, until she could better know what her sisters were thinking.

They arrived back at the resort just in time for the lunch rush. Gail had everything under control and Katie was helping by being a waitress today. She was only thirteen, so she couldn't serve alcohol, but could do everything else as good as any paid staff. She enjoyed chatting with all the different guests and for her it was fun. Plus, she liked making the tips which were hers to do with as she pleased. Josh and Keith were just coming in from ice fishing. They had nothing but rosy cheeks to show for their efforts.

Susan and Janice were with Debbie in the office. Susan was sitting at Mom's desk looking at the year-end financial reports, the latest tax assessment and last year's tax returns. They all knew that the resort was marginally profitable but that any profits were reinvested back into the resort. This was the off season, the time for renovations and upgrades to get done. Henry had already completely winterized two of the cabins and was currently working on the third. By spring, all twelve cabins would have gotten some needed attention. While Susan and Janice were looking at the reports Debbie was putting together a list of people they would have to call.

She asked her sisters, "I know we need to notify family and friends about Mom passing, but what about business associates? Where do you draw that line? Who needs to know and who doesn't?"

"I think you should just follow your instincts on that one. If you think they would want to attend the service than call and if not, they will find out in the newspaper next week along with the general public." Susan offered.

"We should discuss Mom's celebration of life. Which banquet room are you wanting to use for Mom's service?" Janice asked Debbie.

"I don't know how many people to expect so we better use the big room, it will hold a hundred people, better to be safe than sorry," Debbie said. "Chef is going to serve the luncheon in the main dining room. It being a Monday, I wouldn't expect any paying guests and if we do by chance get any we can serve them in the lounge."

In a snarky tone Susan said, "I would expect a huge crowd. After all, the woman lived in this community for the past twenty-five years. I expect it will be standing room only. Don't you think?"

"You're right. I'm not thinking clearly." Debbie sighed. "Don't get cranky with me, I am doing my best here under the circumstances."

"Sorry if that sounded bitchy, I was just trying to point out that I expect a big crowd because mom was well known and well liked." Susan said with more affection.

Janice asked, "Do you have time to come and show me so we can decide on seating and where you want to put the flowers?"

"Sure, but first let's finish the phone calls. I will call Minister Johnson and talk to Chef George about the luncheon. Can you two girls divide the calls up between you? Now that we know the celebration of life is Monday at two p.m. you call tell everyone when you are talking with them." Debbie said. She did not expect them to both agree. Usually there would be an argument about who was doing what but for once, they both followed Debbie's suggestion, no questions asked.

Debbie took the reservation book out to the back kitchen table. She needed a moment alone with her thoughts and with both sisters there, alone time seemed almost impossible. She thought, *'if both sisters moved in, she would never get another moment's peace.'* She admitted to herself that she had her doubts that the three of them could get along without fighting like cats and dogs. In the past there had been times when they didn't even speak to each other but in a time of crisis they all came together just the same. She knew that

Mom's only wish was for the three girls to work together but was that really even possible? What choice did they have? What had Mom done to them?

Janice and Susan needed to be in the office to use the phones. Three more cabins were expected in this afternoon. She had all the rooms upstairs booked for Saturday night for the rally and the hockey tournament and according to the reservation book that only left one other cabin and one of the chalets still available. There was a good chance she would reach 100% occupancy this weekend.

"Wow, you are sure zoned out," Valerie stated.

"Val Oh my goodness, look at you. You are a sight for sore eyes." Debbie got up and gave her best friend the biggest hug she could give her. "I didn't know you were coming. It is just so nice to see you. How have you been?"

"After you called me, I packed my bag and headed home." Val told her. "I thought you might need some moral support."

"I should have known you would come. Let me take the reservation book back to the office and we will get you settled." Debbie had to figure out where she was going to put her. "You have a choice, a cabin way down at the end or if you don't mind sharing my bed you are most welcome to sleep with me."

"Oh, I will sleep with you. You don't still snore, do you?" Val asked.

"Only on special occasions. Follow me and I will get you a key," Debbie said as they headed into the office.

"Oh my goodness, look who's here" Janice got up and gave Valerie a big hug. "Nice to see you stranger."

Susan also got a hug. "Gosh, Val, it has been what? About five years since I have seen you last."

"Yes, I guess it has." Valerie agreed.

Debbie gave her the key to her room. "Let's get you settled and then we can catch up, okay?"

Once Valerie finished taking her luggage up to Debbie's room they went into the bar for a glass of wine. Debbie told her everything that happened with Mom. They shared some tears and Val said, "I just can't believe Mom is really gone. Since I lost my mom back five years ago, your mom was the only mom I had left. Now I truly am an orphan."

"Me too. It really stinks doesn't it?" Mom taught me everything except how to live without her. I guess that is one lesson I am going to have to learn on my own." Debbie said.

"Deb, is there anything I can do to help you?"

"Just being here distracting me is the best help you can give me. So catch me up, I haven't seen you in months, not since you were here in the summer."

"My job keeps me quite busy. I told you I got a promotion, right?" Valerie asked.

"Yes, congrats on that, by the way." Debbie clinked her glass with Val. "How is it all going?"

"The advertising agency I work for just got a new contract with a major cereal company and I am in charge of coming up with some new ideas on how they can sell their cereal. It can get quite hectic and I am usually working against a deadline but for the most part I love my job."

"And how are things going with that new boyfriend? What did you say his name was again?"

"His name is Brian, and we are just starting to date. He works at a travel agency in the same office building as I do. But he lives on the far side of the city, so we tend to go out for lunch more than dinners. He comes over to my apartment some weekends. I guess it is going all right. You may get to meet him this summer. I am planning on coming here for my holidays in August and he may spend part of his holidays here with me."

"That would be nice. I would definitely like to meet him." Debbie told her.

"What about you Deb, any special someone I don't know about?"

"Nope, don't have time for that. You have a boyfriend and I have the resort. I don't have the time or any interest in finding a man to take care of."

"Any chance that you and Doug might get back together?"

"No, not a chance in hell. Actually, I just heard he is getting married this summer."

"Don't tell me he is holding the wedding here at your resort." Val asked.

"No, I doubt that would ever happen. I forgot what a horse's ass you can be sometimes." Debbie said with a smile.

"What are best friends for? No one else in the whole world loves you like I do."

Chapter 5

This was going to be a busy Saturday. The rally was to start from the boat house at nine a.m. and the trucks pulling trailers filled with sleds were already arriving in a steady stream.

"Morning Debbie, so sorry to hear about your mom. How are you coping?" Brad asked.

"Fine I think, Brad, thanks for asking"

Brad came in and gave her a big hug and Debbie started to cry. He held her in his arms until she regained her composure. "Let me know if there is anything I can do. Are you ready for all us crazy sledders?"

"Yes I think so, Chef George is busy cooking up a storm in case anyone is hungry. You may want to let the sledders know that breakfast will be a buffet for twelve dollars per person if anyone is interested." Debbie informed him.

"Oh I am sure you will have some takers, count me in for sure."

Brad Mumford was a general contractor as well as the president of the Ski-Doo club. Debbie had gone to school with him and knew him quite well. They had even dated for a short period of time back in high school. If Debbie was being honest with herself, she carried an old flame for Brad. She had fallen in love with him in high school and every boyfriend she ever had she compared to Bradley Mumford. But high school was a long time ago and that was just water under the bridge. Now Brad was married to his wife Tina who worked in the bank in Clifford. Brad was one of the guys that everyone loved and counted on. If you needed help with something, Brad was usually there helping.

According to Brad, there were seventy-five sleds pre-registered and he expected a few more would join in before it got started. Henry, Keith and even Josh were out there in the cold helping Brad's volunteer's direct traffic. They had the incoming traffic do the drive around in front of the boathouse. The sledders were unloading their machines off to the side of the lake and then going to park their empty trailers and vehicles down by the campground. They were into the final hour and already had about sixty sleds all lined up waiting for the starters pistol.

Most all the sledders came into the lodge for breakfast before they hit the trails, so the dining room was quite busy. Chef George's buffet was popular and it seemed to be going well. He had filled the steam table with bacon, sausage and ham, a big pan of scrambled eggs, another filled with home fries and another pan filled with pancakes and French toast. There was also trays of fresh fruit and trays of pastries and jugs of apple and orange juices. When Chef did a buffet, the guests helped themselves which made feeding a crowd all that much faster.

Gail had two waitresses scheduled to work this morning and at the last minute they both called in sick. It was winter in Ontario and the flu season was in full swing. Debbie asked Susan and Katie if they would help bus tables. Katie was in full agreement, but Susan was looking for any excuse to get out of it.

"Janice is far better at this sort of thing. Why don't you ask her to help bus tables and I will be in the office to collect everyone's money," Susan informed Debbie as she walked away. Debbie thought, *and there it is, big sister is giving her orders just as smoothly as that.* She was not impressed and would have to deal with Susan at a later time. Right now, she had to find Janice.

The waitresses basically served coffee and kept the dirty tables bussed off for the next guests. There were also a dozen hockey players who had stayed over the night before. Most of the team was not checked in yet as a lot were only staying over the one night. Between the sledders and the hockey players you couldn't help but feel the excitement in the air. Everyone seemed in a very festive mood especially for this early in the morning. There were a lot of coffees to go.

While the guests were having breakfast, Debbie went to the office and asked Susan, "Do you by chance have your camera with you?"

"Yes, it is in the cabin," Susan told her.

"Would you consider going out and getting some pictures of the sleds all lined up with the lodge in the background?" Debbie asked. "We could use some good pictures for our winter brochure."

"I'll need to borrow your sled. Is that okay?"

"The keys are hanging at the back door." Debbie was surprised that Susan agreed to go. Usually it would be a big discussion on why she was the one being asked. Maybe because she knew Janet was busy helping in the dining room and Susan was better at taking pictures. She was used to taking pictures of the properties she was selling so she was used to the wide-angle shots and Susan had a good camera that she carried with her almost everywhere she went. As Susan got bundled up Debbie couldn't help but remember when Mom used to say, *take you little victories when you can and appreciate them for what they are.*

By eight thirty, the dining room was deserted. It currently looked like a bomb had gone off, but the staff would have it cleaned up soon enough. Shortly before nine o'clock in the morning, Debbie bundled up in her down-filled parka and snow boots and wandered down to the boat house. She was listening to Brad telling the riders their instructions. The sun was up, but the temperatures were below freezing. Debbie pulled her parka up tighter around her ears. She chuckled to herself thinking there is no way in hell she would be going for any snowmobile ride in this temperature, not even for a chance of winning a ten-thousand dollar prize.

Some of the sleds looked quite expensive. Probably about fifteen to twenty thousand dollars each sat on her lakeshore. When all eighty-two sleds started up, it sounded like a NASCAR race. Brad shot off his starter pistol, and in a flash, they were off in all directions. They were expected back in about five hours and would be cold and hungry. Chef was making big pots of chili and beef stew for when they returned. They had a local three-piece band hired to play in the bar that night and expected some of the sledders and hockey parents would enjoy that at the end of the day.

Debbie announced to Brad and the volunteers that complimentary breakfast was being served in the lodge and they were all welcome to join her.

Susan said, "I know you charge twelve dollars per meal, but what is your cost? How can you afford to feed these people for free? Doesn't that kind of defeat the purpose?"

"No not really, a breakfast buffet cost would be like five dollars a plate. They didn't have to come to our resort to do this run but they did and because of that, we served over a hundred breakfasts as well as rented all the cabins. This same weekend last year we had zero guests. We want this to become an annual event right here at Cedar Grove Resort so feeding a free breakfast to the six volunteers is a good investment in our future."

Susan had to admit, "I guess I can see the logic in that but it seems to me that we give away a lot of free stuff around here. Hop on and I will give you a ride back up to the lodge. I want to show you the pictures I took. I think you'll be pleased."

Henry came in the back door and knocked the snow off his boots. "Damn that is cold enough to freeze the nuts off a bridge."

"Henry where do you get those silly sayings from?" Janice asked him with a chuckle.

"I would say that your breakfast buffet was a huge hit," Brad told Janice and Debbie as he joined their table with a plate full of food.

"Yes, well I thought we would offer it and see if anyone was interested. I would think that almost all of the sledders came in for the buffet."

"I think so too. And now that I am seeing it for myself, I can see why they were all pleased with it. One guy told me now that he had a belly full of food, perhaps curling up in front of the fireplace would have been a better idea that going for a sled ride."

"I don't blame him. It is cold out there," Debbie said. "Chef is making beef stew and chili for the dinner buffet, for sixteen dollars per person."

"I will pass the info on as the riders come back in." Brad said.

"Debbie told me this was the first year the race started from here. Where did the race start from before this?" Janice asked.

"In previous years we started from our clubhouse, but it has just gotten so popular that we couldn't handle it there anymore. The lack of parking was a big problem and our clubhouse only has one small washroom. This has all worked out so much better. There is lots of parking here, which as you can see is needed for all the vehicles and trailers, and the unloading of the machines went so smoothly, I was amazed."

"So I guess we will plan on doing this again next year then?" Debbie asked with a big smile.

"I expect so." Brad told her. "We have also been discussing having drag racing perhaps on the lake sometime within the next month. Is that something you might be interested in discussing? Perhaps you could do a brunch buffet for the races."

"I would be very happy to discuss that with you. Perhaps you could stop in one day this week and we can talk about what that would entail. Any day but Monday would be fine."

After breakfast, the family and staff all congregated in the big banquet room and decided on how it would be set up for the celebration of life on Monday. The Ski-Doo club would be using it later today, but that only required a podium and a head table. Because they were going to need chairs on Monday, they could set some of them up now. Janice had some good suggestions and it all came together quite quickly Susan and Keith had gone into Clifford, the closest little town, to get the pictures developed and Debbie asked them to buy and frame the best group picture in the biggest frame they could buy.

Mr. and Mrs. Silverman, an elderly couple, arrived requesting a room. They came to watch two of their grandkids play in the hockey tournament and they only needed a room for the night. The only available bed left in the entire resort was Mom's, and Debbie hadn't even gone in there since Mom left it. Debbie wasn't ready to deal with all that just yet. Her eyes started to tear up and she chastised herself. Mom would be disappointed with her if she kept falling apart. The only solution she could think of was to put her sister in Mom's room.

"Janice would you consider sleeping in Mom's room tonight so I can rent out the room you're currently in."

"Sure, I'll get Katie and she can help me do the changeover. The room should be ready in a half an hour." Janice assured her. "It's going to be okay."

Debbie went ahead and checked the new guests in. She suggested they could get a coffee in the dining room while they waited. She showed them where the dining room was and since Gail was taking a well-deserved break, Debbie served them both coffee. They told her they used to own a cottage on the next lake over but sold it eight years ago. This was a trip down memory lane for them.

The hockey players were starting to straggle in. Since Chef had the buffet ready, they had a choice of that or ordering al a carte from the menu. Most of them chose the buffet. There was chili and beef stew as well as an assortment of salads and a huge breadbasket full of different kinds of breads, buns, and rolls, most of which Chef had made himself. For dessert, Chef had made a big double layered chocolate cake and three different kinds of pies: apple, cherry and pumpkin. At one point the dining room was full and some of the hockey players had to sit in the lounge to eat dinner. Susan and

Janice were starting to see how much work it took to make it all look so easy.

When the sledders arrived, they had to pass through the dining room on the way into the banquet room for the announcement of the day's winners. The banquet room had a separate entrance that was used for events in the summer. But in the winter, they had to come through the dining room. Most of them passed the buffet table to see what was available on their way in. They were now all cold and hungry and still had the memory of the good breakfast they had all enjoyed there earlier. And here they were tired and hungry again, the aroma of the beef stew was pulling them like a moth drawn to an open flame. It was kind of comical to watch that procession.

Once everyone was seated in the banquet room, Brad called them to order. Each sled had a possible seven cards if they had made it to all the check points on their assigned routes. Now they were allowed to open their envelopes and see what cards they had. They were instructed to choose five cards to make the best poker hand they could. There was the top prize of ten thousand dollars as well as other prizes. There was a big screen TV as well as an ice fishing package donated by the Cedar Grove Resort and lots of merchandise donated from the different Ski-Doo companies.

Brad thanked the resort for taking such good care of them. Susan presented Brad with a framed picture that she had taken that morning. They were quite pleased with the gift and decided the picture would hang at their clubhouse. The day had been a huge success for everyone involved. It was cold but other than that, a perfect day for a sled ride.

Now that the sledders were done with, the room it could be set up for Monday. Henry, Keith and Josh were in charge of setting up the tables and straightening up the chairs. Susan was going to help Gail and Katie cover the tables and set up some picture story boards of Mom's life. Susan and Katie had been working on the picture boards off and on all day. Everyone was busy. Debbie went back to the office and returned a few phone calls, checked on a few deliveries, looked over the next food order, and completed other usual day-to-day things that needed to be taken care of. Business as usual. It seemed strange to Debbie that life just goes on. Here they were planning the celebration of life for their mother, but the people around her just kept going on with their busy lives. For her there was this huge gaping hole in the middle of her world, but life just keeps on keeping on.

Some of the sledders had loaded their machines on their trailers and about forty of them had come back for dinner or to the bar. By nine o'clock, the dinner was cleaned up and put away, most of the hockey kids were tucked in, and the band was just getting warmed up in the bar. Not bad for a slow day in February.

Janice dropped into the chair beside Debbie. "I am exhausted. How do you keep up this pace all the time?"

"Most days are not as busy as this one, but each day is a brand-new adventure. You just learn to roll with the punches and by the way, thanks for helping today and thanks for switching rooms." Debbie told her.

"We will have to clean out Mom's room eventually, but there is no big hurry to do that. I think I will just stay in her room until all the decisions are made, if that's okay with you."

"Absolutely. I will sleep better knowing you're right there on the other side of our adjoining door. Wait, do you snore? If you do you should shut off the monitor, so I don't have to listen to you all night long."

"What monitor are you talking about?"

"Mom and I each have a monitor so that if she needed me in the night she could just call out and I would go over to her side and see what she needed. It is also for security. All the lodge doors and windows have motion sensors so if anyone was to break in, we would know instantly and we could talk to each other if need be."

"Oh, that is a good idea. I don't think I snore so it should be fine left on."

Susan and Keith came in to say goodnight.

"Thanks you guys, for all your help today." Debbie said. "Today was definitely an 'all hands on deck' kind of day and I appreciated all your help.

"We loved every minute of it," Keith said, "but all this fresh air has taken its toll on me. See you in the morning."

Chapter 6

Sunday was check-out day, and all the cabins, chalets, and rooms needed to be changed over. The two cabins that only got cleaned were cabins one and three, where Susan and the Swanson's were staying. The resort did its own laundry in the basement, and change-overs required a pile of linens, sheets and towels. After the guests left, the housekeeping staff went in and stripped the cabins of all linens and towels. The beds were all remade with fresh sheets and blankets. The bathrooms were all cleaned and re-stocked with new towels. The cabins were then dusted and swept and scrubbed all to get ready for the next guest to arrive.

And after the cabins have all been changed over, they still need to get the laundry caught up. Since two cabin girls were also down with the flu, Debbie and Katie filled in. They had the laundry all caught up by supper time. Debbie was actually glad to be a cabin girl for the day. It helped keep her mind off her troubles and away from all the well-intentioned relatives with their hugs and condolences.

Late afternoon relatives were starting to arrive. Her cousin Matt came through the back door and gave her a big bear hug.

"Matt, oh it is so good to see you," Debbie told him while getting the breath squeezed out of her.

"You too, cousin. You're looking pretty good for an old girl," he teased her. He was only three years younger than her and always teased her about being an old lady.

"Geez, thanks a lot. Who else is with you?"

"Just my siblings. Connie, Sharon and Bob. Mom is coming later with Uncle Tom. If I could grab the key, we will get unloaded and then we will have a visit and catch up."

"I'll get the key. I have you guys staying in cabin six. It has just been remodeled."

"Sounds good. Thanks. We'll see you in a little while then."

Most of them were coming tomorrow just for the day, but a few of them were coming to stay overnight. Uncle Tom, mom's brother, was flying in from Calgary and renting a van at the airport. En route, he was going to pick up Aunt Helen and Aunt Jenny, Mom's two sisters. All three of them were going to share one of the chalets. They would also need two other cabins for some cousins that were coming later.

Just before supper, Janice went into Clifford with Debbie and Valerie to pick up the flowers and a few items for Chef George. Debbie had to go shopping for a black dress appropriate for a funeral.

While Debbie was in the changing room trying on dresses, she could overhear Valerie and Janice discussing how they were surprised that Debbie didn't own a little black dress. Between them they decided that they would both have to work on improving Debbie's wardrobe.

"I can hear you all the way in here, and my wardrobe is just fine, thank you both very much." Debbie informed them.

By the time they got back from town, Tom, Helen, and Jenny had already arrived. So had the rest of the cousins. They all had dinner together and then they started telling funny stories about Mom and their many adventures as kids. As everyone was tired, it didn't take long to lock up and settle in for the night. As Mom would have said, *"It won't take much rocking tonight."*

Chapter 7

Before Debbie's feet even hit the floor, her thoughts were on the day ahead. She showered and dressed and when she got downstairs, she saw that Janice was already busy making the flower arrangements for the service. Debbie took her coffee in to the back kitchen table and sat and watched Janice at work. There were red roses, candy striped carnations and daisies. They were mixed in amongst some greenery and baby's breath. Janice sure had a knack for flowers. The arrangements were absolutely beautiful.

"What an amazing job you do with flowers, Janice. You are truly talented. If you're still here on Valentine's Day perhaps I could impose on you to do the wedding bouquets and centre pieces. The bride has already ordered the flowers, but we will have to put them all together that morning."

"Let me get today's arrangements done first." Janice smiled.

Susan and Keith arrived, coffees in hand, just in time to help carry Mom's flowers into the banquet room. Keith and Henry had the chairs all lined up in neat little rows. Janice had made a garland that hung down the front of the podium and had arrangements made for the entrance way, as well as the memorial table where Mom's urn would be displayed along with the picture boards. They would also be playing a video on the TVs hung throughout the room which would be displaying more pictures of Mom and the families. Considering the event, the room looked real nice with all the flowers.

Chef George, who was usually off on Mondays, was already busy in the kitchen getting breakfast started. The only paying guests were Mr. & Mrs. Swanson, and they were already eating. They would be checking out later in the day and there were only a couple skiers reserved until Friday. It was February, after all, and the down time would be used wisely to prepare for the upcoming wedding.

"Sit with us for a moment, if you have the time," Mrs. Swanson said to Debbie.

She freshened up her coffee and joined them. "So, did you enjoy the poker run yesterday?" she asked.

"Oh yes, it was a lot of fun. Cold, but fun. We are glad we did it but sadly, today we must be heading home," Mr. Swanson said. "I have a dental appointment tomorrow and we definitely don't want to wear out our welcome."

"No chance of that," Debbie told them. "I am glad you are staying for Mom's service. I am thinking though that it is going to be a very long, sad, day."

"Try to remember the good times, the funny things, those special things that you shared with her. As long as she is still in your heart, she will still be with you," Mrs. Swanson reached out and patted Debbie's hand. .

"Yes, I still hear her voice in my head. I still can't believe she is gone. I think that may take a while to really sink in. Right now, there is so much going on I haven't had a moment to myself yet and I am afraid that when I get the time, I might just fall apart."

"No, I don't see that happening. You are one of the strongest women I know. Debbie, it is okay to be sad and to grieve but remember grief is only one stage of the process. Let yourself feel the pain, feel the loss, but then move on."

"Thank you for your kind words. If either of you want to say anything at the service, please feel free to do so. You have both known Mom for a long time."

"Yes, she was our favourite Canadian. And you are too, sweetie."

"That's nice of you to say. I hope you enjoyed your trip. You got to do some skiing and sledding both."

"Yes, we enjoyed both, but it will be nice to sleep in our own bed tonight just the same." Mr. Swanson said.

"Well whenever you're ready to check out, just stop into the office and we'll take care of you. I think if I remember correctly you are booked in a chalet at the end of June, so we'll see you again then."

"Yes, so far all the kids are planning on coming with us for two weeks family vacation. I am looking forward to it already," Mrs. Swanson told her.

Gail came over to the table to offer them all more coffee.

"I better get back to work," Debbie said. "I have lots to do today before the service. In case I don't get a chance to see you again before you leave, have a safe trip home and I'll see you in June."

"Okay, Debbie, you take care of yourself."

As she headed back to the office to total up their bill, she decided that she would not charge them for staying last night. They had arrived Thursday and normally would have left yesterday but decided to stay over another night for the memorial service. Debbie made up their bill for three nights stay. The extra night really didn't cost her anything and the goodwill would come back to her eventually. Susan would not approve, but today Debbie just didn't care what Susan would think.

The minister Johnson and his wife, long time family friends, arrived at noon. They enjoyed a leisurely lunch and visited with each of the girls. He met Katie and Josh for the first time. He had seen Susan back a few years ago, but she didn't have the kids with her on that trip. He had saw Janice just last summer on one of her trips home.

Everyone was a little jumpy and anxious. Chef George recruited Susan and Katie to help him make trays of sandwiches that would all be put out in the dining room, buffet style. There was always something that needed to be taken care of when you ran a resort.

They all needed busy distractions and Chef George was thankful for the help. By one thirty, all the food was out on the banquet tables and Janice had added a few small flower bowls on the tables before they were covered with tablecloths ready for their expected guests. When it was time for the guests to eat, all they had to do was remove the tablecloths, unwrap the trays, and they were in business.

By two o'clock, it was obvious that the big room was not going to hold everyone. Henry and Keith opened up the room divider and the big banquet room that held 100 now had an additional sixty seats with the smaller room added in. Debbie was pleasantly surprised to see that they had the foresight to set up the extra chairs just in case. She must remember to thank them later. The whole town was there, and lots of friends from the surrounding towns as well. There were no chairs left. People were standing against the back wall at this point. It was almost two o'clock before everyone was settled. The minister led a beautiful service and shared a couple of funny stories about Mom.

He told them about the time Mom was about fifty years old, and they had a potluck dinner in the church basement. Mom was always cautious of the stairs. He had carried her casserole downstairs for her and after dinner had overheard her asking a young fellow about twelve years old if he wouldn't mind carrying her empty dish up the stairs and out to the car for her. He had told her, "Yes ma'am. My momma tells me that I am to always help old people."

Uncle Tom said a few words about his sister. He told about the Halloween when he was five years old and had dressed up as a scary monster and snuck up the stairs hoping to scare his older sisters, only to find there was no one up there. He came back downstairs, totally disappointed, when Mom jumped out from behind a cabinet and scared him so bad he peed his pants.

Mr. Swanson talked about how his family came up from Watertown every year to enjoy the resort and Mom's hospitality. He told the story of the time Mom had cooked turkey noodle soup and his oldest son about ten years old at the time asked her where all the turkey was. She told him to stick his finger in to see how hot it was. When he did, she told him "There's lots of turkey in the soup now."

Took the young lad a couple minutes to figure it out. He still tells that story.

Chef George and Gail both spoke of working for Mom and how she always made them feel that they were family. She was always quick to offer advice whether you wanted it or not. Gail talked about how she was tough but fair and you always knew exactly where you stood with her. Gail finished off the service with a beautiful rendition of Amazing Grace.

All in all, it was a lovely service. There were lots of tears of course, but a few laughs thrown in made it all bearable. The guests then proceeded into the dining room where the luncheon was served. Chef had made trays of sandwiches and wraps. There were pickle trays, veggie trays, cheese trays, fresh fruit trays and lots of sweets including tarts, squares, cupcakes and fancy French pastries. Everyone just mingled and shared their Mom memories. It was past dinner time before everyone left. Chef George offered to make everyone dinner, but they had all been grazing on the sandwiches and sweets all afternoon and no one wanted any.

Once all the guests were gone, the remaining relatives retired to the bar and had a few drinks. Keith volunteered to be the bartender as Ted had the day off.

Debbie thanked them all for all their help today. "This has been a very tough day for all of us and I just wanted to thank everyone for all their help. I also want to specially thank Henry for having the foresight to set up the extra chairs in the small room."

"I had good help. Keith and Josh pitched in, so it was no big deal. We could have used more seats, but that was 160 chairs and still it was standing room only," he said.

"I told you so," Susan said rather smugly.

Debbie chose to ignore her sister.

"Isn't it amazing how one person can touch so many people's lives? Mom is going to be missed by more than just us, I think." Keith said.

"Well I appreciated your thoughtfulness." Debbie raised her glass in a toast to Mom. "She would have loved the service, all the people, the funny stories, all the lovely flowers and the food. Here's to you, Mom. May you always rest in peace."

Susan and Keith were the first to head off to bed. Keith was finding all the fresh air refreshing, but tiring at the same time. By the time the dining room was cleaned up and all the food properly put away, they were all glad to see the end of this day.

Chapter 8

Although there were no paying guests, there were still people to feed, and Chef George was in the kitchen getting things started when Debbie came down for her coffee. Susan and Janice were sitting in the dining room chatting. Debbie took her coffee over and joined them.

"Morning, dear sisters. You'll be glad to know that today will be a slow day. Perhaps you could go skiing. I am sure the kids would love some time away from the resort."

Susan said, "That is what we were just talking about. Janice doesn't seem too keen, but I am sure the kids would enjoy it."

"I didn't bring much in the way of outdoor clothes," Janice told her.

"What, you mean to say that in all that luggage you don't have ski pants and coats? You are getting too citified, girl." Debbie always enjoyed teasing her sister.

"Besides, I have some calls to make," Janice said. "This Valentine wedding is happening next Saturday, and I am sure you could use some help with things. I noticed the lights arrived yesterday and Henry said he would work on getting them up today. Perhaps I could help him."

"I have volunteered to help him as well," Keith said as he joined the table. Keith didn't ski, at least not downhill. He was a city boy and had never had any interest in skiing. "Susan and the kids are going to spend the afternoon at the ski hill, and Henry and I will install your twinkle lights."

"Keith, you are proving to be quite handy around here. You better be careful, you might get a permanent job." Janice was teasing him now.

"I can think of worse things," he said.

Debbie needed another coffee. "Well I need to do some book work from last weekend and generally work on confirming the wedding details. If you stick around, Janice, I am sure there will be lots of little things you could help me with."

Chef George set a tray of muffins and pastries on the table and they dug right in. Perhaps since none of them had dinner the night before the freshly baked croissants were exceptionally good this morning.

Chef had made them lasagna with garlic bread and Caesar salad for dinner. Technically he should be off today but had just slipped in to make sure they were all taken care of. He showed Debbie where everything was that she would need to finish putting dinner together.

"Thank you, Chef. I have made garlic bread and Caesar salad before you know?" She asked him with a chuckle. "Why don't you stick around and join us for dinner? We'd all like it if you did."

"Sorry hun, but I can't tonight. I already have other plans."

"Okay, another time then. Thank you so much for coming in on your day off just to take care of us. I truly don't think I could do this without you." As she hugged Chef, she was thinking that perhaps telling him that would reassure him that he wasn't going anywhere. She was sure he was concerned about the future of the resort . . . and the future of his job, for that matter.

Over the next few days, things went mostly as expected. They had gotten the tulle and lights up in the banquet rooms. They had ten strings of tulle and lights draped from the centre of the ceiling and hanging down the walls. Janice had fashioned a huge bow from the tulle for the centre piece placed on the ceiling in the centre of it all. It would be a twinkling wonderland before she was done.

Wednesday morning, Susan came storming into the office.

"What's got you so riled up this morning, sis?" Debbie asked.

"Keith's boss called, and it looks like he is heading back to the city today. There is a big meeting with the school board tomorrow morning, and he is expected to be there. He hates his job! It is giving him ulcers from all the stress. I know he's not happy, but what can we do? He's miserable and it rubs off on all of us. When he gets home from work, he is so burnt out that the kids have started to avoid him. I guess if I was being truthful, I avoid him too. What a crappy wife I am, right?"

"Oh Sue, I am so sorry. I was wondering by a few of the comments he had made just how unhappy he was with his job." Debbie asked, "Are you and the kids going back as well?"

"No, we are going to stay over the weekend and help with the wedding if you want us to. And Keith will come back up on Friday afternoon."

"Of course, it's okay. Stay as long as you want. After all, you do own the place now."

"Yeah, I guess so, well at least I own a third of it." Susan chuckled.

Chapter 9

Debbie was in the dining room at the waitress station freshening up her coffee when Brad came through the door. Debbie really wasn't sure who it was until he removed his helmet.

"Oh hi, Brad. You must have come on your sled. Got time for a coffee?" Debbie asked him.

"Yes please, I would love a coffee." He told her. "You got time for a chat about the drag races?"

"Sure, come on in." Debbie told him while she poured him a fresh coffee. "Why don't we sit in the bar as we are less likely to be interrupted in there? I will just need to grab a couple things from the office, and I'll meet you in there."

Janice was on the phone when Debbie went back into the office. She waited a moment until Janice was finished.

"Brad is here and we are going to have a meeting in the bar. Could you watch the office for me for a little while?" Debbie asked her.

"Yes of course. Go have your meeting. I think I can hold down the fort for a while." Janice assured her.

Debbie checked the reservation book to see what the next month's weekends looked like. This weekend there were cabins rented for skiers and next Saturday was the Whitfield Curtis wedding, but the next few weekends after that were available.

Brad and Debbie discussed what the resort was expected to do for the races. It was decided that the Ski-Doo club would rent the boathouse with the extra washrooms. The racers would race in the morning and then take a noon break. The resort would provide a buffet style brunch for the competitors.

Susan came into the lounge. "Is this a private meeting, or can I join you?" she asked.

"Please do," Brad emphasized as he moved his helmet off the chair.

"There's one other thing I was hoping to discuss with you if you have an extra minute." Debbie injected.

"Sure, what's on your mind?" he asked.

"That trail groomer you have, how wide does the trail have to be?"

"Anywhere from twelve to sixteen feet of cleared brush."

"The reason I am asking is the resort has nine acres of bush serving no purpose." Debbie told him.

"Yes, I know. Your property backs onto ours."

"I am thinking of putting in some year-round trails so that hikers and four wheelers could use it in the summer and the sledders could use it in the wintertime," Debbie said.

"You don't do anything halfway, do you?" Brad asked with a chuckle.

"My momma always said, 'go big or go home.'" Debbie told them. "I need to know if I spend the money making the trail that I will be able to recoup my money in, say, five years."

"Oh, I don't know if that is possible, Deb. I image it will cost a small fortune to make and then maintain the trails. The club has some aerial shots of your property if you're interested. I will drop them off so you can have an overview of what you're looking at."

"Thank you, that would be a big help." Debbie nodded

"Just being a good neighbour." Brad gave her a big smile.

Janice stuck her head around the corner. "Sorry to interrupt. Debbie, when you're done, I could use your help in the office."

"I guess that is my cue that my time is up," Brad said. "Thanks for the meeting, Debbie, and we will see you two weeks from this Saturday. Ladies, nice to see you again."

"How did your meeting go?" Janice asked. Debbie who had just entered the office.

"Fine. We are hosting Ski-Doo drag races two weeks from now and providing a brunch buffet." Debbie told her.

"And what is this about trails?" Susan asked.

"Just an idea Mom and I were kicking around. It is still just an idea." Debbie told them.

"Well, before you go making any major decisions, you need to remember that you now have two business partners to consider," Susan quickly reminded her.

"How could I possibly forget?" Debbie answered back, just as quick. "Like I just said, it is in the infancy stage. It may never happen. I would have to find out a lot more information before I would consider going ahead with it."

"Like what exactly? I am just curious." Janice asked her.

"Like the lay of the land, the legalities of cutting trails, the cost of the cutting of the trails, meeting any requirements on how wide the trail needs to be for the trail groomer for the winter, and when the cost is all totaled, how long it will take to recoup the cost of it. Things like that."

"Wow, do you ever stop thinking of ways to improve the resort and make more money?" Janice asked.

"I wouldn't expect us to make any money from a trail through the bush." Susan commented. "If it isn't going to make money, then what is the point of doing it?"

"Like I said, it is just an idea so far. We need to keep coming up with new fresh ideas. If we just sat around here and did nothing the resort would just fall down around us. Business is a living thing. You know that as well as anybody." Debbie said.

"With the flower business it was quite a bit simpler. You bought flowers, arranged them and sold them. That is pretty much the crux of the whole business. Nothing like the resort. I see now what you were saying about all the moving parts." Janice nodded.

"And that is exactly why I never stop thinking about improving the resort." Debbie told her with a raised eyebrow and a pointed finger.

"Well in case you don't know, I am very proud of my little sister and all the improvements you have made to this place. The resort sure has come a long way since Mom and Dad bought it all those years ago." Janice told her.

"Gee, thanks, sis. That was nice of you to say. So, what was it you needed help with anyways?"

"Oh, I almost forgot, the supplier called and there is a problem with the food order. You need to call them back right away."

"Did they say what the problem was exactly?"

"No just that they needed to speak with you about it."

"All right, I will take care of it. Thanks."

Chapter 10

The bride, Jennifer, and her entourage came for lunch on Thursday to check on things. They brought their dresses, makeup bags and things they would need on Saturday. Debbie had provided a room upstairs that they could use for getting ready in. Jennifer was quite impressed with everything. She loved the decorations in the banquet room.

"The banquet room is beautiful. Once we add some flowers it will be amazing." Jennifer told Debbie. "I was also thinking that we would do some pictures in the bar in front of the fireplace, if that would be possible."

"It's definitely possible, but I should warn you it may be hot. That is a real fireplace and the fire will be going."

"We won't be there long, just a few shots of Sam and I and perhaps the parents. I just think it will make a beautiful backdrop for the pictures."

"Okay with me. But you need to know the bar will be open to the public so you may have company. You may have noticed in the banquet room once the archway is moved out of the way, that back wall could also be a good backdrop for pictures. We intend to hang cascading flowers in front of the TV screens in each corner."

"So the archway will only be here for the service?"

"Yes, after your 'I do's' the guests will move out to the dining room while we set up for dinner. The head tables will be along that wall. So if you want pictures before we set for dinner you will need to do them after your vows. After that, you could go do the fireplace pictures while we set up the head tables."

"Oh honey, this is all going to be beautiful," Jennifer's maid of honor, Kelly, said to the bride. Where are we putting the cake?" she asked Debbie.

"There will be desserts on tables along this wall. The cake will be the centrepiece on the desserts table. The cake is in the cold room. I don't suppose you gals want to see it, do you?"

Debbie led the way and the six ladies followed her into the cold room to see the cake. It was a three-tiered cake covered in flowers, with the usual bride and groom on the top. Each layer was stacked on top of each other with wineglasses used as pillars and they were also covered in tiny flowers. The theme of the flowers seemed to be lilies and roses. The bakery in Clifford had done a real nice job, as far as Debbie was concerned. Jennifer seemed quite happy with it. She told Debbie it was a French almond cake. They ladies finished their drinks and headed out.

They would be back tomorrow. The entire wedding party were all going to be staying at the resort for the weekend. Jennifer's parents were expected by noon the next day. Friday night they would have a rehearsal dinner, and then Saturday was the big event. So far, the Whitfield Curtis wedding had booked all three chalets as well as three of the largest cabins.

The resort also had another two couples booked into smaller cabins who were there to do some skiing and enjoy the valentine's weekend. Usually Valentines is a busy day for restaurants, but being so far off the beaten track, they usually only got a few local couples for dinner.

Since the actual wedding dinner was being served in the banquet room, it would not be a problem to accommodate other guests for dinner in the dining room at the same time.

"Gosh, I can't believe how much I am missing Mom. Usually she would stay here at the resort while I run errands in town." Debbie said to Janice.

"Well that is what I am here for, today anyways. Tell me what you want me to do and I will gladly do anything I can to help you."

"If you could hold down the fort while I go to town that would be a great help. Let me show you how to check people in because guests will start arriving after lunch and I am not sure how long I will be gone."

Susan walked into the office at that moment and said, "You might as well show me at the same time. Then we'll both know how."

Debbie spent the next half hour explaining the reservation process to her sisters. She explained how critical it was to make the proper notations in the reservation book so there wouldn't be any confusion if someone else was also taking reservations. The two sisters got their first look at the reservation book and admitted they were surprised by the amount of bookings already booked for the rest of the year. Debbie explained that a lot of their guests came back yearly to the resort for their vacations. Their repeat business had always been quite good. In the spring they did a couple home and garden shows to promote the resort and filled in the book with reservations generated from the shows. Their success depended on filling the cabins. It was still the backbone of their business. Until five years ago, when they did the big addition onto the lodge itself and added the banquet rooms and the bar, renting cabins had been their only source of income.

Although Susan and Janice had basically grown up there, neither one had ever shown any interest in running the place and hadn't ever paid much attention to the day-to-day running of the resort. They just came occasionally to visit. Usually Susan and her family came for two weeks holidays in the summer. Keith loved to golf, and the kids loved swimming. This was the first time either of them had ever shown any interest in the reservations. They got a quick education that morning.

Debbie also showed them the room board. This was a card system. Once the guests had checked in, there was a card printed with all their information and it was placed in the appropriate slot for the corresponding cabin. The card showed check in and check out dates as well as the number of people staying in the cabin. All this information was necessary so the staff knew how many guests to expect for meals and housekeeping knew when to service or changeover the cabins. The entire process depended on everyone involved knowing how the system worked, and it worked very smoothly because they all used the same system.

When Debbie returned it was after lunch. The bride and her bridesmaids had arrived and were currently in the bar celebrating. The groom and best man were not yet there but were expected to be there for dinner. Debbie was introduced to the bride's parents and grandparents. Before the introductions were finished the front door closed with a bang.

"Where's this kickass party at that I'm hearing so much about?" Sam Curtis, the groom, asked as he came flying in with his best man Tony right behind him.

It went through Debbie's mind that perhaps Sam and Tony had already started celebrating.

"I'm looking for the very soon-to-be Mrs. Samuel Curtis," he announced on his way into the bar. He found Jennifer and pulled her to her feet, dipped her backward and planted kisses all over her face.

That Sam was going to be a handful, Debbie thought to herself when she left them.

Janice met her on the way back to the office. Apparently there was no hot water in cabin four, the cabin the grandparents were in. Debbie called Henry at his home. He said he could come take a look at it. It was only twenty minutes or so when Henry came into the office to talk to Debbie.

"The element is burnt out. But I don't really want to spend the money on a new element because that is one of the water heaters scheduled to be replaced before spring," Henry informed Debbie.

"You might as well go into Clifford and get a new tank, but that can wait until Monday. Great way to start off the weekend."

Debbie hoped this was not an omen of how the whole weekend was going to go. She transferred the grandparents to a different cabin. She even sent Henry to help move their luggage from the old cabin to the new cabin. Everything was all good again. The rest of the wedding party arrived, as well as the two couples that were staying for the Valentine weekend. One thing is for sure in this resort, it never rains but it pours. Since Henry was still sitting at the back kitchen table, he volunteered to shuttle the skiers over to the ski hill. The wedding party seemed quite happy in the bar and stayed there for most of the afternoon. They sure were a loud rowdy bunch, and the laughter from the bar was heard all the way into the office. Debbie loved hearing people having a good time. Experience had taught her that the more relaxed and happy people were, the more they enjoyed spending money in her resort. It was good for business. Music to her ears.

The Whitfield party of eighteen ate in the main dining room. Chef George let them order al a carte, but most of them were into the pub foods, burgers, fish and chips, that kind of thing. As he was already busy making food for the wedding tomorrow, he didn't mind the easy menu for dinner.

Following dinner, the wedding party went into the banquet room for the rehearsal and then on into the bar for a few more drinks. The mood was very festive with the wedding and the other Valentine's guests. Jennifer and Sam invited the other guests to join them tomorrow night for their reception. Sam was inviting everyone he met. He seemed like quite the character and was just so happy to be marrying the love of his life. He thought that everyone should be as happy as he was. A few locals stopped into the bar as they sometimes did on a Friday or Saturday night. Sam invited them to his party as well. By eleven o' clock, the bar had started to empty out. Debbie helped Ted the bartender do some cleanup.

Sounded like the wedding party was splitting up for the night. The ladies were all staying in one chalet and the men were all staying in the other, for tonight anyways. Tomorrow Jennifer and Sam would be leaving for their two-week Caribbean cruise. They would be staying in Toronto on Saturday night after the reception, and off Sunday morning for a couple weeks of sun and fun. The rest of the wedding party were planning on going skiing Sunday morning.

Debbie asked Janice, "Do you want to bet on how many of them are going to make it to the ski hill Sunday morning?"

"Gosh I don't know. Out of those eighteen, I would say about ten."

"I think you're over-estimating their ability. I think more like four or five."

"Why do you say that?" Janice asked.

"After two nights of partying hard, they might have a hard time getting motivated to go out and play in the cold."

"Well I guess time will tell."

Chapter 11

On Saturday morning Debbie was having her morning meeting with Chef George and Gail. Two of the waitresses had just called in sick. It was February flu season and Murphy's Law and all that. So now they needed to find additional help. Katie and Susan were already scheduled to work with Gail in the dining room and Janice was helping Chef George. It was too early to start calling in other staff, so they would have to wait to solve that issue. Susan and Keith came in the middle of the conversation and Debbie had to assure them that she had part-time staff that she could call on short notice but wouldn't call until at least nine am. She wouldn't need them until lunch time, anyways.

"And if you can't get someone, then what?" Susan questioned her.

"Then I guess, dear sister of mine, you and I will be filling in." Debbie told her.

Janice was getting things set up at the back kitchen table to do the flower arranging. Chef George had told her he needed his cold room back after breakfast.

Debbie had to laugh at Chef when he complained, "My cold room is supposed to smell like food, not a darn flower garden."

A few of the wedding party strolled in for breakfast. Mr. Curtis, the groom's father, asked Debbie to put any breakfasts and lunches on his tab. The bride's parents were paying for everything else. The wedding was scheduled for two o'clock, so none of the guests were in a rush just yet. Panic didn't start until about noon.

Debbie stopped into the bride's room with a complimentary bottle of champagne. Jennifer had just finished her hair and makeup. She looked beautiful, and Debbie told her so. Jennifer hugged Debbie and thanked her for all the hard work the staff had done on her behalf.

The maid of honor, Kelly, was in a bit of a panic. The hem on her new dress was coming apart. "I forgot to bring a sewing kit, what are we going to do now?" she asked everyone.

Debbie just chuckled. "I think I can help you out with that. I am sure there is a sewing basket around here somewhere. Let me go see what I can find." She was sure there was a sewing basket in Mom's room.

While she was gone looking, Janice brought in the flowers for the bride's side of the wedding party. The attendants had small hand-held bouquets consisting of one large white lily surrounded with red roses and baby's breath. The maid of honor had three lilies in her bouquet and the bride had about seven lilies and a cascade of red roses and rosebuds. They were all so beautiful. Jennifer started tearing up when she saw how beautiful the bouquets were. Janice also had corsages for the two mothers both the same consisting of small lilies and rosebuds.

Debbie had to pull some cardboard boxes off the top shelf of mom's closet to get to the sewing basket. She decided that since she was going to have to clean out this closet sooner or later, there was no point of lifting those heavy boxes back up onto the shelf so she took them over to her living room. She would deal with them later.

When Debbie returned with the sewing basket and saw the bride tearing up, she couldn't help thinking that if Jennifer was tearing up over her bouquet, what she would do when she got into the banquet room and saw all the beautiful flowers in there.

Janice had used the extra tulle left over from decorating the ceiling and the wall and had made small arrangements that hung from the edge of the chairs all the way down the aisle. The archway had flowers cascading down each side. The podium that the minister would use also had a cascade of flowers hanging down the front of it as well.

From the bride's room, Janice and Debbie went over to the chalet where the groom and his attendants were getting ready.

The boutonnieres Janice had done for them were simply elegant. The groom had a small lily, a sprig of baby's breath and two red rosebuds. The best man had one small lily and rosebuds, and the ushers and the fathers had rosebuds.

"Well Sam, this is the big day, are you ready?" Debbie asked him.

"Hell, yeah," he said with a big silly grin. "I have been waiting for Jennifer to marry me for a long time."

"You look very handsome in your suit. Let me get your boutonniere pinned on your lapel for you." Janice offered.

"And I could use some help with this darn tie. I usually get Jennifer to do it but she is not here. Can either of you ladies tie a tie?"

"Here, let me help you," Debbie offered. "Anyone else need help? Once they had gotten all the boutonnieres pinned onto the men's suits and all the ties straightened out, Debbie wished them all good luck.

By one o'clock, most of the guests had arrived. The coat racks were overflowing and the soft jazz music in the background was almost drowned out by all the chatter. By one thirty, the nervous-looking groom was standing beside his best man Tony at the front of the room, anxiously awaiting his bride.

Shortly after two o'clock, Debbie noticed the bride and her father entering the far side of the dining room. She stepped into the banquet hall and signaled that they were ready.

Debbie discreetly stepped aside, and the wedding march started. First came a flower girl and a ring bearer. Janice had made a halo for the flower girl so her little blond curls were crowned in a circle of lilies and rosebuds, with a tail of rosebuds flowing down the back of her long, curly hair. She looked absolutely adorable. The ring bearer had a little boutonniere of rosebuds pinned on the lapel of his little suit. He carried a little red velvet cushion with the rings tied on with white ribbon. Next came the bridesmaids and the maid of honor and then finally Jennifer, the beautiful bride, escorted by her father, made her way down the aisle. It was a perfect wedding. Debbie and some of her staff watched from the back of the room and stepped out as soon as the groom kissed his bride.

"Janice, is that a tear I see rolling down your face?" Debbie asked her.

"Oh, shut up, you know I always tear up at weddings. Everything is just so beautiful, and everyone is all dressed up and looking so nice."

Debbie gave Janice a big hug. "I can't get over how beautiful the flowers are. The little flower girl's halo is so adorable. In a million years I could not have made them look as beautiful as you have."

Janice had also made various vases to put around the bar and the dining room, not to mention the big urns she did at the front door. It really was quite breathtaking.

"The flowers from the archway will go on the head tables, and the flowers on the podium I thought we could put on top of the fireplace for the pictures. What do you think of that idea?" Janice asked Debbie.

"Sounds okay to me. Thanks so much for doing the flowers, sis."

Following the ceremony, the guests wandered into the dining room where Chef George had a variety of hors d'oeuvres and canapes set up for them. Meanwhile Henry, Keith and staff were busy moving chairs and setting up tables for dinner.

The wedding party did some pictures in front of the back wall and then moved onto the bar for their fireplace pictures. The head tables were put into place and the wait staff started setting up linens, dishes, glasses, condiments and freshly baked buns. With the white tablecloths, and each place set with red linen napkins, side plates, wine and water glasses, and cutlery it all looked perfect. Then Janice and the staff brought out flower bowls that went on the centre of each table. The flowers that had previously hung on the trellis were now swags that Janice hung on the front side of the head tables.

They had thought that they wouldn't turn on the twinkle lights until the reception but decided to turn them on for dinner. The lights reflected quite nicely off all the wine glasses so when the guests re-entered the room, it was quite impressive. Debbie asked Susan to get some shots of the banquet room that she could possibly use in a future brochure.

Dinner would be served in the banquet room at five p.m. In the meantime, the wine was flowing, the food was disappearing, and everyone was happily celebrating the beautiful couple.

In the middle of all the confusion Debbie noticed a local couple come in. She went over and greeted them.

"Hi Jeff. How are you Sally? Nice to see you both." Debbie said.

"Wow, looks like a wedding going on. We were planning on coming in for a nice quiet dinner. Is the dining room open tonight?" Jeff asked her.

"Yes, the wedding is in the banquet room. The guests will all be going in there shortly for dinner. Tell you what, why don't you come into the bar and have a drink on me while we wait for the dining room to clear out."

"Sure, that would be fine. We are not in any hurry. The babysitter arrived early so we thought we would take full advantage and come for a leisurely dinner."

"Well come on into the bar and Ted will set you up with whatever you need. Ted, can you take care of Jeff and Sally? The first round is on me. Perhaps they would like to try that new specialty coffee you created."

From the bar, Debbie made her way into the kitchen. Chef looked a little frazzled.

"How's things going in here, Chef?"

"Don't ask. I don't know how we are going to serve this food and still keep it hot. By the time your waitresses get the order and figure out what everyone wants it will be cold."

"I think you should give the waitress four meals at a time, two of each entrée, and they will take them into the guests and give them a choice. You may end up with a couple plated meals extra at the end, but I can't think of a quicker way to serve it. This way the servers don't have to worry about taking orders."

"Yeah, that might work." Chef agreed with her.

"So are we about ready then? I figure it will take a few minutes to get everyone seated. Let me know when you want me to announce dinner."

"You could go ahead anytime. Wish us luck." Chef started pulling inserts from the warming oven.

"Oh Chef, I know you've got this well under control." Debbie gave him her best reassuring smile.

Chef grumbled something under his breath and Janice chuckled at him when Debbie left the kitchen.

On her way through the dining room, she ran into Gail.

"Did you just hear me telling Chef about serving the meal?" Debbie asked her.

"Yes, I think it will work just fine. I will have the staff bring the food in the door on this side and exit from the other door on the far side of the room, so they don't run into each other."

"I was just going to suggest that exact same idea to you. I am so glad you are on this. Thanks Gail. I am on my way to tell the master of ceremonies we are ready to start. Good luck, my friend."

As soon as the announcement was made that dinner was ready, guests made their way back into the banquet hall. Once they were all seated, she asked the master of ceremonies to announce that for dinner they had a choice of maple glazed chicken or a baked salmon with hollandaise sauce. The kitchen staff plated it and the waitresses took the meals to each guest and gave them their choice. Considering there was eighty-five guests, it all went quite smoothly.

The bride had ordered wine for all the tables. Each table had two bottles, one white and one red. The guests helped themselves to the wine while the waitresses were delivering their meals. Dessert was a combination of cakes, pastries, tarts and fresh fruit trays set up in the back corner of the room so that guests could help themselves at their leisure. The wedding cake was the centrepiece on the dessert table and looked quite impressive towering over the other desserts. Debbie noticed the photographer taking pictures of the cake and the whole dessert table as well.

Dinner was a huge success, and the party just carried on from there. The DJ started playing his records around nine o'clock. The new Mr. and Mrs. Sam Curtis had their first dance and shortly thereafter, cut their cake. The bride and groom still had a three-hour drive ahead of them and they left just before midnight. Mr. and Mrs. Curtis senior, the groom's grandparents, had already retired to their cabin, but everyone else had stayed to see them off. Sam came over to Debbie and thanked her for the perfect day. He said they would come for a ski weekend when they got back from the honeymoon. Debbie wished them both all the happiness in the world.

It was going on three o'clock in the morning before everything was cleaned up and put away. Some of the wedding guests didn't want to leave. By the time they all got to bed, everyone was happy but exhausted.

Chapter 12

Sunday morning at seven o'clock when the dining room opened, the only evidence of the previous day's events were the flowers which were now placed around the dining room. And the tulle and lights were still up in the banquet room. Janice said that perhaps they could just stay up unless there was an upcoming event that they wouldn't be appropriate for like a business meeting or something.

The wedding party straggled in for breakfast, but only six of them were still going skiing. Apparently, there was a couple of them feeling a little under the weather this morning. Debbie arranged for Keith to give those that wanted to go out a ride to the ski hill. Everyone was still in a festive mood, but not nearly as rowdy as they were last night.

The bride's father, Jerry Whitfield, came in and straightened up the bill before he checked out. He said how pleased he was with everything and wanted to know if he could book a fishing weekend in July for himself and five of his buddies. He liked his cabin just fine, but wanted a chalet for his buddies. Debbie got out the reservation book and got business all taken care of. There was a standard fifteen percent gratuity already on the bill, but he paused when he saw it.

"Could you make that twenty percent? I can't tell you how impressed I was with the entire event. Your staff is amazing, and they all deserve a big tip."

"Well on behalf of the staff, they all thank you very much. Perhaps you will keep us in mind for your younger daughter's wedding someday."

"Oh geez, don't remind me. I need to get over this one first," he laughed. "But I wouldn't hesitate to hold it here for sure."

"Thanks, that's good to know. I was wondering if you and your wife wanted to take home any of the flowers, and I am sure Jennifer will want the leftover cake. It's back in the cooler."

The bride's mother came into the office just as Debbie was asking him.

"I'll take the cake with me now and perhaps one arrangement of flowers, but as for the rest of the flowers, I'm sure you'll enjoy them around here for the next week or so," she said.

"Yes, we certainly will. They are all so beautiful."

"Yes, the arrangements were gorgeous. Did Jennifer take her bouquet with her do you know?"

"Yes, I believe she did. I remember Kelly handing it to her after she put her coat on." Debbie told her.

Janice came into the office.

"Janice, would you go get the wedding cake from the walk-in cooler for me please?"

"Absolutely, be right back." Janice told them.

Once Janice returned with the cake, they all said their goodbyes. "Thanks again for everything. You made my little girl's special day perfect for her," Mr. Whitfield said.

"It was our pleasure. See you in July," Debbie told him.

When they left the office Janice asked her, "What is happening in July?"

"Just a fishing weekend with some buddies. He just booked a chalet for five of his friends," Debbie told her. "He was so pleased he left a twenty percent tip."

"That was awful nice of him. He must have been pleased with everything then." Janice enquired.

"Yes, he said he was amazed at the flowers and the cake, and the staff all did an amazing job serving and cleaning up the dinner."

"I was pleased with the flowers. I think Jennifer got carried away, but I did end up using them all. I wasn't very impressed with the cake though."

"I thought it was pretty and Jennifer liked it just fine." Debbie assured her sister.

"I guess, I just hate that plastic bride and groom they always put on the top. There are much better options. And the cheap wine glasses were a little tacky. Just my opinion." Janice said with a shrug of her sholders.

"I suppose you think you could have done a better job?"

"Oh I don't suppose, I know I could have. Just saying." Janice said with a smug expression.

"Well Chef is good at baking, but not so much on decorating. For him decorating cupcakes is a pain in the butt." Debbie grinned.

"All-in-all, I think the wedding was beautiful and the fact that we served that many dinners and it only took twenty minutes was amazing. Even Chef was surprised at how smoothly it all went."

"How did it work out in the end? Did he have a bunch left over?" Debbie asked her.

"No, Gail came in with the last order for three chicken dinners, which completed the service. It all worked out very well."

"That's good. Yes, it all went very smoothly. Everyone seemed pleased with the dinner. I noticed some of the empty plates coming back and all they had on them was fish bones."

"One thing I did notice, the big drinkers were going into the bar. The waitresses could have been doing a better job on serving drinks I think." Janice offered her opinion.

"I will mention that to Gail. My guess is that because it was an open bar, they were trying not to overserve some of the guests. I noticed a couple fellows from the wedding party were a bit tipsy, but I wasn't too worried because I knew they were staying overnight and didn't have to drive anywhere. And just so you know, we do have a portable bar that we can set up in the banquet room but the Whitfield's didn't want it."

"Good thing. That one fellow was having enough trouble trying to get his coat and boots on. And that one bridesmaid was doing tequila shots like they were going out of style. I forgot to ask, how many went skiing this morning?"

"Only six made it to the hill." They both had a little chuckle about that.

The rest of Sunday was quiet for the most part. As the guests checked out, the cabin girls completed the change overs and caught up on the laundry. The sisters all had dinner together as Susan, Keith and the kids were all heading home tonight. They talked about their future plans, but no definite decisions had yet been made. Susan had asked Debbie to get a couple appraisals on the resort so they could meet at a later date to discuss their options. Janice was planning on staying another few days. Debbie was sad to see them go, but they had lives of their own outside of the Resort. She was the only one that lived there. Once things quieted down, she would have to do some soul searching and decide what she wanted to do. Although she loved her job, it just wasn't the same without her mom working by her side.

After supper, Debbie asked Susan and Janice to come upstairs with her. They all went into Mom's room and decided on what keepsakes each of them wanted. They went through her jewellery box and each sister picked out a couple pieces. They also each chose a knick-knack as a keepsake from their mom. Debbie didn't feel she was ready to do that just yet, but both sisters seemed glad that they did.

"What will you do with the rest of Mom's stuff?" Susan wanted to know.

"Well I will probably keep some of her sweaters and whatever else fits me, and the rest I will send to charity. Is there anything else either of you want? If you do, say so now." Debbie told them both.

"No, I think you should do with it as you see fit." Susan told her.

"I will get around to it, someday when I don't have anything else to do." Debbie told them.

Chapter 13

After Susan, Keith, and the kids left it was just Janice and Debbie. They headed for the bar and cracked open a bottle of wine. They laughed, they cried and all-in-all, just had some quality sister time.

Janice told Debbie, "I think I might like to come live here and help out. What do you think?"

"I think that would be fine with me, but you realize that there will be no paycheque."

"Well let me figure it out. If I live here and eat meals here, I wouldn't need much in pay compared to the job I have now."

"It's not just that, there is also the idea that because you live here you are available to work twenty-four/seven. Know what I mean?" Debbie looked at her expectedly. "It is not just a paycheque, it is all the other stuff as well. If you're going to make the move, I would like it if you stayed in Mom's adjoining room, but what will you do with all your stuff? Will you sell it or put it in storage? And what about your vehicle? If you come here permanently you probably won't need your car as you could use the company van. When you own a resort you get paid in other ways, not necessarily cash value. Right now, the resort is supporting two people so I know it can continue to do that, but if Susan and her family move back, I am not sure how that is all going to work."

Janice was surprised by Debbie's answer. She expected her baby sister to jump on the chance of having help. "Well, let's just think on it a bit and see how it's going to play out." Janice said.

"I am starting to have my doubts that this can work. I have never worked any other place than here, but I am sure that if I moved on, I would find another job." Debbie could see the look of shock on her sister's face.

"What are you saying? Do you really want to sell and leave? I thought you loved running the resort?"

"I do, but now there will be three of us running things and in the past, we have had problems agreeing on things. I guess I am concerned about our future and I am tired and, it is just not the same without Mom." Debbie continued. "Like I said, I am tired and perhaps this is the perfect time for a change of scenery."

"Oh Debbie, I don't think this place could run without you, certainly not run as efficiently as it is running right now. You have a good handle on things, you have good staff around you, and where else would you want to go?"

"Oh, I don't know, I think I will just wait and see what Susan is planning on doing. There are a lot of moving parts that have to be decided on before I can make any personal decisions. I am tired and going to bed. Hit the lights before you come upstairs, okay?"

"Okay, goodnight, sis. See you in the morning."

When Debbie went upstairs to her living room she just sat there quietly thinking about the past weekend and the wedding they just had. She spotted the two boxes still sitting on the floor beside her couch. Since she was physically tires but not really sleepy tired, she decided to go through the boxes.

Inside the big cardboard box was a wooden box, with a garden scene painted on it. It was full of old family pictures. It was always fun to flip through a box of old pictures as a lot of them were from when the girls were young. Debbie chuckled at a silly one of her and Janice on a swing set. How simple and carefree their lives were back then. As Debbie worked her way into the box, she discovered a stack of letters tied together with a red ribbon hidden at the bottom.

There were six letters in total, all addressed to mom. Four of them were in her mom's maiden name at a different address and two letters addressed to her after she married and moved to the resort. They were all from a Mr. Jefferson Penfold. Debbie sat holding the letters in her hand, trying to remember if she had ever heard that name before. To the best of her recollections, she had no memory of her mom ever mentioning Mr. Penfold. She set them aside on the coffee table in front of her. Should she read them? After all, they were mom's personal letters and obviously, she had kept them well hidden. She wrestled with her conscience if she should open them or not. There was no hurry for a decision and perhaps some time to think was in order. She put the pictures back into the box and thought that her sisters might get a kick out of going through them. The bundle of letters she took into her bedroom and hid them in her sock drawer for now. As she climbed into bed her thoughts were about Mr. Penfold and his letters.

Chapter 14

Another Monday morning was waiting for Debbie. She liked to keep up her routines even though they didn't have any paying guests till mid-week. As Debbie walked through the office to go get her coffee, Janice was already pouring it for her. They were on their own today as Chef George and Gail would both be taking the next two days off. Debbie always found the lodge so quiet without staff there. Chef had left them muffins and croissants and Debbie volunteered to cook Janice breakfast but they both decided on cold cereal so neither had to cook this morning.

Debbie asked Janice, "So, what do you want to do today?"

"What do you normally do on a Monday? Is there anything I can help you with? If so, just name it."

"For starters, I have some book work to do, tallying up all the weekend sales. Then I have to get the bank deposits ready for when I go into town shopping later. I have to do a food inventory and get my food and liquor orders in for Wednesday delivery, just the usual stuff. Any of that sound like anything you would want to do?"

"You mean besides going shopping in town?" Janice asked. "You know I can do shopping real good right? Perhaps we could go out to lunch since we are short our personal Chef today."

"Well, usually one of us would stay here to answer phones, bartend, cook, waitress or whatever is needed in the event that a guest may drop in. I am expecting a sales rep here probably later this afternoon and he will be expecting someone to be here." Debbie said.

Just then, Henry came in the back door. He banged the snow off his boots and headed for the back kitchen table where the girls were finishing their cereal.

"Morning ladies, did you see all the stars out last night?" he asked. "I just love the cold crispness when the sky is clear of nothing but stars. Kind of reminded me of the twinkle lights in the banquet room. Almost seems a shame to have to take them all down."

"We have decided to leave them up unless we get a business event or something that they would be out of place at." Janice said.

Debbie thumbed through the reservation book and told them that there was a baby shower, a cosmetic makeup party, and a few other events coming up. Nothing that would require the banquet room for size, but since it was already decorated, they could use the room for these events. "I think the baby shower in two weeks' time would work for sure so let's just let that ride for today," she said.

"Okay by me," Henry answered. "I have lots of work to do to finish up cabin seven anyways. Deb, could you call the electrician and see what his upcoming schedule is? I need him for about two hours to do the rewiring before I can put up the new drywall."

"His number is in the little black address book on my desk. Why don't you call him yourself, then you'll know what he says firsthand?"

"All right. I'll go do that right now before I get busy and forget."

As soon as Henry disappeared, Janice asked, "Do you know how lucky you are to have your very own handyman? What's Henry's story? I bet that he has had a very interesting life."

"Henry was born and raised here and traveled all over the world with the army for years. He married and had two sons who both now live around Toronto somewhere. Once the boys were raised, he and his wife decided to come home to retire. His wife died from cancer about three years ago and he has been hanging around here ever since."

"Oh, that is so sad. He seems like he enjoys his job. Is he expensive?" Janice inquired.

"No, not really. He gets a small salary. He enjoys puttering and is usually here on a daily basis. Since he lives alone and hates cooking, he comes here for meals. He lives close and is always on call if I ever need him."

"I take it that he doesn't do electrical work."

"For insurance purposes, we occasionally need a professional. Henry can do some electrical, but we are in the process of upgrading hydro in three cabins this year. It is better to have an electrician's stamp on things. Basically, we're just coving our asses in case anything ever goes wrong."

"That is exactly what I was talking about last night. You know all this stuff about the resort and without you at the helm, Susan and I would probably run it into the ground."

"Well you know, as Mom used to say, *'You can't have five years' experience until you've been there five years.'*"

"So, were you serious when you said you were thinking about leaving?" Janice asked her with concern.

"Well, I don't really know how to explain it to you. When it was Mom and I, we usually agreed on almost everything, but you know from past history that we three sisters don't usually agree on much of anything. I guess I am worried that when there is no one person specifically in charge, things will go amuck quickly. As Mom would have said, *'too many cooks can spoil the broth.'*" Debbie let out a big sigh. "I have been manager here for the past ten or so years and I'm not sure if I am up to the task of arguing about every little decision that needs to be made on a daily basis around here. Know what I mean?"

"Well I can't speak for Susan. But I am quite contented to have you stay in charge. You are doing a great job and I don't see why that should change."

"You say that now, but may not always feel that way. And we both know Susan is a take-charge kind of girl. She is already showing her true colours. I don't honestly know what to do. I need to think about it some more."

"Well I have been giving it some thought, and I think I would like to move back and give it a try. Right now, I am working in a flower shop basically for minimum wage, so I am not giving much up to make the move. I spoke with Ann, the owner of the flower shop here in town, and she said that she hires extra staff in the summertime. Perhaps I could work there some as well as helping out here when you need me."

"In the summer when Ann would need you would also be the busy time for us, and the resort would need you at the same time, most likely."

"It was just a thought. I sat down and figured out my expenses. Like how much it is costing me to rent my apartment, hydro, phone, cable and internet and against my wages I am left with about five hundred dollars a month. That is only when I am working full time. Which is not always the case. If I moved back here, I would not have all those expenses so I would not need to be working full time."

"That sounds good in theory, but like I told you before, most times at a family-run resort, you get paid in other ways. The only thing I buy for myself is clothes and personal items."

"Will I be getting any wages?" Janice asked.

"I am not sure. Right now, I take a small wage, but Mom didn't because she was the owner. So now that we are owners, I am honestly not sure how that will all work. I will have to speak to our accountant to see what he suggests." Debbie wrote herself a note so she wouldn't forget to make that call. "You will be basically getting room and board free of charge. That much I am sure of."

"I see, well I know I am ready for a change and I have enjoyed these past few weeks being home. I think I could be a lot of help to you here."

"I am sure you would be a great asset to the resort. We just need to find out the legalities of how all this will work. Perhaps we should, all three of us, sit down and have the accountant explain it all to us. How does that sound?"

"Sounds logical. Next time Susan calls we can run it by her as well."

"However it works out, you know I would love to have you back home with me. Before I forget, besides the salesman, I have two real estate agents coming out this afternoon. One is here about one o'clock and the other is to be here at three."

"Well perhaps I could go to town and run the errands so you can be here to deal with the sales rep and agents. If you make me a list, I don't mind doing the shopping."

"Yeah, that is probably the best idea. I will get the bank deposits ready and make you a list." Debbie got up and headed to the office. She always enjoyed going to run the errands, but it would be easier for Jan to do them. The only problem was now Deb would never have a reason to ever leave the resort. Things were definitely changing in her world.

Chapter 15

Deb had just finished having lunch when she heard the bell on the front door. The real estate agent had arrived early. Deb invited her in, and they sat down to go over the details of the estimate. Deb spent the remainder of the morning putting together the information that agents would need. She had a complete list of all the buildings, she even knew the square footage of all the cabins and the lodge since they had all been upgraded. The agent was very impressed with all the info that Deb had collected for her, including the tax assessments and profit and loss statements for the past five years.

Debbie and the agent spent the next hour touring the grounds. Deb explained all the amenities that the resort provided including the shuttle van and company vehicles. She was impressed and took lots of pictures as they toured the cabins and the lodge.

"I haven't been here in a few years. It is really looking nice," she complimented Debbie.

"Thanks, we try to do upgrades in our downtime, but this winter has been unusually busy so that is proving to be a bit of a challenge."

"Okay, well I think I have all that I need, I will be in touch in a couple of days to give you the estimate."

"Sounds good. I would like three copies of the detailed estimate if possible." Debbie told her as she was leaving.

"Can I ask why you need three copies?" she asked.

"There are three owners involved. The resort belongs to myself and my two sisters."

"I am sure that won't be a problem. I will call you to set up another meeting in a few days."

"Okay, thanks. I look forward to hearing from you."

Janice had arrived back from running errands and Henry came up to help her unload the things she had bought.

"Did you have any visitors while I was gone?" she asked Debbie.

"Just the real estate agent."

"How did that go?"

"Fine, I gave her the ten-cent tour and all the information she needs to do the estimate." Debbie grabbed a bag from the van and headed inside. "She said she would get back to us in a few days."

"And what time is the other agent coming?" Janice follower her inside.

"Should be here anytime." Deb heard a car pulling up out front. "Looks like he is here now. Jan, you should come on the tour with us and have a good look at things."

"Sounds like a good idea. I would like that very much."

The agent introduced himself and extended his hand.

"Well I am Debbie, and this is my sister Janice. While you both still have boots and coats on, why don't we do the tour and then we can do paperwork part when we get back in?"

"Lead the way," he told her.

Janice had been inside the cabins over the years but had not seen any of the upgrades that had been happening. She told Debbie how much she was impressed. When they got to the chalet, Janice admitted that she never imagined it could look this nice. They both had their phones out taking pictures.

Back inside, over a coffee, Debbie gave him all the same information she had given earlier to the other agent..

"You don't have any aerial shots of the property or pictures of the resort in the summertime, do you?" He asked Debbie.

"I don't have any aerial shots yet, but I might be able to rustle you up some pictures of the lodge," Debbie offered.

"It is a little-known fact that summer pictures work for selling properties better than winter pictures do," he told them.

"How many properties do you know of that are for sale in this area?" Janice asked him.

"Right now, within a hundred miles I would guess about ten, but some of them only have a few cabins. Nothing on this grand of a scale. Properties like this one don't come up for sale very often."

"How long before you can get back to us with an estimate?" Debbie asked.

"I specialize in commercial property sales, and that keeps me very busy. I would probably not be able to get back to you with the estimate till next week."

"We will wait to hear back from you." Debbie walked him to the front door.

After he left, Debbie and Janice went to the bar for a well-deserved glass of wine.

"I have to say that I am so impressed with what you have done with this place. Last time I was in a chalet, it wasn't nearly as impressive," Janice admitted. "All the pine on the walls makes it all so beautiful and the new hot tubs are a nice touch."

"Well, that is kind of what I was trying to tell you earlier. On the books we show a very low profit margin because any profits are being put back into the resort for improvements. We had a good last summer and that is why Henry is doing cabin renovations this winter. We do this so we don't end up overpaying in taxes. If we were ever really going to sell it, we would need about two years with no renovation expenses to show the true profits that the resort is capable of."

"The company house is empty right now since you and mom moved permanently into the lodge. I thought you would have that rented out."

"We usually do but the couple that were there decided to move the end of the year and I haven't had any new tenants interested just yet."

"Well," Janice said, "Perhaps if Susan and her family move back, they could rent the house."

"Yes, that is a possibility. And if they don't move back, I will eventually rent it out for two thousand dollars a month. Just another moving part."

"I don't know how you manage to keep it all straight. I see Chef left us some dinners already made up. He sure takes good care of you, even when he is not physically here. Personal Chef, personal handy man, how did you get so lucky?"

"Running a resort has a lot of challenges, but it has some rewards, too."

"Well I am ready to go raid the cold room and see what exactly Chef has made us for dinner," Janice said as she refilled both their wine glasses.

The back door banged shut.

"What did Chef leave us for dinner?" Henry asked while he knocked the snow from his boots at the back door.

"We were just going to go see." Janice told him.

"I think I saw a plate of baked chicken in the cold room. Perhaps I could warm that up." Debbie said. "Do we want to have it with salads, or would you rather have French fries?"

"Salads are fine with me. I know it takes ten minutes to warm up the fryer. Hardly seems worth it just for the three of us." Henry said. "And for that matter, cold chicken is fine with me as well."

"Me too," Janice agreed.

"Okay, I'll get the chicken. Janice do you want to come bring out the salad and Henry, can you set the table?" Debbie asked them.

While they were eating, Henry said, "I saw a couple of real estate cars here today. Are you ladies thinking about selling the resort?

Perhaps I shouldn't ask. It's not really any of my business, but I am curious."

"It's okay, Henry. It is not public knowledge yet, but Mom left the resort to us three girls. We are just getting appraisals to put a value on it. One or all of us have to remain as owners for at least five years."

"Your mom always told me that it was her wish that you three girls would all come home and run the resort as a team. Maybe she will finally get her wish."

"Maybe. Time will tell. But for now, we are keeping this information just between us until we get some decisions made." Debbie told them.

Chapter 16

The next couple of days were fairly quiet. On Wednesday they had the weekly bridge ladies for lunch. This consisted of eight gals who came to the lodge for the afternoon to play bridge. Chef made them a lemon drop cake which was a huge hit. Chef always had a dessert tray ready for them and often did a pie or a cake to entice them. Janice was hoping for a leftover piece, but there wasn't any. One lady bought the last two pieces to take home for her husband. Janice had to settle for a cupcake.

The real estate agent arrived just as the bridge ladies were leaving. She had an estimate prepared for them to see. Debbie suggested they retire to the lounge, as she didn't want Chef George or any other staff to overhear their conversation. Janice grabbed a coffee and joined them.

"Well, I have been running the numbers and researching other commercial properties in the surrounding areas. I think you'll be pleasantly surprised. As you will see, I included some other similar type of listings for you to compare."

"Wow that is interesting. You have showed properties in different price ranges. Very impressive," Janice told her. "Where do we fit into this list?"

"When you take into account all the cabins, the lodge, the house and the boat house I would estimate you at the higher end of the scale. I would estimate your property at two and a half million dollars. That would be a fair asking price. I would suggest we list it a little higher and leave a little wiggle room to play with, unless you're in a hurry to sell."

"That is definitely higher than I expected." Janice said. Deb, what do you think?"

"Sounds about right. I am not surprised. I did a little research of my own and comparing apples to apples I expected it to be between two point five and three million somewhere. Also, we pay taxes on a three million assessment."

"Of course you did, Deb, I should have known you'd be on top of this." Janice commented.

"Thank you." Debbie said to the agent. "We appreciate your efforts."

"Are you looking for a quick sale, or are you willing to wait for the right buyer?" she asked.

"We haven't decided. At this point, we are just exploring our options. We still need to discuss it with Susan, our other sister, before any decisions can be made."

"Oh okay. Well, when the decision is made, I would be glad to help you with the listing." She told them. "I would suggest you shoot for end of April if you are thinking about a quick sale. That is when potential buyers will be starting to look at commercial properties for sale."

They both thanked her for her work and after she had left Janice asked, "Should we call Susan?"

"No, not yet. Let's wait till we hear from the other agent and see what he thinks. I also would like to suggest that we should have a third appraisal and then average out the three estimates. Susan only asked for two, but I would feel better if there were three."

"Okay, that makes sense. Do you have an agent in mind?"

"I thought I would call the agency in town, you know, the one beside the flower shop. Grant Agency, I think it is called. That way we will have a local agency, a bigger out of town agency, and the commercial agency. I think that would give a clear fair picture of all our options."

"Sounds good, go give them a call."

"No, I think I will make a trip into Clifford tomorrow and go in and speak with them in person." Debbie told her. "The beer truck has just arrived. Tony is bringing in the liquor order. We will need to check the inventory once he gets it unloaded. Janice, you should come see how this is done. You will want to put on a sweater and meet me in the basement in about fifteen minutes."

By the time Janice got downstairs, Tony had all the liquor boxes unloaded and was now bringing in the twenty-eight cases of beer.

Debbie liked Tony. He was quite friendly, and more importantly, he was usually on time. He had been delivering her booze order for the past five years at least. When Janice came down, Debbie did the introductions.

"Tony, this is my sister Janice. Janice, this is my friend Tony."

"Pleased to meet you, my dear." Tony stuck out his hand.

"The pleasure is all mine," Janice said with a silly grin.

Debbie showed Janice how to receive the inventory and how to check everything off against the invoice, and when Tony was done bringing in the beer, they finished checking it off as well. Tony locked up the truck and pulled it ahead to park it out of the loading bay so as to not block any other deliveries. He came in and got a coffee. Debbie was surprised as he had never come in for a coffee before in the five years she had known him. Janice and Tony were actually flirting with each other! Debbie excused herself and went to file the invoice in the office.

"Who is that hunk and where did he come from?" Janice asked as she came into the office. "He certainly is a charmer, isn't he?"

"I don't really know much about him other than he delivers my liquor order most every Wednesday."

"Well I think I might need to know more about him than that. He sure is cute, isn't he?"

"I guess, if you're into that handsome rugged type." Debbie teased her sister.

"I would be happy to receive the liquor order on Wednesdays. Just to help you out, you understand."

"Gee, thanks. You are just a little transparent, dear sister of mine."

Chef George poked his head around the corner to ask what the ladies wanted for dinner. He suggested chicken fingers, as he already had the fryer warmed up. "Sounds good," they answered in unison.

Debbie took all three copies of the proposal upstairs to her private room. Most things went into the office, but this was something she didn't want to share with the staff, not yet anyways. The staff were constantly in and out of the office. Chef and Gail would both sit at her desk and use the phone to place food and liquor orders. She didn't need them to accidentally see the real estate estimates. It was impossible to keep a secret of any kind around here and although it wasn't a big secret, it did not need to be common knowledge either.

Early Thursday morning, Debbie took a trip into Clifford. She had to stop and pick up a flat of eggs and a few other things Chef George had forgotten to put on this week's food order, and a few things she needed. She went by the Grant Real Estate office and was pleased to see that John the owner was in. He was the only one in the office and they had a chance to have a visit. Debbie and her mom had met John once at a Chamber of Commerce meeting a few years ago.

After they finished the small talk, she explained what she needed. "Mom left the resort to us three girls and we are trying to decide if we want to keep or sell it." Debbie told him. "I was hoping you would come out and take a look and give me your opinion on what it is worth."

"If you are going to sell, now would be the time. Potential buyers start looking at commercial properties usually about this time of year," John told her.

"Do you sell a lot of commercial properties?" Debbie asked him.

"I have sold a few. It is a little different than selling a home or a cottage. When you sell a business, you have to put your financial information out there for the world to see, and as an agent it is my job to weed out the curious from the serious buyers."

"How long does it take to sell a commercial property in this environment?"

"Gosh, that depends on so many different things. It is just too hard to predict. Last summer I sold a bed and breakfast almost immediately, and a small property with six rental cottages took about five months to sell. It just depends on finding the right interested buyers. Basically, it is a crapshoot."

"Would you be interested in coming out to see the resort and giving us an estimate?"

"I could probably come out tomorrow."

"I would rather you come on Monday when there would be no staff there." There was no need to get the staff all upset if she could help it.

"How about I come Monday at one o'clock?"

"That would be fine. Thanks John, see you Monday."

Debbie spent the drive home trying to think of all the possible ways this could play out. The three sisters had to all work together or buy each other out. She didn't have any personal savings to speak of, so that put her out of the running to buy her sisters out. She could sell them her share and move on to something else. But what would she move on to? She loved working in the hospitality industry and would probably open a restaurant or another resort someplace else. If that was the plan, why not stay and work the Resort they already had?

Could the three sisters run the Resort together? Janice had said she would be happy if Debbie stayed on as the manager, but she didn't expect Susan to be so agreeable. Being the oldest sister, Susan thought that automatically put her in charge. In the past, the three sisters had a history of disagreeing on many things. Debbie just didn't think she wanted to spend the next five-plus years constantly arguing with her sisters. If they would be happy to let her carry on managing the resort that would be one thing, but if they were going to micromanage every decision she made, it would drive Debbie crazy.

There were so many unanswered questions and Debbie didn't have any answers. In a perfect world, both sisters would move home and help with the work and agree with everything she said. But here in the real world, things don't usually work out that way.

Chapter 17

Friday was proving to be a good day. They had one chalet and three cabins booked for the skiers and three more cabins booked Saturday for some hockey games at the local arena. The skiers required a fancier menu, but the hockey players were quite happy with the bar menu consisting of burgers and fried foods. Thankfully, Chef George was very good at satisfying both.

The salesman that was supposed to be here Monday finally showed up today. His "plans ended up changing" was his only explanation as to why he didn't show up when he said he would. Debbie looked over his sale flyers since she did need to order some new syrup jugs and bar glasses, but there was no hurry, and there was nothing that she couldn't do without for now. She also wanted to order some more flower bowls. She needed a dozen, enough for all the tables in the dining room. She was so impressed when Janice had done the flower bowls for Mom's service and the wedding that Debbie thought they would be a nice change for the dining room tables this summer. The man was hoping to make a sale, but Deb was so unimpressed with the guy that she didn't buy anything today.

Some local folks stopped in for lunch and while chatting with them, she learned about the upcoming races that were being held next weekend at the ski hill. She must remember to call Nancy and Robert at the hill and get the details, as it may bring in overnight guests. The local businesses were good about helping each other, especially in the winter. When the ski hill was doing well, so were the other local businesses. That was the nature of the beast, so to speak, when your livelihood depended on tourism.

They had a crowd in the bar tonight. The jukebox was going steady all night long. The guests were keeping Ted the bartender busy at the bar mixing drinks, and he hadn't had a chance to pick up the empties for a while. Deb went in around ten o'clock and helped him for a half an hour. She picked up empty bottles and glasses and bussed off some empty dirty tables. When she left, Ted had just done a tray of tequila shots and was now mixing up a tray of B52s for another table. Everyone was having a good time.

Debbie was always interested in the different vehicles in the parking lot. Tonight, it consisted of cars, trucks, four-wheeler ATVs and a few Ski-Doo's or sleds, as they were now called. She had just learned that the big crowd that was buying all the shooters in the bar were staying at the Nicholson cottage across the lake. They were the ones traveling by sleds. Because the back side of the Muskogie Lake had no public access road, most people who lived across the lake parked down by her campground and accessed the lake from her boathouse.

"What are you looking at?" Janice asked as she came up behind her sister.

"Just checking out the vehicles in the driveway. I see we have a four-wheeler and a few Ski-Does both here tonight." Debbie indicated with a wave of her hand.

"Where is that big group from?" Janice wanted to know.

"I just found out they are staying at the Nicholson cottage across the lake."

"I noticed a lot of vehicles and trailers parked down by the campground. Would that be them parking there?"

"Yes, it is. We let them park down there year-round." Debbie nodded her head.

"What do you charge them to park there?"

"Nothing, they park for free."

"Free? Why? You could be making a fortune on parking. You are usually all in if it makes money." Janice enquired earnestly.

"I do charge them for boat docking. We even put in a special dock just for the cottagers and they do pay for parking their boats, but the parking lot doesn't cost me anything. We have lots of room, so it is no big inconvenience or anything. And because they park there, they come in and use the dining room, the bar, the boat house, the variety shop and other amenities. So although we make zero money on the parking, we made up for it in other sales."

"Guess that makes sense," Janice said. "I find it interesting how we seem to give so much away hoping it will come back tenfold."

"Usually it does," Debbie told her.

Chapter 18

Debbie was woken out of a deep sleep by ringing telephones. The office extension in her room was ringing and so now was her personal cell phone. It was four thirty in the morning.

She answered the cell phone first because it was the closest. Janice came in and grabbed the business phone. It was Nancy from the ski hill telling her the snow plow truck had been in a terrible accident just down the road. Apparently, the plow caught the corner of a guardrail and flipped the truck, sending it down over an embankment. The driver was trapped, and help had been called. She thought Debbie might want to know.

"I'll go down and put a pot of coffee on," Janice volunteered.

"I am not sure what we can do to help, but perhaps we could take some coffees up to the crash site. I imagine all the volunteer firefighters and first responders haven't had a morning coffee yet. You better make a few pots. Nancy said the first responders had just arrived and the ambulance and two tow trucks were on their way."

"I was just talking to Robert Martin from the ski hill and he said it would be a miracle if the driver made it out alive," Janice said.

"Here Janice, fill this up with coffee." Debbie gave her sister a big portable insulated coffee urn. "If I remember correctly, it will hold ten pots of coffee. While you're doing that, I will get the cups, creamers, and sugars together. I wonder if we should take some muffins."

"I know Chef baked muffins yesterday. I can wrap them while I am waiting on the coffee if you like." Janice offered.

"Thank you, I would appreciate that."

While they loaded everything in the van, they could hear sirens going by on the road above them. Debbie and Janice arrived with the big urn full of coffee and a box full of muffins, Henry was already there, and he came over and helped serve the coffee. They served it right out of the back of the van. There were quite a few men working on getting the truck rolled back over. They needed to get the truck out while there was no traffic on the road. It was currently upside down, about twenty feet below the roadway. Henry explained that they had to turn the truck back right-side up and then pull it back up the bank. The volunteers were grateful for the coffee and muffins. The temperature was somewhere below freezing, and Debbie was right, most of the guys hadn't had their morning coffee fix yet this morning. There were already four inches of fresh snow on the road, and more still falling fast.

Nancy and Robert were there, although there was nothing they could do to help. They came over and accepted coffees from Debbie.

"Hi guys!" Debbie handed them each a steaming cup. "What a night, eh? This is my sister, Janice. Janice, these are friends of mine, Nancy and Robert Martin. They own the ski hill up the road. And I think you both know Henry." Debbie did the introductions.

"I think we spoke earlier on the phone," Janice said to Robert.

"Yes, that was me. I didn't realize Nancy was on the other phone calling at the same time I was. Anyways I am glad we called. The guys sure seemed to appreciate the coffee."

"How did they ever get the driver out of that tangled mess down there?"

"They had to use the Jaws of Life to open the cab of the truck up. They opened it up like you would open a can of soup. It took quite a while but then they pulled the driver out and got him onto a stretcher and then we pulled him up the hill," Robert told them.

"Robert helped. He is my hero." Nancy gave him a pat on the back.

"Did the paramedics say anything about his condition?" Janice asked.

"Just that he was in bad shape, but alive. He was in and out of consciousness when they loaded him into the ambulance," Robert brushed the falling snow off his coat.

"They were meeting the air ambulance at the strip just outside Clifford. From there they would be flying him to Toronto," Henry added as he walked away.

"I hope he is ok. While I am talking to you, I hear that you folks are having some ski races next weekend," Debbie said to Nancy.

"Yes, I was going to call you about that," Nancy said. "We already have thirty-five contestants signed up and a lot of them are from out of town. Some of them may want to stay over as we are racing both Saturday and Sunday. You know we have the resort featured on our website, so don't be surprised if you get some customers."

"If you want to email a copy of the flyer or whatever you are using for advertising, we will add it to our website as well. Well, good luck with the races." Debbie told them both. She announced last call for any coffee and once that was served, she and Janice headed home.

Chapter 19

It was past seven o'clock before they got the snow plow tuck pulled out of the ditch. Some of the guys stopped in for breakfast. They reported that the driver was taken to Toronto. He broke his hip and his leg quite badly, as well as a few ribs. He was currently in intensive care. Apparently, a broken rib had punctured his left lung. As soon as they could get him stabilized, he would have to have several surgeries. Besides all the cuts and scrapes they were hopeful he would eventually make a full recovery. The truck, on the other hand, did not fare so well. The general consensus among them was that it would probably be written off.

In the afternoon, her hockey team stopped in for their usual trays of chicken wings. Whenever the team that the resort sponsored played at the home rink, they would invite the visiting team back to the lodge for wings after the game. It ended up being a dining room full of rowdy teenage kids and a handful of parents. The wings and pop for the kids were free. A couple of the parents ordered burgers and fries as well.

Today there were thirty-five kids and seven parents. Chef always did them up trays of wings garnished with celery and carrot sticks and dip. The volume in the dining room was almost deafening, but it always did a heart good to see kids having fun. Charles the coach went into the kitchen to thank Chef for the wings.

When the teams left, Janice helped clean up the mess and do all the dishes. "They sure are a noisy bunch, aren't they? How long have you supported the team?"

"Only for the past five years. As you will notice in the picture hanging there, we provide their jerseys with our logo on them. It is great advertising," Debbie explained. "The wings are a great way to get the visiting team through our doors. Now that they know where we are, they will come back on their own for summer holidays or whatever."

"It amazes me how much free stuff we give away."

"I overheard one of the hockey dads tell his wife that this would be a nice place to spend their anniversary weekend. So, who knows? I made sure to give them our brochure to take home with them." Debbie continued, "I should also tell you we sponsor a soft ball team in the summer but we are way too busy during the summer ball season to have wing nights for them. We do a big banquet for them instead in the fall."

"I see in the pictures it looks like some of the same kids are both in hockey and baseball. Lucky kids." Janice commented.

"And some of them work here part time in the summer as well. Small towns are like that."

"Yeah, I can see how that would happen." Janice agreed.

Chapter 20

Janice was starting to get the feel of how the Resort run. By the time Debbie came down, Janice already had the coffee made.

"Morning, sis. How are you this morning?" Janice asked her baby sister.

"It's Monday and still too early to tell."

"Here's your first coffee, and the reservation book. What is on the agenda for today?" she asked.

"Not too much. I need get bank deposits ready, pay some bills, and meet with John the real estate agent at one o'clock" Debbie took the coffee and had a sip. "Henry wants me to go see something in one of the cabins this morning, too."

"I forgot to tell you Susan called yesterday. They are coming up next weekend" Janice gave a little smile. "I should also tell you that she asked about the real estate agents and I told her what the agent had said."

"And what was her reaction?"

"She agreed with you that we should get three estimates, and she also wants you to send her the package of information as she would like to do some research on her own."

"I was surprised that she didn't ask for all that before she left, but she didn't" Debbie shrugged "so then I thought perhaps she was going to stay out of it."

"You have met our sister Susan, haven't you?" Janice chuckled. "When has she ever stayed out of anything?"

"You're right. I will make another copy and you can mail it when you're in town." Debbie started opening the necessary files.

"I don't mind going to town, but I would like to be back when the real estate agent is here." Janice told her.

"Then you best be getting the errands done and hustle back."

"I will leave here by nine or so, after the school buses" Janice stated. " Do you want carrot or a banana muffin this morning?"

"Debbie always has carrot, and I'd love a banana muffin please." Henry said as he joined the ladies. "Are either one of you going to town today? I need to pick up some sandpaper and a couple other things at the hardware store."

Debbie nodded. "Janice is going, make her a list of what you need." Then she turned to Janice. "We have an account there, so you just charge it and they will send the bill at the end of the month."

Henry reminded Deb, "Don't forget I need your opinion on the bathroom renovation in cabin seven this morning. Perhaps we could go look at that after our muffins."

"You should come too, Janice, to see what Henry is doing." Debbie suggested.

Janice only had a light winter coat that was not adequate for this cold weather. She would definitely take a look in town to see if she could come up with something more appropriate.

Once inside the cabin, the first thing they noticed was that the bathtub, the sink, and the toilet were all sitting on a tarp in the middle of the living room floor.

"Really like what you have done with the place," Janice teased Henry. The walls had been stripped back to the bare two-by-fours.

Henry squatted down to straighten the tarp. "Part of this year's upgrade was to winterize three of the cottages. When they were all built some fifty years ago, they were for summer use only." Henry pointed. "This is where the fixtures used to be and the sink had more spider cracks in it once it was removed."

"And what exactly is it you want our opinion on?" Debbie asked him.

"I would like to suggest that we consider replacing the sink, and if we do, I think we could go with a much smaller vanity as well. Then the plumbing and the light would need to be moved over. I need your decision before the electrician arrives later today."

"I can see it would give the whole room a little more much needed space," Debbie told him. "What was the original cost estimate for the renovation, Henry can you remember?"

"Not off the top of my head," he said.

"Is this the only revision to the original estimate? How much extra will the sink and vanity cost?" Debbie asked.

"I would never go over the estimated expense without your approval, Boss, you know that. Probably add another hundred and fifty bucks for a sink and vanity I would expect." Henry told her.

"What do you think Janice?" Debbie asked her sister.

"Well, it makes sense. Now would be the time to replace it. Besides, you wouldn't want to put that old cracked one back in a nice new bathroom anyways." Janice said.

"Well, okay Henry, you got your answer, go ahead. And perhaps we could replace the light with something smaller as well so add another fifty bucks for a light then." Debbie told him.

Henry gave Janice a list of what he needed at the hardware store and sent them on their way so he could get back to work.

"So, how does it feel? You just made your first executive decision!" Debbie nudged Janice on their walk back to the lodge.

"Good, I think it is going to look real nice when it is done."

At noon, there was a table of four that came in for lunch. They were heading to the ski hill for the afternoon. Debbie was the waitress and the cook today and thankfully they ordered off the bar menu, which was much easier to prepare. They ordered two burgers, one fish and chips and one plate of chicken fingers, all with fries. They were done eating but still sitting when Janice got back from town. Henry came in and they all had fish and chips for lunch since the fryer was already on.

"Your new sink vanity and light and everything else on your list is in the van." Janice told Henry.

"Thank you so much, my dear. I hate having to go into town, it always wastes at least two hours of my time," he told them.

Just as they were finishing their lunch, the real estate agent, John Grant, came in the back kitchen door. "Guess I should have come in the front door, I used to work here as a teenager and old habits are hard to break."

"No problem, come on in." Debbie rose to greet him. "John, this is Henry our handyman and Janice my sister."

Once the introductions were made and Henry got back to work, Debbie went to the office for the information for John to look over while Janice cashed out the table from the dining room.

They all did the tour and John and Janice both took lots of pictures of the cabins, the chalets and the lodge. He seemed quite impressed. John said that he hadn't been here in ten years and things were certainly looking up from what he remembered. When he worked here as a kid there was no ski hill or golf course, so the resort relied mostly on fishing.

He took his pictures and the information Debbie had given him and headed back to the office. He wasn't gone ten minutes when the commercial agent came in. He was there to give them his estimate.

"Well ladies, I have been busy looking into things for you," he said. "With the ten acres, the house and the rest of the resort including the trailer park and the campground, I would list your property at three million. We could list higher if you're willing to wait for a buyer. I should also tell you that I currently have a client looking for a property just like this. Your Resort is bigger that he is looking for but trust me, it checks off all his boxes and then some. I spoke with him and mentioned that I may soon have a property, your property, for sale and he was quite interested to hear back from me."

"Good to know, but we haven't decided if we are selling or not. At this point in time we are just evaluating our options. No decisions have been made yet. There are three owners involved so it won't be a quick decision," Debbie explained.

"No pressure, I assure you. I'm just letting you know that if and when you do decide to list it, I hope you choose me to represent you and know that I have a potential buyer on the hook. I sell a lot of commercial properties and trust me, my reputation speaks for itself."

"Thanks for letting us know," Janice offered.

"I would advise if you are going to sell, that we get on it sooner rather than later. Trust me, anyone looking into Resort type properties will start looking as soon as spring hits. At least that has been my experience."

"Thank you so much. We will all discuss it and get back to you." Janice said as she got up to see who had just come into the dining room.

Two more customers stopped in for lunch on their way to the ski hill. Janice was the waitress and Debbie w the cook this time. They ordered one banquet burger and fries and one jumbo hot dog and fries. The bar menu was working out fine when Chef George wasn't around. Chef liked cooking fancy dishes, but Debbie was glad they chose easy things to cook from the bar menu.

As Janice joined Deb in the office she commented, "I thought that agent was a little pushy. I take it you didn't tell him that we're not selling, why is that?"

"He wouldn't have given the estimate otherwise and yes, I thought he was a little pushy too." Debbie agreed.

"I didn't like that he kept saying 'trust me.'" Janice said. "Like mom used to say, *'never trust anyone who says, trust me.'*" They both quoted mom in unison, then laughed at each other for having the same shared thought of Mom at the exact same time.

"I see you bought yourself a down-filled coat today." Debbie commented. "You won't regret buying that for sure, if you're seriously going to move back here."

"Yes, I have been giving it a lot of thought and I will need to go back to Ottawa and clean things up. I am sure I will miss working in the flower shop, but I will survive. Looking through the reservation book, I am thinking the week after next looks quiet. Perhaps I will go then. What do you think?"

"Sounds good to me." Debbie told her. "I will try to pack up Mom's room while you are gone. You do plan on staying in that room right? Susan said she was coming for the weekend, and I assume the whole family is coming with her."

"She never said. I guess we'll just have to wait and see. Or we could call and ask her. And yes, I would like to stay in Mom's old room. I feel close to her there."

"Will you be able to handle packing everything up in Ottawa? Will you need help?" Debbie asked her sister.

"I really don't have much to do there, just get rid of some furniture and pack my personal stuff."

"What about your job? Don't you have to give your employer notice?"

"I already have. She is okay with me leaving. She always knew I was only there temporarily until I got my own shop again, anyways."

"I told John that we would pick up his estimate on Friday so when Susan is here, we will have all three to compare."

"It's going to be an interesting weekend for sure." Janice said.

Chapter 21

This was going to be a typical off-season week. The bridge player ladies were in on Wednesday afternoon and they had a few customers mostly going skiing.

Janice asked, "Is there a liquor order being delivered today? If there is, I know how to check it off the invoice for you."

"No, sorry, no order today. Maybe next week if we have a busy enough weekend."

"I could start drinking more, if that would help." Janice said.

"Very funny, but you don't pay for your drinks, sis. When we drink, we are literally drinking up the profits." Debbie stood looking out onto the frozen Muskogie Lake, watching the trail groomer out on the ice.

"Look at the size of that machine! I never realized it was that large," Janice joined her at the window. "What are they doing?"

"Getting the racetrack ready, I suspect," Debbie said.

On Friday, they had one chalet and four cabins booked for the weekend. Two rooms upstairs were also booked for Saturday night.

Susan, Keith, and the kids arrived on Friday night about eight o'clock. Debbie suggested they stay in the house, as the cabin they used last time was booked. The house was at the other end of the property, so not quite as convenient as the cabins, but it would give them an idea of what it would be like to live there if they decided to move back up north permanently. Susan agreed. She thought it was a good idea.

Debbie told the kids about the ski competition. They wanted to go first thing in the morning and see if they could get in on the fun.

"According to the advertisement, there are races for different ages, with cash prizes for the winners." Debbie told the kids.

Susan suggested, "While the kids are at the ski hill, perhaps we sisters could get together tomorrow to discuss the real estate estimates."

Debbie reminded them, "Tomorrow we have the sled races. Perhaps we could do it on Sunday. I will give you the estimates now, if you would like time to read them over before the meeting. Let's meet Sunday afternoon at the house so we can have a private discussion without interruptions. Chef George and Gail are both working, so I am confident we could get away for a while without too much fuss."

Chapter 22

Brad was standing at the back door first thing Saturday morning when Chef arrived. Janice and Debbie were at the back kitchen table having coffee when they both came in.

"Morning, ladies," Brad said. "Looks like it is going to be a fine day for racing."

"Morning, Brad. You got time for a coffee?" Janice asked him as she got up to go get his coffee. "How do you take it?"

"Double cream," Debbie told her. Then she turned to Brad. "So how many racers do you have signed up for this morning?"

"So far, forty-six, but some more may join in when they get here. Hard to say, this being our first time doing it and all. I am also expecting we are going to have a lot of spectators as well."

"And what do they win for the races." Debbie asked.

"Cash prizes for first, second, and third place. The amount they win will all depend on how many enter. I honestly think they would pay to race just for the fun of it."

"Well, I will give you the keys for the boat house. Henry set up a couple big tables and some chairs for you. The washrooms are open, and the heat is turned on. You will see on the wall beside the light switch, just inside the door that there is an intercom. It is connected to the office up here so if you need anything you can try calling on that. If anyone is in the office, they will answer you."

Again Henry, Keith, and Josh helped direct traffic and it all went off without any problems. The machines were all unloaded, the vehicles and their trailers were all parked and the riders were all revved up and ready to race. Some racers came for breakfast, but most just came in for coffee. Once the races started, the dining room emptied out again. Gail and Chef worked on getting the buffet set up for brunch.

Debbie noticed the spectators were on lawn chairs down the side of the racetrack. She chuckled when she heard her mom's voice inside her head saying, *"only in Canada would you find people sitting in lawn chairs in a snowbank."*

Brad called up on the intercom and Debbie heard him, so she answered.

"Hello Brad, how's things going down there?"

"Oh, fine. I just wanted to tell you that we will not be breaking for brunch until about twelve thirty if that is okay."

"Yes, that would be fine," she answered.

"See you at twelve thirty then. Over and out"

Debbie had to smile at Brad's over and out. It was an intercom, not a CB radio. She went out to the dining room to see how the buffet was shaping up. She told Chef and Gail that Brad had just called and they should expect about ninety people for brunch at twelve thirty.

She looked over the buffet. In the steam table she saw breakfast items like the bacon, sausage and ham. There was an empty insert which Gail told her was for quiche, pancakes and waffles in the next insert and western omelets in the last pan.

There were also lunch items like salads, including Greek, Caesar, and tossed salad. There was a big basked of buns and crusty rolls. Chef had also done trays of fresh fruit. There was also a tray of fruit cocktails made up. And of course, the apple and orange juices by the jug. Henry and Keith came in the back door and knocked the snow from their boots. "Thought we should come up and set up some tables and chairs in the banquet room in case you need them." Henry told her.

"Oh Henry, you are truly the best. I was about to ask for volunteers to help me set them up," Debbie said.

"How many will we need?" Keith asked.

"Enough to seat thirty should cover it, I would think," Debbie told them. "Thanks guys. I really appreciate your help."

Chef got Debbie's attention. "I could use an extra pair of hands here for ten minutes, please."

Debbie grabbed an apron off the hook, tied it around her back, went to the sink, and washed her hands. "What do you need me to do, Chef?" she asked.

"I need you to transfer these quiches into that insert while I get the next tray ready for the oven," he told her. Debbie watched as he poured the egg mixture into the pre-formed pastry shells.

Debbie grabbed the egg lifter and started filling up the deep insert that would go out to the steam table. When she had a layer covering the bottom of the insert, she put a shallow insert in on top for another layer of the little quiches.

"We will stack the rest in another insert and leave them in the warming oven. Once the guests start coming in, they will go quite quickly." Chef said.

"So there is one insert with thirty-two in it and the rest are here to go into the warming oven." Debbie offered.

Gail came into the kitchen and grabbed the insert just as customers were starting to come inside.

"Anything else I can do at the moment, Chef?" Debbie asked him.

"You could run back into the cold room and grab me the waffle mix. We will probably need to make more waffles. They are usually quite popular."

When she got back, Chef was just pulling the other batch of quiche out of the oven.

Debbie grabbed the egg lifter and started stacking them into the insert Chef had just pulled back out of the warming oven.

When she finished, Chef put his hand on her shoulder. "Thank you, my dear. I do so appreciate your extra pair of hands sometimes. Now you better get that apron off and go check on your guests."

"No problem Chef, glad to help," she told him as she hung up her apron. Debbie walked out into the dining room and saw that everything was going fine. Gail had things well under control. Debbie went to the cold room and returned with two more jugs of orange juice. Gail gave her a thankful smile.

Within a half an hour, all the guests had been through the line at least once and were happily eating their meals. *Wow,* Debbie thought, *it sure was a full house in here today.*

Brad came up to Debbie and suggested she might want to make an announcement on how she wanted them all to pay as they would probably all leave at the same time..

Debbie told him. "Brunch is fifteen dollars each. With tax it will be seventeen dollars, so if they are paying cash, they can give it to Gail and if they need the debit machine, they will need to go into the office to pay there."

Brad made the announcement and went back to finish his brunch. Susan went to the office to run the debit machine, and Debbie helped the waitress pick up empty plates. She asked a few of the guests how was everything and they all said it was good. A few people went back for seconds. By one thirty, the dining room was empty, and the staff sat down to eat.

Debbie told Chef, "These quiches taste as good as they look, Chef, they are definitely a hit. Everyone liked them. We are really getting good at these buffets don't you think, guys? Buying that steam table has sure proven to be a good investment." Debbie addressed the staff in general.

"Yes, it is working out very well," Gail told her. "And I like how people can go down both sides at the same time. We could use a smaller table at the starting end because all it really needs to hold is the silverware tray and a couple stacks of plates."

"And that would free up more room at the end of the buffet as well. It seems a little tight at the end. Do we have any smaller tables downstairs anywhere, Henry?" Debbie asked him.

"I think there are, but I'll have to look," he said. "But first, I will go take the chairs and tables down in the banquet room. Will they need anything for their awards ceremony, do you know?"

"They didn't ask for anything, but I would suggest leaving them at least one table since it is already there." Debbie told him.

About four o'clock, Debbie and Susan got all bundled up and headed down to the boathouse. Susan took her camera to get some pictures of the races. She got some very good shots of the riders flying over the finish line, some from behind them and some pictures in front of the finish line as well. Debbie saw that there was a photographer there from the local Clifford newspaper. She went over and introduced herself. She asked Susan to get some pictures of the crowd of spectators sitting in their lawn chairs in the snowbanks surrounding the racetrack. Debbie stopped at the boat house to see how things were going there. She did a quick check on the bathrooms and everything seemed fine although it would need a good scrubbing tomorrow.

They went back to the lodge and with fresh coffees sat warming up in front of the fireplace. They were still sitting there a half hour later when Brad came in. He joined them beside the fireplace for a moment. "The races just finished, and the riders are loading their machines onto their trailers."

"So how did it all go? Was it as good as you thought it would be?" Debbie asked him.

"Yes, I think so. Everyone had fun. I was just wondering what you wanted to do about dinner if anyone is interested. Are there any announcements you want me to make?" Brad asked her.

"Do you think anyone will come in for dinner? You were late coming in for lunch and it seems a little early to be thinking about dinner. Has anyone asked about it?"

"I don't know. I was kind of busy, so I didn't get to talk to too many people really."

"Let me just go quickly and speak with Chef and I will get right back to you." Debbie found Chef in the cold room. "Chef, the races have just finished, and Brad was asking if we are going to offer a buffet or just do al a carte for dinner if anyone is interested."

"Yes, I have a pasta buffet ready to go. I planned for about fifty people."

"Oh, that is fantastic. I am sorry I have been so busy today I haven't even had time to speak to you about this. What will the cost of the buffet be?"

"I would think sixteen dollars per plate should be about right." Chef told her. "I guess I should start putting it out now then if the races are over."

"Is everything ready to go out now?"

"Of course it is. I know what I am doing," he said a little sarcastically.

"Oh please, I have absolutely no doubt that you do. I just meant that this is earlier than I expected them to be done racing and ready to eat again. They just ate a big brunch four hours ago."

"Yeah and I think that might deter some of them from wanting dinner, but it is all ready to go out. How be we say dinner buffet will be served at five o'clock and if anyone is wanting to stay, perhaps they will enjoy sitting in the warmth of the bar while they wait."

"And we have some skiers that may also come for dinner. Henry is still bringing guests back from the hill. I will go ask Brad to make the announcement." When Debbie located Brad, he was in the banquet room meeting with some of the racers. When he saw her he came over to her.

"So, what is the verdict?" Brad asked her.

"Pasta buffet will be served at five o'clock. Sixteen dollars per plate if anyone is hungry."

"I am sorry we were so late for brunch, but it wasn't logical to stop the races at noon. I am not sure if anyone is hungry yet, but I will gladly make the announcement for you. And Debbie, thanks again for hosting us today."

"My pleasure, Brad. My pager is vibrating. I will catch up with you later." Debbie told him, and then headed to the office.

"What's going on in here?" she asked Janice and Gail as she entered the office.

"We were just tallying up the lunch bills and Gail did a head count while everyone was eating and when the bills are all totaled, we are two short. Two people didn't pay for their lunch."

"Did Brad and his wife Tina pay for their lunch?" Debbie asked Gail.

"Tina was not here today and yes, Brad paid for his lunch. We are still two short."

"Are you sure?"

"Yes, we counted a third time." Janice told her.

"Okay, I will ask Brad to mention it to his racers." Debbie told her. "Gail, Chef is starting to put out the dinner buffet. He says he will be ready for five o'clock. You may want to finish up here and go see if he needs any help."

Debbie went back into the banquet room and caught Brad's attention. He came over and stood at the back door with her.

"What's up? Is there a problem?" he asked her.

"Just a small one. We have just tallied up the bills from lunch and according to our head count we are short on payment for two meals." Debbie said with a shrug. "I was wondering if you could make an announcement and just tell them that two people forgot to pay for their lunch. Hopefully someone will remember and come and pay for it."

"Well if they don't, I guess the club will have to cover it." Brad placed a reassuring hand on her shoulder.

"Whatever you think is fair. I just think you should make the announcement first, and we'll see what happens okay?"

"We are just about to start, why don't you stick around for a few minutes?"

"Sure, okay, I can do that."

Brad walked up to the front of the room and called for everyone's attention.

"First I would like to say a big thank you to all the riders for coming out to play today. I think we all had fun. Didn't we? And now we need to take care of some business quickly before we award the winners their prize money." He held up the prized envelopes for the riders to see. "I would like to say a big thank you to Debbie and her staff, and the Cedar Grove Resort for hosting the races today. Can I get a round of applause?" He hesitated until the applause died down. "And Debbie has just informed me that when we were in here earlier for brunch there was two people who forgot to pay for their lunches. I am hoping that whomever it was, will remember and get their business taken care of before they leave here today. Also, Chef George has put together a pasta buffet for sixteen dollars per person, and will be starting to serve at five o'clock. I heard a rumor that there is going to be lasagna, so I know I am in." Brad rubbed his tummy.

A rider from the group stood up and announced "Sorry guys. I think I was the one that didn't pay for lunch. My wife thought I paid, and I thought she paid. I do apologize. So sorry Debbie. I will come out to the office in a minute and take care of it."

Debbie nodded to him and left the room. As she left, she heard Brad saying, "Mystery solved. Bob, your age is starting to show, old buddy, when you forget to pay for the lunch you just ate." She could hear the room laughing at poor old Bob.

The dinner buffet was served to thirty-six people who all seemed to enjoy it. Half of them moved from the dining room into the lounge. They had a band in that night, and everyone was having a good time.

It was after two a.m. before Ted got all the rowdies out the door.

"That was a good night. I made almost a hundred bucks in tips." Ted told Debbie, who was helping him clean off the tables and wash the glasses.

"I must remember to have Nancy and Robert over for drinks one night this week," Deb said. "I also wanted to comment on your new cocktail. It seems quite popular. Ted, you are doing a good job, and I just want you to know that your hard work is not going unnoticed."

"Ah geez, Boss, you're going to give me a big head. Thanks so much. Oh, and before I forget, would you ask Henry to take a look at the pulley in the dumbwaiter? When I tried to bring the beer up earlier, it seemed to be slipping or something."

The dumbwaiter was so handy for bringing up beer or taking down empties to the basement. When they did the big addition onto the lodge the bar is on the opposite end of the building from the stairs going down to the basement, so they had installed the dumbwaiter for convenience. It was basically a platform held up by a rope system that worked from a pulley that was located up in the attic. They were having problems with the pulley sticking. Last time Henry looked at the pulley he said he thought they needed a bigger sized pulley and if they kept having trouble, he would replace it.

"Okay, I will mention it to him on Monday. Leave me a note with the night's cash drawer so that I don't forget."

"I have already started the next liquor order. We had a run on wine tonight so we will need to get restocked, and also Bailey's Irish Cream because of the new drink."

"Thanks Ted. Good night." Deb went to lock up the front while Ted finished locking up the bar.

Chapter 23

Sunday morning there were guests already on the doorstep, waiting to come in for breakfast. Gail opened the door, let them in, and gave them coffee. Chef George wouldn't start cooking breakfasts until seven thirty, but everyone was happy to be in out of the cold.

The whole day seemed to stay busy, which was how Debbie liked it. Time always passed quickly when they were busy. Henry was shuttling guests to and from the ski hill all day long.

Gail stuck her head in the office to tell Debbie that Tony was there. In her memory, she couldn't remember his ever stopping in unless he was doing the liquor delivery. She couldn't help but smile as she walked out to say hello.

"Nice to see you Tony, you must be lost." Debbie told him.

"I might try skiing. Robert said he would give me some lessons so I thought I might come check that out."

"Oh sure. You might even run into my sisters, Susan and Janice, at the ski hill, but I don't think Robert will have time to give you lessons today. They are having some races over there today so he's probably a little busy."

"Oh, I didn't realize that. I couldn't have picked a worse day to come then." Tony said.

"I think you should still go over and see what's going on. I see Henry is getting ready to take another couple over to the ski hill right now. If you want to, you can leave your truck here and catch a ride in the van with him. When you come back, you should plan on having dinner with us."

"Sure, that sounds great. I think I will. See you later then."

Just before lunch, Henry brought Janice, Susan, and Keith back to the lodge. Janice got a big bottle of wine and four glasses from the bar, Debbie went into the office to get her notes, and they all walked together up to the house. As they walked up, Janice commented on how beautiful the whole resort was covered in a blanket of white snow, and how beautiful it was when the sun danced on the crystals in the snow.

Once they all got settled around the kitchen table, Debbie asked Janice, "Did you see Tony at the ski hill this morning?"

"I sure did. What a nice surprise."

"He has been coming around doing deliveries for at least five years and this is the first time I have ever seen him here on his day off. I think perhaps he is smitten with our sister." Debbie winked at Susan. Janice was smiling from ear to ear.

"Ok let's get down to the task at hand, shall we?" Susan asked, trying to get them focused on their purpose.

Keith asked the girls, "Is it okay for me to be here, or would you rather I wasn't?"

"No that's fine," Debbie told him "You are as much a part of this as we are."

"Okay then, let's get down to it. Debbie, can you explain the three estimates to us all?" Susan asked.

"Certainly. The first estimate suggests we could list for two and a half million. Then there's, the commercial agent who thinks we could get an even three million and may already have a buyer. And last but not least, John from the local Grant Agency in town says that we should get two point six million, so they are all in the same ball park."

"That sounds good," Keith said.

"So if we average the three that would be two point seven million then, right?" Janice asked.

"Looks right," Susan said. "I did some research and similar properties in better locations are a bit higher, but I think two point seven is an agreeable number for our purposes. So, do we all agree on that number then?"

"Yes, I guess so." Janice said.

"I agree." Debbie said.

"Yes, me too." Keith said.

Susan pointed out, "It is unanimous then! Two point seven is the magic number. So that would make each of our shares worth nine hundred grand each. That makes it all very simple."

"Let's drink to that!" Janice said as she opened the wine.

"So that was the easy part. Now we all need to know how we all feel about what we are going to do." Debbie said. "First off, is either one of you thinking you want to sell your share?"

"Keith and I have been discussing it between us, and also with the kids over these past couple of weeks. Keith hates his job. It is making him sick from all the stress. You know how much the kids love the summers up here. And I can sell real estate anywhere so, we have decided we would like to move back up here and give this a try." Susan told them. "The only problem is that Keith and the kids are in the middle of their school year for another four months, so we wouldn't be able to move permanently until then."

"Mom would be so proud of us right now," Janice said. "I have decided I am also going to move home and give it a go as well. I still have to make one final trip back to Ottawa to finalize things there, and then I am moving back also."

"Can the resort sustain five more people?" Keith asked.

"No, it can't, not really." Debbie said. "Right now, it has been sustaining two people. Mom, as the owner, did not take a salary but I have a small salary for being the manager. Honestly, I think four more people could be a real strain. It may put us in the red for quite some time, but we could figure it out."

"I plan on getting a part time job at the local flower shop in town, so that could help." Janice offered.

"And like I said, I can sell real estate anywhere." Susan pointed out. "And Keith could look for other work in the area. He is quite a handy fellow for a city boy."

"Gee, thanks," he told Susan.

"So, let me get this straight, you all want to move back home but are all going to get jobs outside the resort. Have I got that right?" Debbie asked.

"Don't you think it could work?" Susan asked. "I will need to get associated with a local real estate company, but I work mostly from home. There may be times when I have to go show properties or even do open houses but when I am not doing that, I could help out at the resort as needed. Hopefully Keith will get a teaching job in one of towns close by."

"Only time can tell if it will work." Debbie said. "And if you all have outside jobs, how will you want to be paid for the time you help out here? Should we set an hourly wage or a maybe a small salary? Who is going to keep track of how many hours each of you works? I work twenty-four/seven and I only take a small salary. Will you all expect the same?"

"All I am looking for is basically a place to sleep and eat my meals," Janice said.

"But from a business perspective you are only one person, I am four people," Susan pointed out.

"Yeah, I never thought of it that way," Janice told her.

"Are there any other things we need to be concerned with?" Keith asked.

"One comes to mind," Debbie said. "Another important question that needs to be answered, who is the manager going to be?"

Janice said "I think Debbie should stay as the manager and we will both have to respect that. What do you think Susan? Can you live with that?"

"I don't see why not, you're doing a fine job right now and I know that every business needs one definite leader. I think we should discuss any major issues like say, renovations or major purchases, that kind of thing, but as for the day-to-day operations, Keith and I are both quite happy to let Debbie stay at the helm."

"And what happens in the event that you are unhappy or disagree with my decisions?" Debbie asked. "What then?"

"We will just have to cross that bridge when we come to it," Susan said. "We have three votes, so the majority vote will always rule."

"I just hope that doesn't divide us, you know, two against one. I might feel like you're both ganging up on me like you used to do when we were kids." Debbie pointed out.

"Well, we are all fully grown, intelligent adults now, so hopefully we are better equipped to handle any potential disagreements." Susan told them.

"So, it's settled then, we are all moving back home. I am sure we can make this work if we all put our minds to it. I have owned my own flower shop and Susan has her real estate business so we both understand basic business issues. I think we can do this. That's just my humble opinion." Janice exclaimed.

"Deb, do you have any other concerns? If you do, now would be the time to express them," Keith said.

"I will need a little time to think this all out in my head. I think it is great that you're all taking an interest now and for you it is all new and exciting. I have been down here in the trenches for a long time and perhaps it has made me a bit jaded. I have seen resorts go under from too much overhead, like trying to support more family than it can withstand." Debbie continued, "Take this past year, for example. We had a very good summer, and because of that, we decided to reinvest the profits into renovations and winterizing three of our biggest cabins. And so far, this has been a better-than-average winter but with any tourist driven business, or any business that depends on Mother Nature, we are always on the edge of surviving or going under. It is just the nature of the beast."

"But we are a team! We have our superpower on our side," Janice pointed out.

"That's all well and good, but sometimes things are out of our control," Debbie said. "Like the weather for one and the tourism industry is closely linked to the local economy, things like that. Let's just leave it here for now and give me some time to mull all this over in my head. I look forward to making this work but work it will be, hard work, and we will have to be very thrifty."

"You do the heavy lifting and we will be the support holding you up," Susan offered.

"The wind beneath your wings," Janice added.

"And when we get all of the details worked out, I think we should get the lawyer to draw up some official agreement between the three co-owners." Debbie asked. "Agreed?"

"Agreed," they all said.

"So, Janice will stay in Mom's old room and Keith, the kids, and I will stay here in this house. All any of us are asking for is room and board. Debbie, you will continue to get a salary for being the manager and the rest of us will work just for the perks. We will be able to use the business vehicles and such. Is that what we are all agreeing to here?" Susan asked.

"Yes, I believe so. I know I am in agreement." Janice said.

"So, this house belongs to the resort but I would like to know if it is okay for us to paint it, or renovate it or whatever. If we are going to live here permanently, we want to make it comfortable for us." Susan wanted to know.

"This entire house was just painted last year. What kind of renovations are you thinking about?" Debbie asked.

"I may want to put on a small addition to somehow make a home office." Susan said.

"Is there any reason you couldn't use Mom's desk in the office at the lodge? That way you could be helping out and still have an office. We already have fax machines, internet and what not hooked up there already. If you need a separate phone line, we could add that as well and there is room there if you needed your own filing cabinet." Debbie suggested.

"I think that is a great idea," Janice said. "That way if Susan is in the office, she can basically be doing two jobs at once.

"Yeah, I guess that could work. Let me take a good look at the office and see what I can do with it." Susan nodded in agreement.

"So, if that is all, meeting adjourned. Who is pouring the wine?" Debbie asked.

Janice refilled everyone's glass and offered a toast. "As Mom would say, "here's to looking up your new address.' Cheers."

The dining room was busy for dinner and the skiers were all tired and hungry. Brad and his wife Tina also came in for dinner.

"Hello, you two. How's things?" Debbie asked them.

"Fine. We are tired and Tina didn't feel like cooking, so we decided to let you cook dinner." Brad told her.

"Well I can cook, but Chef does it so much better than I ever could. Have you tried his maple glazed chicken? It is quite good, and he does an excellent job on charbroiled steak if that is more to your liking."

"There are just too many good things on the menu. Last time I had the pork tenderloin in apple butter, and it was amazing," Tina offered.

Janice was walking through the dining room, so Debbie did the introductions. "Brad I know you have met Janice, but I don't think Tina has."

"Yes, we met the day of the poker run. And I also met your other sister as well," she told them.

"Yes, Susan is here this weekend as well, but they are staying up at the house. Her kids were at the ski hill for the races today. Josh won one of the races in his age category. He is strutting around like he is the king of the mountain," Debbie told them.

"We were there today as well, just as spectators though," Brad said. "They sure had a big crowd. I would say there was over a hundred spectators. Nice to see them so busy. Robert and Nancy are doing a great job over at the hill."

"Yes, and I even got some overnight guests because of it. I just love those win/win situations, don't you?" Debbie asked.

Brad looked at Janice and asked "how are you enjoying being home in the winter?"

"Better, now that I have a nice down-filled parka," she told them.

Debbie noticed Gail standing off to the side holding menus. "Well, we are holding Gail up, I think she is wanting to take your drink orders. You two enjoy your dinner."

The races were all over at the ski hill and Henry had just dropped off six more hungry guests. He didn't even come into the lodge, just dropped them off and headed back to the ski hill to pick up some more guests. Debbie was standing with her back to the door, talking to Janice who all of a sudden got a big grin on her face. Debbie had to turn to see who she was looking at and there in the doorway, looking lost, was Tony.

"Well, what are you waiting for, sis?" Debbie asked. "Why don't you bring him over to the back kitchen table?" Debbie couldn't help thinking it would be nice if Janice and Tony became a couple. After her nasty break up with her ex-husband, Janice had been a little gun shy about getting into another relationship. But that was well over a year ago, so maybe it was time. Deb was happy for her sister. Susan, on the other hand, didn't look as impressed.

Debbie went to the office to answer the phone. She was only gone a minute, and when she came back into the kitchen Janice was putting on an apron.

Debbie asked her, "What are you doing?"

"Looks like Chef could use some help."

"Thanks anyway, but we've got it covered. Why don't you and Tony go sit in the bar and have a drink. When the dinner rush is over, we will have a family dinner, okay?"

"Are you sure? I don't mind helping."

"I know, but we are fine. So, go! Have some fun. Tony didn't come all this way to sit and watch you work."

Susan had overheard the conversation and when Janice and Tony left, she asked Debbie, "Who is this guy and where did he come from? And how did he ever meet our sister?"

"Tony is the guy who delivers our liquor orders and they met here while he was unloading the truck. Now you know as much about him as I do. I think it's kind of cute. She sure seems taken with him."

"You think? I didn't realize she was even looking for a boyfriend," Susan said sarcastically.

"I don't think that she was, but then this handsome rugged guy just walked into her world and that was that."

"He certainly isn't hard to look at. I just hope she doesn't get hurt."

"Janice is very level-headed. I think she will be cautious. I am just enjoying seeing her happy again. It wasn't that long ago she was going through hell with that nasty divorce. It's about time she had a little joy in her life, don't you think?"

"Yes, I agree with you there. I just don't want to see her getting hurt again," Susan said.

After the dinner rush was over Debbie invited them all to join her for dinner.

Gail served them in the dining room. The staff seemed to enjoy when the boss actually let them serve her dinner, and now they had three bosses to impress. It gave all the staff a chance to show off their skills.

When all the paying guests had left, Debbie invited Chef, Gail and Ted to join them for a drink. Ted made the three sisters his new drink. He wanted them to try it. He called it the Cedar Grove toddy. It came in a clear glass coffee mug rimmed with sugar, and consisted of coffee, Baileys, Kahlua, and some liquid cedar smoke topped with whipped cream and a chocolate swirl.

"While we are all here together, I have an announcement to make," Debbie told them. "As you may or may not know, we have read Mom's will and the resort now has three new owners. Susan, Janice, and myself. We are all now equal partners."

"I don't think I can handle three bosses. One is more than enough." Chef George admitted. Everyone chuckled at his comment.

"Let me finish. I will still be the manager, so you only have one boss. Sorry, but you're still stuck with me."

"Think of us as silent partners, or maybe not so silent in the case of my sister," Janice said with a grin. They all laughed when Susan made a shocked face.

"Just so you all know, Janice is moving into Mom's old room, effective immediately, and Susan, Keith, and the kids will be moving into the house as soon as the school year is out." Debbie informed them. "You may also want to know that they will all learn every job at the resort, just like we all did, so that they can step in and help when and wherever needed. I am counting on you three to show them things they would need to know to be able to step in to help you." Debbie asked looking at Gail, Chef and Ted. "Any questions?"

Gail said, "Your mom would be so proud. She told me many times that was her only wish, that all her girls work the resort together."

"Yes. She had told me the same thing" Chef George added.

"Even I knew that. And I am just the delivery guy," Tony added. Everyone laughed at that.

"Okay, I guess that's everything then." Debbie said. "I knew you all had questions and until now I didn't have any answers to give you. I am hopeful for the future of Cedar Grove and look forward to working with the whole bunch of you. Let's stay open and honest with each other and if any issues come up, we will deal with them straight away, together as a group. Agreed?"

"Agreed," they all said in unison.

"I'll toast to that," Ted said, and they all stood up and clinked glasses. "So, what do you think of my new drink?" he asked Debbie.

"I like it. It is creamy with a kind of woodsy taste all at the same time. I can't identify the taste, kind of like cinnamon or something." Debbie told him.

"It is a secret ingredient. I could tell you, but then I would have to kill you," Ted told her with a chuckle.

"Okay, then. I guess that will have to just stay your little secret," Debbie said.

"But didn't you just tell us that we all had to learn how to make the drinks in case we needed to step in to help?" Susan pointed out.

"Well, alrighty then" Ted threw his hands up in the air. "It is impossible to keep a secret around here anyways,"

Susan and Keith got the kids all packed up and headed back to the city. Tony left shortly after they did.

Everything was cleaned up, and the staff all said goodnight. This was Debbie's favourite time of the day. Her quiet time. She invited Janice to join her for a coffee and Bailey's in the bar.

"So, 'fess up, girl," said Debbie. "Tell me all the details. You seem to really like Tony, if I am reading you right."

"Oh Deb, he is really something, isn't he? I definitely have a crush on him. I was so surprised today when he showed up at the ski hill. And I am going to see him again next Sunday—that is, if I am back by then, oh who am I kidding, I'll be back. I guess I will have to buy some ski pants and maybe a warmer pair of boots."

"Perhaps by then you will be able to wipe that silly grin off your face." Debbie was enjoying teasing her sister. It was so nice to see Janice happy again.

Chapter 24

Janice sat in her little apartment in Ottawa. She was really doing this. She was uprooting her life, such as it was, and moving back home. She could not help but feel a little sad for her old failed life. She had loved Fred and had trusted that he loved her, but was proven wrong, so very wrong. She was absolutely heartbroken when she discovered what a rat he really was. How can you love someone so much that you can't see their faults?

Because they had mortgaged their house to buy the flower shop, she ended up selling both of them to be totally finished with Fred. If she never saw that man again, she would be better off. The breakup had truly broken her, both mentally and emotionally. Physically, she went into a deep depression and really struggled for the next six months. It was just now that she was getting back on her feet. Moving back home would be a fresh start, a whole new beginning. She really had nothing to lose. She did have a few friends here that she would miss, but other than that, she decided to go ahead full steam.

Back at the resort, Debbie spent the next few days getting some book work caught up. She wrote letters to the three real estate agents stating that they had decided not to sell at this time but if and when they did decide to sell, she would certainly keep them in mind.

It was eerily quiet at the resort. Since they had no reservations, the staff had the day off and she was the only soul in the whole place, except for Henry. He was always in and out, always in for meals. It was comforting to Debbie to know that he was around. Debbie even cooked him spaghetti for dinner on Tuesday night because she knew it was his favourite.

It was Wednesday before Debbie got up the courage to face her mom's old room. She had to decide what to keep, what to throw away and what could be donated to charity. Gail was watching the dining room and taking care of the bridge club, which meant Debbie could do this hopefully uninterrupted.

Since Janice was bringing her own bed, Henry had already moved mom's old bed down to the basement for storage. The room looked as empty as it felt. She started the three piles and opened the closet. Since Deb and her mom were the same size, she would keep all the sweaters and any tops that would fit her. The keep pile grew quickly. Once she had all the clothes removed from the closet, she started pulling down boxes full of Mom's treasures. Perhaps she would find some more hidden secrets in all those boxes, she was about to find out.

There was a beautiful wooden carved box that Susan's kids had given her for Christmas one year. Perhaps Susan or Katie would like to have it back. Inside there was some jewellery pieces and some old newspaper clippings back from when her parents had first bought the resort. Debbie moved the box into her room. She was thinking that perhaps she would frame the clippings to hang in the dining room.

The next box was a plain box full of things from when they were kids. Mom kept the craziest things. There were two old envelopes browned with age but still clearly marked with Susan and Janice's names on them. Inside were baby bracelets, locks of hair, and even baby teeth. Who knew that Mom was that sentimental? Why wasn't there an envelope with her name on it, she wondered? Oh well, she would make sure her sisters got their treasures from the box. That box got moved into her room as well, but she left it out on her coffee table. Debbie quickly realized that a lot of boxes were going to be moved from Mom's closet into her closet, which was already full. When she was done with Mom's room, now Janice's room, she would have to do some downsizing in her own room.

Inside another cardboard box was more treasures including a small trinket box, one that Debbie had not seen in quite a while? It had four little gold-plated feet and a matching clasp. Deb had once, long ago, told her mom how much she liked this particular box. It had flowers painted on the lid, and Deb remembered how beautiful she thought it was as a little girl. Mom had told her that someday she could have it. *Well I guess someday had come* Debbie thought to herself.

When she opened the box there was a folded note laying across the top of the box. ***This box belongs to Debbie*** was written on the note in Mom's handwriting. Tears started rolling down her cheeks. She never realized her mother had taken her seriously when she had admired it years earlier. It was just like her mom to remember something like that little detail. Opening the note she saw that it was dated over two years ago. Debbie sat down on her couch and read it.

> *Deborah,*
>
> *If you are reading this, I am probably gone. Thank you for being my business partner, my caregiver, my confidant, my baby girl, and my best friend.*
>
> *I have kept this box especially for you. You were always fascinated with it as a little girl. My mother passed it on to me and now I pass it on to you. I bet you had forgotten all about it but I didn't. Please accept it now, with all my love.*
>
> *I hope in years to come when you think of me you will have nothing but happy memories. I will now be watching over you from heaven. Be good to your sisters, and always stay humble and kind.*
>
> *Yours truly,*
>
> *Mom*

Debbie just sat there and let the tears flow. She was so sad and missing her mom, she felt like her heart was literally breaking in two. Life was surely going to go on for her, but not the way she had it planned. She thought she would have another twenty or thirty years with her mom. How could she be gone? Gone so suddenly. Just like that. One thing for sure, life wasn't fair. She refolded the note and returned it to the pretty box. This box was going into her room, right on top of her dresser, not hidden away in the closet anymore. Every time she would look at it, she would remember her mother's love. Beneath the note was a small envelope browned with age just like the ones she found marked for Susan and Janice containing Debbie's baby bracelet from when she was born and a lock of hair from her first haircut. There were a few small broaches and an old report card from grade six. Debbie had gotten straight A's that year. Mom must have kept it to remember the only year Debbie got straight A's.

Well at this rate she was never going to get this job done. Reading moms note made her think about the Penfold letters still safely tucked in her sock drawer. She was still wrestling with the decision of what to do with them. Should she show the letters to the other girls? Yes, she thought they had as much right to read them as she did, if they wanted to. Maybe she should read them first to make sure there was nothing bad in them. Why had Mom kept these particular letters bundled and hidden all these years? Common sense told her that there must be something in them to warrant the secrecy. Debbie always thought they had an open relationship and she and her mom told each other everything. But mom had never ever, not even once mentioned any letters or anyone named Jefferson Penfold.

Once Debbie finished cleaning out the closet, she moved onto the dresser. By the time she was all finished, she had two big bags of clothes she was keeping, one bag of personal things for the landfill and three bags for charity. Kind of sad to see what was left from someone's life. Just some clothes, a few personal items and a whole lot of memories.

As long as Debbie drew breath, her mom's memory would always be alive. One of Mom's favourite sayings was *'May your memories always keep you warm.'* Debbie didn't truly appreciate what that meant until now.

Thursday there was no reservations, so Debbie offered Gail and Chef the extra day off, which they both gladly agreed to take. This meant she was alone, or as alone as she could be. Henry was onsite somewhere, probably down in one of the cabins. She was feeling restless and decided to put her coat and boots on and go see what he was up to.

She found him splattered with drywall mud. The bathroom was finished, and he was right, the smaller sink looked nice and freed up extra space in the room. He pointed out that the new light it had a dimmer switch in case people wanted to use it as a nightlight.

"Both Chef and Gail are off today, so I am making lunch. How does tomato soup and a grilled cheese sandwich sound?"

"Fine by me, but I want to finish mudding the drywall in this room before I clean up for lunch. I'll only be another half hour, it that okay with you?"

"Sounds good, I'll see you back at the lodge in a half an hour then."

While they were eating lunch Henry asked, "So have you girls decided what you're planning to do with the resort? If you don't mind me asking?"

"No not at all. According to Mom's will, we are all now equal owners. Both of the girls are going to move back home and help me run things. Janice is hoping to get some work with the flower shop in town, and Janice will probably join John Grant at his real estate agency, either that or she will start her own agency. Who knows? Keith will try to get teaching in a school in one of the neighbouring towns. There is going to be some changes, but nothing too drastic."

"Are you still the boss, or do I have three bosses now?"

"You're still stuck with me. They have both agreed to that. I will consult them on any major decisions like any major purchases or major renovations, but they agreed to let me manage the day-to-day operations."

"Well, I think that was a wise decision for them to make. You do a good job, and it shows everywhere you look."

"Thanks Henry. Susan and Keith won't be making the move until the kids and Keith finish the school year. Then life is going to get interesting. I should warn you that Keith likes to stay busy, and he may offer to help you occasionally."

"Oh, I wouldn't mind that at all. I really like Keith, and he is a good helper. Josh is very much like his dad, but with a shorter attention span."

Just then a small U-Haul truck backed up to the back door. It was Janice. "Honey, I'm home," she called as she came through the back door.

"Welcome home, sis. I suppose you'll need help unloading that truck. How did things go in Ottawa?" Debbie asked.

"Better than I thought they would. My boss told me she was sad that I was leaving, but wished me the best of luck. She even wrote me a nice referral letter in case I need it for my next job. Remind me and I will show it to you later. I gave notice on my apartment which is still mine till the end of next month. I sent most of my furniture to an auction house and the rest of my life is in the back of that truck." Janice asked, "Did you get around to cleaning up Mom's stuff yet?"

"Yes, I did it yesterday. It is all cleaned out and I even did some house cleaning. The room is all yours, sis. We'd better go help Henry. He is already unloading." Debbie took the first armful of boxes upstairs and deposited them onto the couch in Janice's living room. Once everything from the truck was delivered upstairs, Janice had to take the truck back to town. She had rented the truck there on Monday and had to return it back and pick up her car.

When she got back, Debbie had dinner ready. Janice brought her a bouquet of daises and carnations, both her favourite flowers. They shared a bottle of wine, and Janice told Debbie all the details of her trip.

"Welcome home to the Cedar Grove Resort." Debbie raised a glass to her sister. "I hope you never regret making this decision."

"Thanks, I really didn't leave much behind, so the move really doesn't seem to be a big deal. I thought I might miss the hustle and bustle of the city, but after spending a few days there, I would have to admit I actually was missing the quiet and beauty of home all the time I was gone. I am just glad it is done and now I am home to stay."

Although Debbie was missing her mom, she also had to admit to herself that she was glad Janice was here. This place was very big and lonesome when she was there all by herself.

Chapter 25

Saturday proved to be a busy day. The hockey team sponsored by the resort was hosting an open-air hockey tournament on the lake in front of the lodge. Debbie had agreed to provide the required two rinks, and with a lot of help from Henry and the volunteer fire department, they got them made. The fire department came and flooded the ice three days in a row and with the weather being so cold, it froze perfectly.

On Saturday morning, the dining room was full of excited kids and tired parents. They had three cabins rented out for Friday night. Two cabins were families for the hockey tournament and one cabin was two couples staying for some skiing. All but one cabin and one of the chalets are all rented for Saturday night. This was the first year for this open-air hockey tournament, but Debbie had everything planned out and things went smoothly for the most part. Charles, the team coach, had the teams all scheduled and he had also taken care of all the advertising. If this was as successful as they hoped it would be, this may become an annual event. The spectators brought folding lawn chairs and sat around the new rinks. It was cold, but the sun was shining on them which helped ward off the chill.

Since Susan wasn't there this weekend, Debbie got all bundled up and took her camera down to the rinks. She was not a professional photographer by any stretch of the imagination, but she wanted to get a few shots for advertising purposes. She used pictures like these for her brochures for the resort.

Chef George did a pasta buffet for dinner. There was spaghetti for the kids and lasagna for the adults. There were both Caesar and tossed salads, freshly made garlic bread, some with cheese and some without, and an assortment of tarts, cupcakes and cookies for dessert.

They hired a local band to entertain in the lounge that night, and they rocked the place till two o'clock Ted was quite busy there for a while, and Debbie had gone in several times to help pick up empty beer bottles and dirty glasses. There were two different groups of local guys from Clifford. Tony stopped by, and he and Janice danced the night away. It was nice to see Janice so happy.

Sunday morning, the brunch buffet was very popular. The kids had playoff games to play today and then the awards ceremony. So far, her team was still in the playoffs. The trophies were already ordered. The store in Clifford was just waiting for the call to tell them the names they wanted engraved on the trophies for the winning team and the most valuable player before Keith could pick them up. He was already there in town waiting for them.

One of the spectators came into the office. She had taken the brochure with her at brunch and now said, "Hi. I am hosting a girls' weekend for some of my friends. I was wondering if it is possible to see a large cabin and a chalet."

Debbie met the lady out in front of the lodge, and they walked down to cabin six, which had just been newly winterized and renovated. As they walked Debbie asked her, "Do you have a date already in mind for your weekend?"

"Probably towards the end of April, I am thinking. We usually get together once a year for some fun away from husbands and kids. This year it is my turn to organize it."

"Oh, that sounds like a good group of friends to have. Do you mind if I ask what you'd have done in previous years?"

"We have had shopping trips, spa trips, and trips to casinos to see shows . . . that kind of thing."

"Do any of the ladies like skiing? There is a good ski hill just up the road from here."

"Yes, I know, I have skied there myself. I don't think all of the ladies ski though."

"This is cabin six. It had just been newly renovated. As you can see, it has two bedrooms, both with two double beds and one set of bunkbeds. So, if you ladies wanted to share a bed, you could sleep ten in here."

"Nice. I like the little kitchen area. These girls are drinkers and there are sure to be blender drinks involved. This would do quite nicely."

"Okay, now back on the other side of the lodge I can show you a chalet."

As they walked, Debbie asked her about the spa weekend. "I have been thinking about putting a pampered ladies' kind of weekend package together to offer my guests in the wintertime. What would you suggest are some of the things I should include? Besides manicures, pedicures, and facials what else would you expect to be available?"

"I would say massages for sure, perhaps a reiki treatment or a meditation session."

"Okay, I can show you the first chalet here." Debbie started up the stairs. "They are all the same inside. We just built them a few years ago. Watch your step, it could be a little slippery."

"Wow, this is absolutely gorgeous. I am glad I don't have to clean all these windows" She opened her arms wide. "I can see us sitting here beside the fireplace watching the sunrises and sunsets."

Debbie removed her boots, and the lady followed suit. "Down the hall here is a small bathroom with a stand-up shower" Debbie opened a door. "This is a storage closet with extra fold-up chairs, towels, blankets and pillows. This room holds the washer and dryer for your convenience." As they moved forward Debbie continued, "This is what we call the library room. Those couches will fold out into beds if needed." She went up the stairs into the kitchen. "You will notice it comes equipped with fridge, stove, microwave and dishwasher" Debbie opened the broom closet to. "The table has eight chairs around it but can be extended out to seat twelve." She indicated the extension boards.

"This is amazing," she commented. She followed Debbie down a carpeted hallway.

"Up here, you will find three bedrooms. The master bedroom has one king size bed. The other two rooms each have two double beds. And here we have the bathroom."

"Is that a hot tub?" She asked as she followed Debbie into the bathroom. "Oh, I am so impressed. This is incredible. The girls would absolutely love this."

"The hot tub can hold up to eight people and the towels racks in here are heated" Debbie walked over to the far wall and opened a cabinet. "This cabinet is also heated, and in here you will find terry cloth robes and large bath towels."

"This is so nice," she said as she followed Debbie back downstairs. "I love the gift baskets. That is such a nice touch."

"All three executive chalets are basically the same. You could sleep ten, and with the fold-out couches in the library you could sleep four more."

Debbie headed back to the door and put her boots back on. The lady sat down on the couch facing the window.

"I could sit in here and watch the hockey game." She smiled at Debbie as she reluctantly got up to put her boots on. "Thanks so much for showing me the cabin and the chalet. I sure have a lot to think about now."

"Here's my card if you have any questions or want to call and book a weekend." Debbie handed her the Cedar Grove Resort business card. Then she went back the lodge and the lady went back to the hockey game.

It started to snow during the final hockey game, but the kids didn't seem to mind one little bit. As soon as the games were over and the winners had been decided, they headed back into the lodge for pizza. By the time the kids were done with their pizzas, Keith was back with the trophies. The home team that Debbie sponsored came in second place. All in all, it was a huge success. Coach Charles presented the trophies and thanked Debbie and the Cedar Grove Resort for hosting the event. "See you all next year," he told them all.

Chapter 26

Debbie was busy in the office doing book work when Janice came in. She had already decided that today, while Janice was gone to town, she was going to open those six letters her mom had kept hidden away. With Janice here looking over her shoulder on a regular basis she was finding it hard to find any solitude. Her last roommate used to have afternoon naps. Mom always went upstairs after the lunch rush was cleaned up. But Janice was so eager to learn what she could about the business that Debbie was starting to feel suffocated. Debbie couldn't help but think it would only get worse when Susan, Keith and the kids move in.

"How long until you have the bank deposits ready?" Janice asked. "I would like to get to town and back before it starts to snow. Just heard the weather report and they are calling for possibly six inches."

"Give me another half hour and it will be ready." Deb told her. "I got sidetracked comparing this February to the past few years. We did exceptionally well this year. But I expect things to quiet down now till the end of April."

"I was looking at the reservation book and see we have that baby shower Saturday. What are we required to do for that?"

"Chef George will make sandwiches and veggie trays. They have asked us to provide a cake as well. Chef loves baking but hates decorating. Hey, didn't you take a cake decorating class in college?"

"Yes I did, and I love decorating cakes. Do you think Chef would let me decorate the cake? I wouldn't want to step on his toes."

"I am quite positive he would let you decorate the cake."

"All right, I will mention it to him when he is here on Wednesday. For now, I will leave you alone and let you finish the bank deposit."

Janice was becoming very useful. Deb was pleased on how well she was fitting in to the resort routines. Managing a resort was not rocket science, but it did take dedication. Her friends always teased her about how organized and detail-oriented she was, but that was precisely why everything worked so smoothly. Experience had taught her to plan for worst and hope for the best.

Charles, the hockey coach, called to thank her for all she did for them over the weekend. The kids had a lot of fun, and he got a lot of positive feedback from the players and the parents. He was looking forward to doing it again next year and thanked her for putting it all together.

Janice had just left for town and Debbie had just come downstairs, letters in hand, when she heard the bell on the dining room door. She quickly hid the letters under a pile of papers on the desk and went through the kitchen into the dining room to see who had come in. The letters would have to wait.

It was Becky Shafer, the expecting mom-to-be, her mother and her best friend. They were there for lunch and to talk about the baby shower scheduled for this Saturday.

"Oh my goodness Becky, look at you. You're absolutely glowing. How is everything going?" Debbie asked her.

"Fine I guess, as fine as I can be with these two little ones kicking me from the inside out." Becky told her.

"Two little ones, are you having twins?"

Becky nodded. "Yes, two, apparently one boy and one girl. Figured if I was going to have a baby I might as well have two and get it all over with all at the same time."

"Becky never does anything the easy way," her mom said.

"Congratulations, that is so exciting. Well, let's decide what you would like for lunch and we can chat later."

Debbie was both the waitress and cook today and when they were finished lunch, she showed them the banquet room.

"We had a Valentine's Day wedding here and thought we would leave the lights up and have your shower in here. Becky, what do you think about that idea?"

"I love it. It is so pretty. Basically all we need are some chairs in a circle and a few tables for the food, the cake and the gifts. This is amazing. I would love to have the shower in this room."

"I was thinking of hanging some streamers and a few baby decorations to make it more personal for your shower," Debbie told her.

"That would be wonderful," Becky smiled..

After they left, Debbie called Janice on her cell phone to tell her that Becky had been in and she was having twins, so pick up some decorations and streamers in both pink and blue. She suggested Janice check out a couple different stores, hoping it would detain her longer in town.

So now was the perfect time to open those letters. Henry had been in for lunch and he was back down in one of the cabins installing insulation. She did not expect to see him again today.

She quickly did her walk through the dining room, lounge, and banquet rooms and even took a quick check on the parking lot. The coast was clear. She was the only one around.

She sat down at her desk and withdrew the letters she had hiding. It was now or never. As she undid the red ribbon, she said a prayer to her mom.

"Mom I am sorry if this is a mistake, but I have come to the conclusion that you wanted us to find out whatever secrets you have hidden. Please forgive me if I am wrong." She spoke the words out loud to the universe and hoped Mom would hear her.

She gently turned them upside down and opened the bottom one first. She thought that was probably how her mother would have stacked them, with the oldest being on the bottom. Debbie was like her mom that way. It kept things better organized when things flowed in proper order.

She carefully opened the bottom letter first. They had originally been opened with a letter opener, so they all opened from the top of the envelopes. There was no date or greeting. It was handwritten on a small single sheet of paper. It simply read:

> My dearest love
>
> It was so good to see you again. I trust that you are fine after our last night together. I hope you didn't get caught in our little deception. It was so wonderful that your cousin Agnes covered for you so we could be together. I can't wait till I can make love to you again. Write and tell me when we can arrange to be together. Until then.
>
> Yours truly,
>
> Jefferson Penfold

Debbie read it twice to make sure she didn't miss anything. This Penfold guy must have been an old boyfriend of her mom's before she met Dad. She carefully put the letter back into its original envelope. Debbie looked around nervously, like she was about to get caught with her hand in the cookie jar, so to speak. She opened the next letter just as carefully as she had opened the first one.

> My darling,
>
> Congratulations are long overdue. I ran into Agnes yesterday. She told me that you are now married with a new daughter already. I remember you telling me how much you wanted

a family someday. Looks like your wish came true and I could not be happier for you.

You must know that you broke my heart when you chose him over me, but I do understand why you did. You wanted a home and a family, and you needed the stability that this traveling salesman just couldn't give you.

I hope your new family makes you very happy. I will always love you, but now I must love you from afar. I will be passing through your town on the fifteenth of next month. I need to see you. I have some questions that only you can answer for me. Could we at least meet for a coffee? Is there any way you could slip away even for an hour? If you can make it, I will be at our favourite café at ten a.m. If you can't make it on that day, then you choose a day when we can meet, and I will be there. I look forward to seeing you.

Yours truly,

Jefferson Penfold

Wow, Debbie thought. *He sure made it sound like they had some sordid affair.* Debbie wondered why Agnes would have helped her hide the fact that she was with Mr. Penfold without anyone's knowledge. Way to go, Mom. Debbie couldn't help herself feeling somewhat proud of her momma.

Just then, Debbie heard the back door. She was so lost in reading the letter that she hadn't noticed or heard Janice arriving until she was already inside the back door. Debbie quickly put the second letter back into the envelope and, along with the ribbon, she shuffled them under the stack of papers on her desk.

When Janice got back from town, she explained that she had found streamers and some crepe paper, but did not have much luck buying baby decorations so she picked up some smaller ribbon to match what was already in the banquet room. Using artificial baby's breath along with pink and blue ribbon, she could make some lovely decorations. Debbie didn't doubt her for a moment. Janice was the most creative person she knew, and Debbie knew she would create something amazing. The first chance Debbie got, she took the letters upstairs and hid them in her bedroom dresser.

Wednesday when the bridge ladies were there, one of the ladies, Margarete, asked about holding a fiftieth wedding anniversary dinner and party there.

"What date are you thinking?" Debbie asked her.

"Our actual anniversary date is on Wednesday March 25th so either the Saturday before or the Saturday after," Margarete told her.

"Okay, let me go get my reservation book and see what is available. I'll be right back."

When she returned, the ladies were finished playing bridge and were enjoying their coffee and sweets.

"I have an opening for the third Saturday in March," Debbie said. "Are you wanting a sit-down dinner or a buffet? And do you want us to provide the cake and bar service?"

"Gosh, I hadn't thought that far ahead. I guess I should ask the cost per person and yes, if you could provide the cake that would be wonderful."

"Didn't I hear that you and Barney are going to renew your vows? Why don't you have it like a regular wedding reception? Debbie asked her.

"Oh, I like that idea. What do you ladies think?" Margarete asked her friends. They all agreed that would be a great idea.

"Okay then, I'll book the Snider wedding anniversary reception for Saturday, March 28th." Debbie made the notation in the reservation book.

"I was originally thinking about just a dance, not dinner. What do you ladies think?" Margarete asked her friends.

They basically talked her into the dinner. They thought they could all use a nice night out and if they were going to have to get all gussied up, they might as well come for dinner too. Besides, one of the ladies reminded her, she was rich, it wasn't like she couldn't afford it. And she was only going to do this once, or in this case once again.

They all had a good laugh over that. Margarete said, "Go ahead and book it, but I wouldn't know the exact number of guests till closer to the event."

"Can you give me a guess for now? I wouldn't need to confirm the number of people coming until the Tuesday before the party."

"I would think at least fifty people. I know I will have to invite all these nice ladies here and their hubbies, as well as my family and a few other friends. Maybe more than that. I will have to make a list and get back to you."

"Oh, no worries. And do you want me to hire the band?"

"Why don't I just leave that all up to you, my dear, if you don't mind?"

"No problem, I don't mind at all. That's what I'm here for." Debbie told her. "I'd better get to work on this. You ladies enjoy the rest of this beautiful day. I will see you all next week. And Margarete, if you have any more questions or concerns you can always give me a call." Debbie handed her the Cedar Grove Resort business card.

When Debbie got back to the office Janice asked her, "Did the bridge ladies just book some kind of event?"

"Yes, Margarete Snider just booked an anniversary party for the 28th. That doesn't give us much time to prepare."

Chef George came into the office. "Deb, you got a minute to chat?" he asked her.

"Yes of course Chef, what's on your mind?"

"I wanted to ask what you think about buying some hamburger ahead for the next few months," Chef told her. "I see that our supplier is having a big sale next week. I was wondering at these prices if we should buy some for the freezer. I was just looking back over last year's invoices and I see that we are going to need at least thirty-five cases to get us through the summer. It would be a big expense now, but would be quite a savings over the next six months. What do you think?"

"I think that is a good idea, and we have had such a good month that now would be a good time to buy. As long as you have room in the freezer, go ahead and order what you think we will use."

"Okay, done. By the way, did Janice tell you she is going to decorate the cake for the baby shower? I am so relieved. You know that is not my forte."

"I know, and she is good at it so why not let her do it? In fact, if you sweet-talk her she would probably decorate cupcakes and other cakes for you as well."

"Oh, I am all for that. I will bake them, and she can decorate all she wants."

"I just took a reservation for a fiftieth wedding anniversary dinner on the 28th. They want us to do dinner and the cake. I was thinking since they are renewing their vows, perhaps we could do a three-tiered wedding cake."

"I can bake it if Janice can decorate it. For how many people, do you know?" Chef always asked that question.

"Guesstimate was for fifty, but I expect it will be more. We can give them two entrée choices and serve it just like we did for the Whitfield wedding. I will call her in a few days and confirm some details. As soon as I know, I will let you know."

Saturday morning when Debbie came downstairs, Janice was at the back kitchen table already decorating the cake for the bridal shower. Chef George had baked two cakes and shaped them side by side into the shape of two baby booties. Janice was icing one pink and one blue. It really looked cute.

"I will want to get a picture of that when you are finished." Debbie told her sister. "It would be good to have to show potential clients."

"Will I be decorating a cake for the fiftieth wedding anniversary party coming up?"

"Yes, I think so. A traditional, three-tiered cake would be expected."

Later that afternoon they had the baby shower which was a success. There were twenty-eight ladies in total. Chef George had put together fresh veggies and fruit trays, some finger sandwiches, pickles, and a cheese and cracker tray. Becky was so pleased with the cake she didn't want to cut into it, but they finally convinced her that after they took a hundred pictures of it, it was time to taste it. Apparently, it tasted as good as it looked. When Becky's mom came into the office to pay the bill, she commented on how pleased she was with the whole thing: the decorations, the food, and especially the cake.

It was always interesting to Debbie that when people came to her to celebrate the major events in their lives like weddings, birthdays and anniversaries they had an expectation of what the party would look like and Debbie tried each time to surpass their expectations. It usually didn't take much, just attention to the minor details.

Chapter 27

It was a few days before Debbie had a chance to look at the letters again. Although they had been on her mind constantly, she was determined to keep them secret until she had them all read. After they closed the dining room Debbie faked a headache and asked Janice to stick around until Ted closed the bar.

Once safely in her room, she dug the letters out of her sock drawer and settled back in bed to read the rest of the letters. She opened the third letter.

> My dear friend,
>
> What happened? I waited two hours, but you did not show up. As I said in my last letter, I need to see you. Please don't just ignore me. I have some questions to ask you and I need some answers. Please write and let me know when a good time would be for me to come to visit you. I would love to meet your new husband as well as your new daughter.
>
> Or perhaps we could meet at our favourite café? Please write soon as I am anxious to hear from you.
>
> Yours truly,
>
> Jefferson Penfold

Well. Debbie though to herself. Her mom must have had two fellows on the hook at the same time. She was not really surprised as her mom was a very beautiful woman especially when she was young. She put the letter back into its original envelope and opened the next letter.

Hello my dear,

It was so lovely to see you again. Thank you for coming and letting me meet my daughter Susan. She is a beautiful little girl, just like you said she was.

I will respect your wishes and not interfere with her upbringing. I will forever keep our beautiful secret. I do have one request, however. Would you send me photographs of our daughter occasionally? This way I can at least watch her grow up in pictures.

I would tell you to take care of our little girl, but I already know that you will do just that. You are a very good mother.

Yours truly,

Jefferson Penfold

WHAT? Her dad was not Susan's dad! She was shocked. Debbie didn't know what she was expecting to learn from reading Mom's hidden letters. She thought there might be a secret or two, but nothing as devastating as all this. Susan was only a half-sister. What did this all mean? It kind of made sense, if she stopped to think about it. Susan was so much taller than her or Janice and Susan's natural hair colour was auburn where both Janice and she had black hair. Reflecting on a few of these differences, Debbie could in fact now see the obvious differences that she had never noticed before.

Debbie was now anxious to read the rest of the letters. She was about to remover the next letter when she heard Janice entering their adjoining bathroom. She quickly tucked all the letters down under the covers. Damn, this was getting good, and she was anxious to finish reading them.

"You still awake?" Janice said loudly through the closed door.

"Yes I am. Did you have any problems locking up or setting the alarm?" Debbie asked her.

"All done." Janice said as she poked her head in through the door. "Look at you, all snug as a bug in a rug."

"I expected I would be sleeping by now, but this headache has other ideas."

"Call if you need me. Night, sis. See you in the morning." Janice closed the door behind her.

"Good night."

Debbie waited patiently until she was confident Janice was in bed. Knowing her sister, she would be asleep in under five minutes. While she waited, she debated with herself what she would do now with her newfound knowledge. Should she tell Susan? After all, she lived the first forty years of her life secure in a loving family. What purpose would there be in telling her? It would only hurt her now. Perhaps she should tell Janice and the two of them could discuss it and decide together about telling Susan or not. When Debbie felt that Janice would be asleep, she pulled the letters back up on top of the covers. Debbie noticed that this letter had different postage on it and was addressed to mom here at the resort. She carefully opened the next letter. She had to see where this was going.

Hello stranger,

I hope this letter finds you well. I have written many letters that were returned, address unknown. I happened to run into your cousin Agnes the other day, and she told me you moved to the Muskoka area. She also told me that you now have three beautiful daughters. By my calculations, Susan must be fifteen by now. I think of you and her often.

I wold love to see you both. Perhaps I could come to your lodge for a holiday, even though I don't care for fishing. We need to get caught up. Did you ever tell Susan or your husband about me? I doubt that you have. Our little secret is still safe with me.

I am still the single traveling salesman that you fell in love with all those years ago. I still love you and will till the day I die.

Please write me and send some pictures of you and Susan.

Yours truly,

Jefferson Penfold

Debbie couldn't believe that her mom hadn't stayed in touch with Susan's real father all those years. She wondered if her dad knew that he was raising another man's child. And, if he knew, did he care? Debbie couldn't remember any time that Susan was ever treated any differently than her and Janice. Well one more letter to go. Perhaps it could answer some of her burning questions.

My dear old friend,

First off let me apologize for showing up unexpectedly. I just needed to see you and Susan for *myself. Your husband seems like a nice enough fellow. He has taken good care of his family and you need to respect that in a man.*

You are still a beautiful woman and you still take my breath away. It was so good to see you and Susan. It was very hard for me not to tell Susan that I am her real father, but I held my tongue. She appears to be healthy and happy. She seems like a smart, well-adjusted young lady. You have done a fine job raising Susan and her sisters. I always knew you would be a good mother. You should be very proud of yourself.

Please stay in touch, as I cherish your letters and the pictures you send. Perhaps one day you will decide to tell her that I am her real father. As always, I leave that decision entirely up to you.

Yours truly,

Jefferson Penfold

Well that didn't answer any of her questions. Did Mom ever tell her dad or Susan? Debbie didn't think so. She believed that Mom and this Mr. Penfold were the only two people that knew the truth. And now she knew. So, what was she to do with this new knowledge? She would definitely have to think about this. Debbie put the last letter in its envelope and retied the six letters back together with the red ribbon. She got up and took the letters to hide in her dresser drawer until she could decide what to do with them.

Now, halfway through March was historically the resort's quiet time, Debbie's creative time. This time of year was when she put together some advertising files and worked on a new brochure. Over the year, she had taken pictures of different events at the resort. As the pictures were taken, Debbie downloaded then onto her computer. She would then pick out one picture of the event and print it out for reference for the advertising file. The resort had all the latest computer technology, but Debbie still liked old school ways for backups. Honestly, she just didn't have much confidence in anything electrical that could just crash or quit working. Many times when the hydro went out she was glad for the paper trail, so she could still take care of her guests.

The kitchen appliances were all propane, which was stored in big drums out behind the lodge. All the fridges, stoves, ovens. fryers, and even the walk-in cooler were all run by the propane.

They had two huge gas generators back there as well. They could run the entire lodge, but in a power outage Debbie would just leave on the security locks and lights. When you live in rural Ontario, you learn you need to be prepared for anything. It was not uncommon to lose your hydro in a winter blizzard or a summer thunderstorm. The people that lived there were quite used to it. For them it was just a way of life. For guests there were always emergency candles and flashlights available.

As Debbie scanned through the advertising folder, it brought back a lot of memories of the past year. There were a few good pictures of Mom. They should have been included on the picture board for her celebration of life. Oh well, too late now. Just seeing the pictures was all it took to swamp Debbie. She was sitting there with tears running down her face when Janice walked it.

"What's the matter? Why are you sitting here crying?"

Debbie handed her the folder and had to just walk away until she could get a hold of her emotions. She walked out into the kitchen and Chef George stopped what he was doing.

"Just need a moment," she told him as she walked by.

Janice came up behind her and gave her a big hug. When Debbie turned around, she saw Janice had tears rolling down her face also. Chef George discreetly left the room.

"What a pair of saps we are," Debbie said as she handed her sister a box of Kleenex.

"What is that file all about? There are a lot of pictures in it, including some nice pictures of Mom." Janice asked.

"Oh, that's just my advertising file. I was going to take a look at it, but I just started missing Mom too much."

"Yeah I understand, it had the exact same effect on me too. Maybe that file can wait till another day."

"I think you are definitely right on that."

Debbie walked away thinking about what just happened. That was like what you would imagine it would feel like being hit by a tidal wave or a mac truck. Naturally she thought about her mom a lot, but at that particular moment, she was not thinking about her. The instant that she saw Mom's happy, smiling face in that file, the floodgates opened instantly. People kept telling her time would heal the pain of losing her mom, but honestly Debbie didn't see that happening any time soon, or probably ever.

They had only two cabins rented for the upcoming weekend for some skiers. The ski hill was starting to slow down. Although there was still plenty of snow, when the days started to warm up to above the freezing mark, the snow changed consistency. The local guys were starting to gather sap to make their famous maple syrup. Debbie had a standing order with Sanford Bradley, the neighbour who lived just up the road. She bought syrup from him for the resort as well as honey from him in the summertime. The tourists really liked the local flavours on the menu. Chef George did a chicken breast glazed with a maple sauce that was quite popular, and even the local residents came for breakfast to have fresh local syrup on their pancakes. Debbie stopped in to have a talk with Sanford.

"How's things going? I see you've starting tapping already this year." Debbie handed him a cheque for the past few month's sales of his products in her gift shops.

"Yes, the sap is just starting to run. I think the colour might be a bit darker than it was last year. Want a taste?"

"Yes, please." Debbie was grinning like a kid in a candy store. "Mm, that is good."

"What are you grinning about?" he asked.

"I was thinking about the time I told my mom that my favourite tree is the maple. In the summer it gives shade, in the fall when the leaves changed colour that same maple tree gives great beauty to the world and then in the spring that same maple tree gives sap that makes maple syrup. Now I ask, how could a person not help but admire a tree that can do all that? I remember Mom laughed at me and told me most people would have never given it a thought."

"Well when you're right, you're right," Sanford said. "I assume you want your usual order this year?"

"For sure, but you may want to increase my order and send me more of the little pint jugs for sale. We had to get more before the summer was over, remember? That size sells very well in the gift shops. Quite popular with the tourists. And I have orders from Chef—he needs another gallon for the kitchen now, please."

"Mary tried the maple chicken the last time we came in for dinner. She let me try it and we both really liked it. You are so lucky to have Chef George. He is an amazing Chef."

"Oh I know, and he always goes above and beyond to take care of me and my family. I am grateful to have him for sure."

"So, what did you think about the sap? Taste all right?"

"Yes it does, thank you, I just stopped in to bring you money."

"Now what more could a man ask for than a pretty lady bringing him money?"

"Sanford, you are flattering me. Well I best be getting back to work. See you folks soon."

Later that evening, Janice and Debbie were sitting chatting about the resort in general. Debbie told Janice that she had dropped the cheque off for Sanford.

"How are they doing?" Janice asked. "I have always wanted to see how he makes his syrup. I bet there is a real knack to getting it just right. I wonder if I stopped by if he would explain it to me. I wonder why he doesn't give little tours and charge people who are like me and would love to see his operation."

"I don't think he would have the time. He is busy keeping the wood fire going under his sap pan. But you could ask him for a tour, if you like," Debbie told her sister.

"Next time you go there, can I go with you? Or better yet, if you feel up to it, we could walk up there right now. Everything is under control here at the moment."

"All right. Get your coat." Debbie totally expected Sanford would think they were crazy for even suggesting such a thing. But Janice was keen on the idea, so let her ask him.

"Twice in one day," said Sanford when they walked in. "Are you bringing me more money? And who is this pretty lady you brought with you?

"Sanford, Mary, you might remember my sister, Janice. She has just moved back home."

"Nice to see you again, Janice. It has been a long time since we have seen you, dear." Mary said.

"I have a question for you sir if I may?" Janice addressed Sanford.

"Go ahead, I'm all ears." Sanford said. "By the way, I heard that your outdoor hockey tournament was a huge success and I also heard about the poker run. A couple of friends of mine were riders in the race. They said it was a lot of fun and they will definitely be doing it again next year."

"Yes, it has been a good winter. Best February the resort has ever had, actually." Debbie offered.

"That is good news. You are doing a wonderful job down there." Sanford smiled at the girls. "You must be missing your mom. She was such a nice lady. I always liked her. She is why you get your syrup cheaper than the rest of the world" Sanford looked right at Debbie. "But you just remember, young lady, that price is only in effect for the next three years and then we will have to renegotiate."

"Good to know." She knew he was just teasing her. He loved the fact that she featured his products in her dining room and sold them in her gifts shops as well.

"So, what is your question girl?" Sanford asked Janice.

"Well I was wondering why you don't have tours of the sap boiling house?" Janice asked. "I know I would love a tour, maybe even a demonstration."

"You mean the sugar shack? I have considered it, but it seems like a lot of work with no reward," Sanford told her.

"If you had it set up right, you may be able to sell some of your products right here," Debbie said.

"I don't need to sell from here. You do that part for me." He smiled.

"Yeah I guess I do. I am one of your many store fronts. I bet that I sell more than any of your other locations do, because I have it promoted on my menu. Am I right or am I right?"

"How many people are you thinking will want to see the sugar shack?"

Janice looked at Debbie for some help.

"That depends." Debbie stepped in to help her sister. "I am think-ing we could talk to farmer John about a horse-drawn sleigh ride. Perhaps he could take guests for a ride around the property, and if we cross the road back there, past that first corner they could literally go from our property to yours and the guests could come and get a look at a real live maple syrup making demonstration."

"Sounds good, but you would have had to start packing the trails for the horses from the first snow fall. I have trails around the sugar bush for my tractor and I know John has trails around his property for his sleigh rides, but they take time to build. You see my sleigh there with the two big drums. I pull that with my tractor and collect my sap into those drums and then I bring it back to the sugar shack to boil down into syrup," Sanford pointed out.

"You're right. I never thought of that," Debbie agreed. "Would you be willing to give a tour and a short demonstration on the whole process? We could use the shuttle van and just drive guests over here and then they could come back to the lodge for a pancake breakfast."

"I might be interested. My wife Mary has been after me for years to give tours of my sugar shack." Sanford told them.

"Well I am thinking we would advertise the sugar shack tour and an all-you-can-eat pancake breakfast and see if anyone would be interested. I think the sleigh ride would have added some excitement to the whole thing but maybe we can add it next year, if we can get this part of it off the ground." Debbie told him.

"So you're thinking about paying me so much per person, or so much per group? How many folks are you expecting?" Sanford asked.

"No idea. That is the unknown part of this. We could advertise for the Saturdays and Sundays for the next three weeks. Hopefully the sap will run that long. Let's say we offer the tour from ten till two o'clock. Henry will shuttle them up here, you give them a ten to fifteen minute talk explaining how it all works, and perhaps you could do the hot syrup on the cold ice demonstration. Then we will shuttle them back to the lodge for the pancake breakfast. The question then becomes, how much would fifteen minutes of your time be worth, Mr. Bradley?" Debbie asked.

"I don't rightly know. My wife tells me I am priceless," he said with a silly grin.

"We haven't got all the details worked out yet. At this stage in the game, we are just wondering if it possible and feasible for that matter." Janice injected.

"Well, the pancake breakfast on the menu right now goes for eleven fifty and a buffet usually costs me a little more, say thirteen bucks so if I charged fifteen dollars a head that would leave two dollars per person profit for you. We can take seven passengers at a time in the shuttle bus so that would be roughly fourteen dollars per tour. If we draw a big enough crowd you could potentially do up to six or eight tours each day. Fourteen times say six tours you're looking at over eighty dollars potentially a day for four hours work or twenty dollars an hour, and all you have to do is talk." Debbie pointed out.

"When you say it like that it all sounds good. Let me think about it, talk it over with Mary and see what she thinks. I have to take my syrup off the fire right now. Tell you what, Mary has been bugging me to take her down to the lodge for dinner so we will do that tonight and we can talk about it then. That okay with you, my dear?"

"Sounds good. We will see you and Mary later then." Debbie said.

When Debbie and Janice got back to the lodge Janice was all fired up about the idea. She couldn't understand why they had never tried this idea before. Debbie explained that up until the last few years they didn't have much winter business. It had only been since the ski hill opened that they were getting winter guests, and she didn't think the local folks would be that interested. Some of the locals were busy making their own syrup. And if this could happen, they would need to decide on all costs involved. They agreed to sleep on it and discuss it with Chef tomorrow.

When Debbie was getting ready for bed she thought about Janice's idea. On one hand, she was happy that Janice was taking an interest and coming up with new ideas, but on the other hand, what if it was a flop, a big failure? She felt that her sister was still quite fragile and didn't want her to get hurt.

The next day, the girls cornered Chef after the lunch rush. Janice told Chef her ideas and he agreed it all sounded good.

"Chef what would be a ballpark cost per breakfast for an all-you-can-eat pancake buffet?" Debbie asked.

"The cost for the pancake and sausage breakfast on the menu is like six dollars and fifty cents. If you're thinking a buffet with sausage, bacon, ham, and perhaps some fresh fruit, tea and coffee included, milk or orange juice for the kids I am guessing about eight dollars per plate." He told them.

"So if we charge fifteen dollars per adult, ten dollars per kid kind of thing, this would give us a seven dollar profit per plate to split with Sanford Bailey." Janice was figuring out loud. "Gotta like that."

"Sounds like it. But don't forget you'll need a driver for the shuttle bus so there is that cost as well." Debbie pointed out. "If we do this, I would also like to have some maple products for sale. Chef, I know you spoke before that you have a good recipe for maple fudge and maple cookies. I think the guests might like to buy something to take home." Debbie commented.

"For sure, be glad to. I will pull out some old cookbooks and see what else we can come up with."

"Thanks Chef. You are the best."

Susan had arrived alone late Friday afternoon. She was planning on staying for the week and then Keith and the kids would be joining her for the following weekend.

"Do you want to stay up at the house? It's still available if you want it," Debbie asked Susan.

"I don't think I want to be way up there all by my little old self necessarily."

"Tell you what, why don't you stay upstairs with Janice and me and then when the family arrives next weekend you can move up to the house with them."

"Perfect. Sounds like a good plan," Susan agreed.

When Sanford and Mary arrived for dinner, the dining room was quite busy. Debbie went out and welcomed them and suggested that they could talk after dessert. While Gail was getting their drinks,

Debbie introduced them both to Susan and Janice. Sanford pointed out that they had met them both before, but they hadn't seen Susan in years.

When they finished their dinners, Debbie suggested they talk at the back kitchen table. This wold be more convenient for Chef to join them when he had a moment and it was a good practice to not hold business meetings in the dining room while people were trying to enjoy their meals.

Debbie let Janice tell Susan her idea. Starting Saturday, they were going to try sugar shack tours and see how it would go over. Susan thought it sounded like a good idea.

"Chef is going to make fudge and cookies to sell. I expect we will sell some syrup as well." Debbie told them.

"Am I going to have to collect money from each person?" Sanford asked.

"No, you don't have to. If you trust me, I will keep track here and the guests can pay me and when it is done, I will cut you a cheque for your share of the profits." Debbie assured him. "I am selling it as a package deal, the breakfast and the tour, so it won't be a problem to figure it out. That is, if you trust me."

"Should I? I don't know about that." Sanford said.

Mary gave him a poke in the ribs. "He is just teasing you, of course he trusts you by now."

"Oh here, you both need to try Ted's new drink. He is calling it the Cedar Grove toddy. The drinks are on me, okay?" Debbie said while Ted was setting their drinks down in front of them.

"Thank you so much. I already had a beer with my dinner. After this, I might need a ride back up the hill," Sanford said.

"That looks interesting." Susan pointed to the drink. "Ted, could I have one of those? I need to know if it tastes as good as it looks."

"Me too, please," Janice added. Debbie knew that Ted would record the four free drinks in the complimentary book. They kept track of any drinks the boss comped for guests as a way of controlling inventory and discouraging any possible theft.

"Would you like one too, boss?" Ted asked Debbie.

"Sure, why not, since you're in the business," she told him.

"Umm that is just yummy," Mary said. "It tastes creamy and woodsy all at the same time. Just please don't tell me how many calories are in it."

"We also have a rum drink with a shot of maple syrup in it you should try sometime." Debbie told them.

"Rum and maple syrup, two of my most favourite things," Sanford said with a smile. "I will definitely have to try that next time we are in for dinner. Mary, don't forget to remind me to do that."

"So, are we all in agreement about the sugar shack tours? Sanford, all you have to do is a short ten or fifteen minute speech explaining the process. You could give a demonstration on how you tap the tree or how you, I don't know, how you do any part of the syrup making process. Your demonstration is totally up to you."

"I'm a shy guy you know. I might get all tongue tied or forget what I am supposed to say," Sanford told them.

"Oh fiddlesticks," Mary said. "You could talk the ear off an elephant. I am sure you will do just fine, you old fart."

"Well I guess it's all right with the boss here, so I will agree to do it for this year. Then we can discuss next year depending on what results we get now." Sanford said.

"I can't make any guarantees on how many guests we will get. It is really quite late for the advertising. I will get it in the local papers for the next three weeks and I can put it on our website, but other than that there's not much else we can do this late in the game." Debbie told him. "Are we still in agreement for the next three Saturdays and Sundays from what, ten till two?"

"Okay with me," Sanford agreed.

After Sanford and Mary had left, Janice asked, "Would you like me to put it out on social media, like Twitter and Facebook?"

"No, I don't think so. Because of the time frame we will be lucky to get local folks interested. It is hard to say how well it will go. My guess is the local folk will be in for breakfast anyways. Traditionally, pancake breakfasts at the lodge get quite popular around syrup time."

"How will you be able to tell if they are local or tourists?" Susan asked.

"Well if anyone wants to have the all you can eat buffet and go on the tour, the price is fifteen bucks and if they just order pancakes off the menu, it's twelve fifty and has nothing to do with Sanford."

"You're very good at all this, I must say. I am glad you are on the job." Susan told Debbie.

"This is all Janice's idea," Debbie told Susan.

The rest of the week was relatively quiet, which gave the three girls time together. Susan asked for a tour of the chalets and boat house which she hadn't been inside since the renovations had been done. Janice give her the tour. Janice had also taken her down to cabin six which was now finished its renovation. When they got back to the lodge, Susan told Debbie how impressed she was with the renovations.

Thursday afternoon they had no cabins rented. When the three of them sat down to lunch Chef told them, "Looks like it is going to be a quiet afternoon, why don't the three of you go skiing and have some fun?"

"That sounds like a very good idea." Debbie agreed with him. Susan loved to ski and had already been a couple times this week, but Debbie had only been there once this winter when the girls were home for Christmas.

At the ski hill, Debbie did three trips up the chair lift and down the hill. They both laughed at Debbie when she wiped out. Debbie had enough skiing and went into the ski hut for a warm drink.

"I saw your fall, are you okay?" Robert asked her.

"Yes, I am fine. I just wanted to give my sisters a good laugh. They are both way better skiers than I am." Debbie told Robert and

Nancy both. "I think I am done for the day, but they both went back up for another run. I would love a coffee."

"I assume you are getting some extra overnight guests this year because of the ski hill. How's that going?"

"Fine. Henry shuttles them over and then comes and picks them up when they call back that they are done. We had a few stay the weekend of the races you had over here."

"That's wonderful. Glad to see both our businesses doing well this winter. I hope it snows for another month at least," Robert commented.

"Well I expect the season is starting to wind down for you guys. Do you have any plans for the summer?" Debbie asked them.

"We are going to take the motor home and tour down in the States some. I have a sister in Arizona, and then we'll visit our son who lives in Kentucky. If we have time, we may go see Robert's brother in Nova Scotia as well. We have the whole summer to ourselves so why not go enjoy it while we can." Nancy told her.

"For sure. I don't blame you one bit. You deserve the break. Do you have anyone to keep an eye on things here while you are gone?"

"No, not yet, I was going to ask you if you would have any suggestions." Robert said.

"What about Henry? He is trustworthy. And he could almost walk here from his house."

"I thought about him, but I know he stays busy working for you."

"Henry putters around doing odd jobs and I pay him with food. He likes Chef's cooking better than he likes his own. If you want to ask him, don't stop on my account." Debbie told them.

"Okay, thanks, I will." Robert said just as Janice and Susan came in. They were done skiing and ready to go home. Debbie paid for the chair lifts and they said their goodbyes.

On Friday, Susan and Debbie went into Clifford to do some shopping. Susan wanted Debbie to introduce her to John at the real estate office. She introduced them and then left Susan there to talk with John while she went shopping next door.

On the way home, Susan said that she thought she could work with John and had a good feeling about it all. She was starting to get excited about moving back home permanently. She said Keith was more excited than anyone. He absolutely hated his job teaching where he was. The kids where he currently taught were rude and unruly and the administration didn't seem to care. At the beginning of the school year, one of his students had gotten stabbed.

Susan told her, "Keith has a meeting with the high school here on Monday."

"Oh, that is good news."

"Yes, they will need a grade nine and ten English teacher, so it is right up his alley. He is a good teacher, and if he had any faults it would be that he cares too much and the city kids take advantage of his kindness."

"I would imagine kids here would be a little less street smart than the city kids would be" Debbie suggested. "Not to mention giving up that one-hour traffic jam he has to endure twice a day."

"Keep your fingers crossed for him. I know he would feel a whole lot better about the move and about a lot of things if he had a job already lined up," Susan said.

Debbie was starting to believe that this was all really going to happen. Both her sisters were finally ready to move back home and help her run the resort. She felt a little scared and a little relieved all at the same time. She knew that a family-run resort was usually successful only if it had a family to support it. She needed their help. If she had to pay staff instead of free family labour, it would be very obvious on the profit and loss statement. But on the other hand, could she work with her sisters on an ongoing basis? Susan, who always wanted to be in charge and Janice, who was very creative but also very scatterbrained would both be a challenge for her. She didn't know if she was up to the challenge.

Friday night, there was two big groups of sledders in the bar, and they kept the juke box going till two a.m. Most of the guests were from the Nicholson cottage across the lake. Mr. Nicholson senior came into the office to talk to Debbie about reserving the banquet room for his daughter's upcoming wedding in June. He thought there would be close to a hundred people. He also wanted to know if the resort could provide a shuttle boat to get his guests across the lake before and after the party. Debbie told him that she did not have insurance for that, and she didn't have a big fancy yacht like he did. Perhaps he could hire a local guy to drive his yacht for the night. He agreed that would probably be a good idea, and perhaps she could suggest someone responsible that he could hire for the occasion. She told him to leave it with her and she would give it some thought.

She pulled out the reservation book and showed him that the last two Saturdays were still open, but he should get back to her as quickly as he could to confirm which date he wanted as the summer was starting to book up quickly. He promised he would get back to her soon. He just needed to speak with his family first to confirm which date the wedding would be.

Chapter 28

Saturday morning dawned. It was going to be a beautiful day. The sun was shining, the temperature was slowly creeping up above freezing, and Chef was humming a tune to himself when Debbie came downstairs to get a coffee.

"Morning, boss," Chef said. "How are you, this fine morning?"

"So far so good, but the day is still early," Debbie told him.

When she walked into the dining room, she could see that Gail already had the steam table in place and the small table that Henry unearthed from the basement was now covered in a clean white tablecloth with silverware and plates stacked on it.

"New table is going to work better on the start of the buffet, don't you think?" Gail asked Debbie.

"Yes, it looks fine and it will free up a space at the end of the line. Good idea, girl. You are more than just a pretty face." Debbie told her as she put her arm around her shoulders and gave her a little hug.

By ten o'clock, there were at least thirty people in the dining room waiting for a ride to the sugar bush for their tour. Since the buffet was ready, Debbie suggested that some of them might like to eat first while they waited for their turn. That seemed to work out fine. In the next four hours, they served a total of fifty-five buffets as well as twenty other guests who were just there for breakfast and were not going on the tour.

Sunday was a cold snowing day and they only had forty guests for the tour. At the end of the day, Debbie took her sled and drove up to see Mr. Sanford Bradley at the sugar shack.

"Well, how did everything go for you up here, Mr. Bradley?" Debbie asked him.

"Okay, I think. Did you hear any comments from any of your guests about the tour?" He asked her.

"Just that they liked to see how syrup is actually made and they enjoyed the syrup toffee on the ice."

"So, do you have any idea of the number of people that were here tramping through my bush?"

"Yes, we had fifty-five yesterday and forty today. I really didn't expect that many because it didn't even hit the newspapers until Wednesday. I expect next weekend could be busier. If need be, we may have to go past the two o'clock shut off time. You all right with that?"

"I guess I'll have to be," he told her. "So you said we had how many, ninety-five people these past two days?"

"Ninety-five times two bucks a head is one hundred and ninety dollars. What do you think of our big idea now?"

"I like your big ideas. Got any more up that sleeve of yours?"

"Not today I don't. Have a good week."

When Debbie got back to the lodge, Henry, Susan, Keith, and Janice were all sitting around the back kitchen table talking. Debbie grabbed a coffee and joined them.

Just then, Gail walked in.

"So how did everything go in the dining room? Was everyone happy to eat while they waited?" Debbie asked her.

"I think it was fine. If they ate first, when they returned from their tour they didn't come back into the lodge. But the ones who did the tour and then came in to eat stayed longer when they were finished. We sold all the fudge and I think there might be one bag of the cookies left. I had to send Keith down to the boathouse to get more syrup from the gift shop. We only have three of the small syrups left."

"Wow, I better let Sanford know that I will need some more before the weekend. I saw your display table set up, was that your idea?"

"No, actually, that was all Janice. She set it up and it worked very well. People went into the office gift shop to buy the stuff in there. The display just let people know that we had the products for sale." Gail told her.

"Good, so we will do the same thing next weekend, only expect a bigger crowd. Good job everyone. Now I am going to go in and call Sanford before I forget."

On Sunday night, Susan and the kids went back to the city. Keith stayed because he had the meeting with the local school board. On Monday evening, Debbie and Janice waited for him to get back from his meeting so they could all have dinner together. Chef had left them beef stroganoff and freshly baked rolls for dinner.

As soon as they sat down to eat, Janice was anxious to ask, "So, how did it go?"

"Okay, I think. It is a small school, only 500 kids. I met with the principal and two ladies from the school board. They showed me around. It seems like a nice little school," he told them.

"But did you get the job?" Janice asked.

"I don't know yet. They were meeting with a couple other teachers, so I have to wait to find out. Technically I am over-qualified and would be taking a big cut in pay, but I would do it just to get out of the rat race I am currently in."

"Susan has told me that the school you are teaching in right now is kind of a rough neighbourhood. How many kids go to your current school?" Debbie asked.

"It has about 1,200 kids from grades five through eight, and the kids are like little monsters. There was a stabbing at the start of this school year and so far, there have been two different bomb threats. Quite frankly, I can't wait to get out of there."

"I can certainly see why," Debbie told him. "Are you staying overnight, or do you have to go back to the city?"

"I either have to leave here by five o'clock tomorrow or go right after supper. They are calling for snow tomorrow morning, so I think I will go tonight." Keith replied.

They finished their meal, and then Keith headed back to the city. Debbie sure hoped he got the job. She couldn't imagine working in the environment he described. No wonder he was stressed and always medicating for ulcers. Susan called at about nine thirty to say that he was home safe and sound.

Debbie fell asleep thinking about the sugar shack tours. She really expected Sanford would say no to Janice's idea. But he agreed and because of it, they were busy making money. That was always a good thing.

Chapter 29

As predicted, this was going to be a quiet week. They had the bridge ladies on Wednesday afternoon and the Snider fiftieth wedding anniversary dinner on Saturday night. As well, they were expecting big crowds for the sugar shack tour on the weekend. Debbie had called Mrs. Snider and confirmed details like the menu, the band, the bar and the decorations. The guest list grew from the original estimated fifty people to now seventy-eight. Debbie had asked her if by chance she had a picture of her wedding cake and also suggested that if she had a wedding picture, they could display it in the banquet room for the party.

When the bridge ladies arrived on Wednesday, the party was all they could talk about. Mrs. Snider had brought in the pictures Debbie had asked for. The big portrait would display nicely on the centre of the back wall behind the head table. The picture of the cake was a three-tier white cake, plainly decorated.

Tony delivered the liquor order and then came in for a coffee. By now, even the bridge ladies knew that he was sweet on Janice. They were teasing him that his deliveries seemed to be taking longer and longer these days. He took it all good-heartedly. Debbie told Janice later how cute he was when he blushed. His face turned red and he got the cutest little dimple in his cheek when he smiled.

The evening was quiet, so Debbie and Janice were sitting in the office. Debbie was at her desk and Janice was sitting at Mom's old desk.

"There is something I would like to discuss with you, but it is very personal and private. You must promise to keep this a secret. Can you keep a secret?" Debbie asked her sister. "I can remember as a kid you couldn't keep a secret if your life depended on it."

"Yes, I can keep a secret." Janice told her with a scowl on her face. "I have grown up, in case you haven't noticed. So, what's the big secret?"

"I found some letters in Mom's treasures when I cleaned out her room."

"What kind of letters?" Janice asked inquisitively.

"Love letters. And not from our dad, either."

"Oh, what fun? Can I read them, too?"

"Yes, you can. But you have to promise to keep them to yourself until we can discuss them and decide what to do." Debbie handed her the pack of letters.

Janice turned the pile upside and started with the oldest letter first. While she was reading the letters, Debbie went out to freshen up her coffee. She heard voices coming from the lounge and wandered in and said hi to the two fellows sitting there. She recognized them from Clifford but did not know them by name. By the time she returned back to the office Janice had finished reading the letters and was just sitting there, dumbfounded.

"Holy moly. What the hell are we supposed to do with this?" Janice asked. "Why didn't Mom tell Susan after Dad died? Why did she still keep the secret? Are we going to tell Susan now, or let her carry on blissfully ignorant? Why did Mom leave this up to us to deal with? I think she has a right to know, don't you?"

"I don't know. I have all the same questions you have." Debbie told her.

"Well put yourself in her shoes, wouldn't you want to know?"

"I think I would, but this is Susan we are talking about. She doesn't like it when things get complicated or messy. She may not take it well."

"Yeah, you're right about that. What do you think we should do then? How long have you known?"

"Since shortly after I cleaned out Mom's room. I debated about even reading them, but my curiosity got the better of me."

"Oh, I would not have even hesitated." Janice chuckled. "I would have read them instantly."

"The problem is, now that we know, what do we do? I have been thinking about nothing else and my only conclusion is that I want to go see cousin Agnes. Perhaps she could shed some light on this."

"That's a very good idea. I want to go with you, if that's all right."

"Fine, but let's just keep it between us for now. Sleep on it and remember we can only discuss it when we are alone together, okay?"

"Okay, I got it."

On Saturday, the kitchen and dining room were hopping. The sugar shack tour brought in seventy guests and there were another twenty locals just in for breakfast as well. Everyone knew their jobs and things were busy but running smoothly. It was going on three o'clock before they were finished with the tours, and now they needed to get ready for the party.

They had done everything they could do on Friday in preparation for the party. Janice had already decorated the cake and it looked exactly like the original cake did. She also hung the decorations. Mrs. Snider didn't want to be bothered much with flowers, but she did want a bouquet for herself and a boutonniere for her husband Barney. Janice did the flowers to match Margarete's original bouquet as best she could from the portrait. It consisted mostly of red roses and pink carnations. Janice did a vase for each table with a single carnation and a bit of baby's breath.

Chef was making two entrees for them for dinner. They had a choice of roast beef or maple-glazed chicken, and they served it hot right from the kitchen. Most people would ask a Chef to prepare something a little fancier than roast beef, but apparently that was Barney's favourite meal, and it was his party after all.

Dinner was to start at six o'clock, and the guests began to arrive around five o'clock. Margarete's grandson brought in balloons and more balloons. He had to make four trips to his van to get them all. Mr. and Mrs. Snider, the bride and groom of fifty years, arrived about five thirty. She was in a very elegant white dress with a matching jacket and he was in a dark grey suit. Debbie told her she was still a beautiful bride.

The dinner went off with only a small hitch. Two of the waitresses had called in sick at the last moment. Debbie and Janice helped deliver the meals. The bride cut her cake and they had their first dance. Later in the evening Margarete came and found Debbie in the office.

"Is everything okay? Is there something you need, Margarete?" Debbie asked her.

"No dear, I just wanted to say thank you all so much. This has been the best party ever."

"Oh my goodness you are most welcome. I am so glad you are enjoying your special day."

"Oh, I certainly am. I wanted to thank you especially for the flowers and the cake looking like they did on my wedding day. That was so thoughtful of you. I just wanted to say thanks. I am so glad we had the party here."

"It has been my pleasure. Now go enjoy the rest of your evening."

By midnight, most of the party guests had cleared out. A few stragglers had moved over to the lounge where they joined some locals and they stayed until Ted escorted them out at two o'clock in the morning.

On Sunday, for the sugar shack tour, they served another sixty-five for the pancake buffet. Janice walked up the hill and watched one of Sanford's presentations. When she got back, she explained it all to Debbie.

"So do you think the demonstration was worth the effort? Do you feel now that your curiosity has been satisfied? Debbie asked.

"Yes, and I am not the only one who thinks so." Janice told her.

"That all went pretty smooth I thought," Henry said as he sat down to join the girls. "But I think Sanford looked relieved when I told him the traffic was starting to slow down. I hope we don't wear the old guy out."

Debbie got a chuckle out of Henry's statement, as Henry was older than Sanford by about twenty years. "I can't believe we sold out of all the fudge and cookies by noon, and I am not sure how many bottles of syrup are left, but I am going to have to get more before next weekend again." Debbie told him. "I think Sanford is surprised by the number of people that want to see how syrup is made. I recognized quite a few folks from Clifford taking the tour."

"Do you expect next weekend to be as busy as this one was?" Janice asked.

"It's possible. We'll just have to wait and see." Debbie told them both.

Chapter 30

Sometimes, it amazed Debbie how time passed so quickly. She liked being busy. It kept her focused and didn't give her time to dwell on the past, like her losing her mom. This time last year Debbie and her mom had taken a weekend trip to Toronto to go see Phantom of the Opera. They did some sightseeing and some personal shopping. Gail and Chef had managed the weekend so they could get away for a couple of days. Debbie had convinced Mom to get a message and a manicure and Mom even agreed to have her nails air brushed. Mom picked out a little tiny evergreen tree for her nails that was close to the Cedar Grove Resorts logo. She had a picture of that somewhere. Debbie couldn't help but smile at the memory.

When the bridge ladies came to play cards, they were still talking about Margarete's party. Everyone had been impressed with the dinner, how it was so good and served piping hot. Margarete was beaming from ear to ear. She knew how to throw a good party, she told them, and they all agreed. And they also commented on how much they had enjoyed the band. They had played golden oldies all night long. One of the other ladies, Mary Beth, informed them that her fiftieth anniversary was coming up in November and she thought she might like to have a party also. Debbie assured her that she was sure they could help her out with that.

By Saturday, they were back in the pancake buffet business again. Chef complained, "I will be glad when this weekend is over, I am getting tired of making pancakes."

"But Chef, you do them so well. Everyone loves them, and your fudge is certainly a hit. I think we should offer that year-round in the gift shop," Debbie suggested to him.

"You think I don't have other things to do?" he asked her.

"Well you could make a batch occasionally and when it all sells, you could make another batch," she suggested.

"I'll get right on that," he told her. She wasn't sure if he was going to do it or not, but she would ask again in a couple weeks' time. Today he was tired of pancakes and anything maple and she really couldn't blame him. Looking around at the crowd of people Debbie couldn't help but think it looked like it should be July, not April.

"Henry, there are still another twenty people waiting to go on the sugar shack tour. Why are you sitting here drinking coffee, may I ask?" Debbie inquired.

"Sanford asked me to give him fifteen minutes. He has to take the syrup off the fire and will restart another pan of sap. So I am just waiting till I hear from him before I take the next load of tourists up to his place."

"Oh. How's things going otherwise?"

"Good, but I think Sanford will be glad when this day ends," Henry told her. "There is a lot of work to making sap into syrup. More than even I realized."

"Sanford sure does a good job of it. In the past three weekends we have sold at least fifty bottles of syrup," Debbie told him.

Just then Henry's cell phone dinged a text message. "That was Sanford, he is ready for the next group." Henry headed to the dining room to round up his next load of guests.

"Henry, I would like to take the last group up so I can see the demonstration for myself, if you don't mind."

"Not at all. By now I have heard the speech so many times I can almost recite it and I am counting sap buckets in my sleep." He was chuckling on his way out the door.

Debbie was in the office when Henry came in to tell her that the last five guests were waiting in the van, ready to go to the sugar shack.

Sanford was surprised when he saw that it was Debbie driving the van. She watched and listened while he patiently explained the process of how he tapped the trees. On a piece of wood, he demonstrated how he drilled the hole and inserted the spigot. Then he explained how he collected the sap from the buckets and even let any that wanted to, have a taste of the sap. He told of how the sap was filtered in case there were any leaves in it. He went on to explain how the sap was boiled on a slow even fire until it became syrup. He also explained that it is filtered again before it is put into bottles.

He had a pan of syrup boiling over a propane burner that he drizzled over a big cube of ice and snow that he had in a big plastic tub. He then took a Popsicle stick and showed them how to twirl the sticky toffee like treat so they could all have a taste.

While they were having their maple Popsicle he asked if anyone had any questions. One guest asked about why syrup came in different colours.

Sanford explained, "The first sap run in the spring when it is still real cold will produce the lightest colour or grade of syrup. As the days warm up, so does the sap and the next run will be a little darker. And the next run is darker still. By the end of the last run, the sap will be quite dark. The darker the syrup, the stronger flavour it will have." He showed them a collection of bottles from this year. The first bottle was golden, and the fourth bottle was quite noticeably darker.

The group actually applauded Sanford before they left.

"Good job, Sanford. I would like to invite you and Mary down for dinner one night this week. My treat."

"That would be nice, how about Wednesday? And if there is any of the fudge left, could you save me a bag? I have been hearing some good things about the fudge and I would love to try it for myself."

"Absolutely. See you on Wednesday then."

Chapter 31

On Tuesday, Jake and Sally Nicholson stopped into the dining room for lunch. They owned the big cottage and Bunkie on the far side of the Muskogie Lake. They had been at the cottage for the weekend and were heading back to the city. Janice served them coffee and took their lunch order. Debbie got to be the cook today. Jake had a cheeseburger and fries and Sally had a clubhouse with a tossed salad.

When they finished eating, Debbie took the reservation book out and joined them at their table.

"Mr. and Mrs. Nicholson. How are you today?"

"Oh please, call us Jake and Sally, after all these years of knowing each other we should be on a first name basis by now," Sally told her.

"Of course, and this is my sister Janice. I don't think you have met her yet." Debbie did the introductions when Janice, today's waitress, came over to refill coffees. "Janice, this is Jake and Sally Nicholson.

"Nice to meet you," Janice said. "I have met your kids Kirk and Shelby already."

"So, have you picked a date for Shelby's wedding then?" Debbie asked.

"Yes, we would like the last Saturday in June if it is still available," Sally told her.

"I will make the notation in the reservation book. Can I get a rough idea on the number of guests?"

"Gosh I don't know, let's say for now we will reserve for a hundred people." Jake suggested.

"Noted. Now, will you be wanting to book any cabins for that weekend?"

"We never thought of that, but yes I think we should. Are any of the chalets still open that weekend?" Sally asked.

"One is already booked, which leaves two available."

"Okay, let's book the two chalets for Friday and Saturday night for us then. We can figure out who will stay where, as the time approaches." Jake suggested.

"Done. Two chalets are reserved as well as the banquet room for Friday the 15th for the rehearsal and Saturday June 27th for the wedding. Would you like to see the banquet room?"

Debbie showed them the rooms. The room divider was open, so they saw the whole space including the small stage and dance floor. She explained where the head table would go and discussed the possibility of the portable bar, told them that they could provide the cake and do the flowers as well.

Jake admitted "I didn't realize you could take care of all those things. This is going to be easier than I imagined."

"We try to offer services that you will need to make Shelby's day special. Now let's talk about the menu. Will you want wine already on the tables for toasting the bride and groom?"

"Wine on the tables would be fine" Jake suggested. "I was actually thinking about a BBQ. Perhaps ribs and chicken all smothered in BBQ sauce."

"NO. We are NOT having a BBQ for our daughter's wedding day, Sally told him. "BBQ sauce is not a good idea when everyone is in their Sunday church meeting clothes."

"Well, fine then. Choose whatever you want," Jake said.

"Perhaps we could do BBQ ribs for the rehearsal dinner on the Friday night," Debbie suggested.

"Now you're talking." Jake smiled at this wife. "That would be all right wouldn't it dear?"

"Yes that would be okay, Jake. We don't need to be dressed up for the rehearsal." Sally agreed.

"Debbie, did you come up with any ideas on who I could get to drive the boat to shuttle my guests across the lake?" Jake asked her. "And can we rent a parking spot on the main dock for that weekend as well?"

"I am sure that could be arranged. Let me make a note on that. As for a driver, Keith, my brother-in-law will be here, and he would be happy to help us out. Would you like me to hire him or would you prefer to meet him, and you and Keith can work something out?"

"You best send him over to me so we can take the boat out for a spin and I can see if he knows how to handle her before I hire him," Jake told them. "Sounds like this is all going to work out fine. I am sure it will all cost me a small fortune, but Shelby is my baby girl and I want nothing but the best for her."

"We will do everything we can to make her special day as beautiful as she is," Debbie assured them both.

"Thanks Debbie, we will be in touch to figure out all the little details. The next time Shelby is up, we will come in for lunch. I don't think she has seen the banquet room yet," Sally told her.

"No problem, stop in anytime."

Jake paid the bill, shaking her hand. "I look forward to doing business with you."

Chapter 32

Wednesday night, Sanford and Mary stopped in for dinner. They both had the baked salmon with hollandaise sauce. Sanford even remembered to try the new drink. Ted called it rum sunrise. It consisted of spiced rum, orange juice, and maple extract, topped off with a shot of grenadine and garnished with a cherry.

"How was dinner? Sanford, how did you like your drink?" Debbie asked them.

"Fine, everything was fine as usual," he told her. "The drink is a little sweet for my taste, but I liked it just fine."

"Well, after you're finished your dessert come on back to the kitchen table and we can talk business."

"We'll be a few minutes, Mary ordered Chef's crème brûlée for dessert," he told her.

When they finished Debbie was already waiting for them. "I have a cheque here for you, sir. We sold a lot of syrup these past three weekends."

"Thanks. I have a great fondness for ladies who give me money." Sanford had a big smile on his face.

"So, how did your sugar shack tours work out for you? I saw the last one and I thought your demonstration was very good." Debbie told him.

"It was okay. I was surprised at the amount of people that came. People are a curious bunch for sure," he told her.

"I know, and that was just local, last-minute advertising. I think part of it too is that spring is just around the corner and people want to get out and enjoy the nice days. Is the sap still running? Do you want to do another weekend?"

"Yes, and hell no. Yes, the sap is still running but has slowed down so I may only get one more pan and no, I don't want to do any more tours, at least not this year. What was the final tally on how many folks we had?"

"346 tours at two dollars each. That's almost seven hundred dollars in your pocket. Did you ever think you could make that much money just for talking?" Debbie asked.

"Just think, he talks to me all the time for free. Some days I would pay him just to shut up!" Mary laughed.

"The rest of the cheque is for syrup sales. Chef says we should add an extra gallon to our usual order for the kitchen as well because his maple glazed chicken is becoming very popular, so he needs more syrup. And I am trying to convince him to make fudge for the gift shops. Before I forget, here is your fudge I promised." Debbie handed him a bag of fudge

"Oh, thank you." Sanford immediately opened the bag and sampled the fudge. "Oh, my goodness this is good. It just melts in your mouth. If you start selling that, I would most likely be your best customer."

He passed Mary a small piece for her to try.

"Thanks for the taste," she said, "now give me a bigger piece!"

He reluctantly passed her the bag.

"So, Sanford, do you think we should do the sugar shack tours again next year?"

"I don't see why not. We both made a good profit, and no one got hurt. I do think a horse-drawn wagon ride would have been a nice touch. I could have given tractor rides, but I was kind of busy doing all that talking."

"Well maybe between now and next year we can get that figured out. I am thinking seriously of putting some trails in those nine acres of bush down there at the end of the campground."

"You know Ski-Doos and horses don't mix well. If you have trails, I guarantee that the Ski-Doo club will use them. I figured that sooner or later you would figure out something to do with that bush."

"It's still in the very early stages, but I am going to look into it seriously this summer." Debbie told them.

"Good luck with that. I imagine it would cost you a small fortune to cut the trails out. Do you have anyone in mind yet to do the clearing?"

"No, not yet. You got any suggestions?"

"Well I would be interested in the wood and could take down some of the trees for you but only if you don't want it done in a hurry."

"I'll have to get back to you on that. I would first have to decide on where I want the trails. Brad Mumford told me that he has areal pictures he is going to give me copies of. It may not even happen. So far, it is just another one of my big ideas."

"You surely do have some big ideas, girl." Sanford complimented her. Then he turned to Mary. "Well, old girl, are you ready to go home?"

He handed Mary the cheque and she reluctantly handed back the half-empty bag of fudge. Debbie couldn't help but smile at them. They were such a cute couple.

Chapter 33

The rest of April the resort was relatively quiet. The ice fishing was slowing down as the ice on the lakes started to become unstable. The weather was very unpredictable at this time of year. But as they say, April showers bring May flowers. It was just part of the joy of living in Canada. Debbie always enjoyed the four seasons. Each season had its own charm. She loved the spring, when everything was coming anew. The trees all budded out and the flowers were all popping their heads above the soil. Of course, she was going to lose business when the ski hill closed. They had a snow making machine, but still needed actual snow for it to work and with all the rain, it would not last much longer. That was just the nature of the beast.

Next would come summer and around the resort, they would be so busy that the next five months would be just be a blur. Debbie had to get some new brochures ready and update the resort website. This quiet time was when she usually did her advertising and promotion things.

This was the first weekend in three months that there were no cabins booked at all. Chef and Gail were both enjoying having some well-deserved extra days off. But Chef had made sure there was leftovers for Debbie, Janice and Henry to eat while he wasn't there to take care of them. They would both be in to work on Sunday for the Easter Dinner. So far, they had twenty-two reservations. Susan and Keith and the kids would also be there for the long weekend. Susan was already starting to move things into the house. They brought a car full every time they came up to the resort.

Friday evening the three sisters, Keith, and Tony were sitting chatting at the back kitchen table. They were discussing the next couple of months.

"I guess I should take another look at that advertising file." Debbie admitted to her sisters.

"Not if it's going to make you cry again." Janice told her.

"I am prepared now, but the last time I opened it, it just hit me that Mom isn't here anymore. God I never imagined I could miss someone so much. It's like my left arm is missing."

"Yes, we are all missing her. I think I miss most that I can't call and chat. Mom was always my sounding block. With the advertising file what exactly do you have to do? Is there anything I can help with?" Janice asked her.

"Well we need to make up a new brochure that we have to give to guests to inform them of different services that we offer." Debbie took a sip of her coffee.

"Why don't we have a ladies weekend package?" Susan asked. "I love getting away with a group of friends once in a while."

"A lot of ladies do that sort of thing," Janice commented. "I occasionally get together with a group of my friends and we go away for a weekend without husbands and kids. But I have been too busy for the past couple of years and haven't seen any of the girls in a while. I guess now that I am home to stay, I will probably lose touch with them altogether now." Janice sounded sad.

"You should make the effort. It is not good to lose friends," Debbie told her.

"Yeah you're right. So, what options do we have available?" Susan asked.

"I am not sure. We would need to find out if there is anyone in Clifford or one of the other little towns that has a person who would come here to the resort to pamper our guests," Debbie told them. "We would need someone to do manicures and pedicures. Also, perhaps someone who could do massages. Maybe someone to do facials. I don't really know what is available. We would need to know if it is possible and what the cost per person would be."

"Why don't you let me work on that? I could make some phone calls, look into that for you." Janice offered.

"Sure, that would be a big help. And I will work on the brochure. We will also need to update the website. I hate doing that, but it needs to be done occasionally."

"Susan is better at that than I am, but I could probably help you with that." Janice offered.

"I would love to help with the website," Susan told them.

"Well I'm not ready just yet, Susan maybe you could look at it the next time you're home. I will try to have some new things to add to the site ready for you by then. I will work on that first."

"So, I will work on the ladies weekend idea and you're going to work on advertising and Susan will work on the website. That sounds fair," Janice said.

Janice and Debbie spent a lot of the next week working in the office. Debbie chose some new pictures that should be added to the website. She called her sister Susan and discussed what was currently on the site and what they should delete and add. Susan had some suggestions and seemed quite interested in helping out. Susan asked Debbie to email her the pictures and she could work on it from home. Debbie preferred she do it at the office so she could work with her, one on one. It would be so much easier to explain it all in person. Debbie could do the website, and had been doing it previously, but honestly, it frustrated her to no end. If Susan wanted to do Debbie was more than happy to let her.

Debbie also called the local newspaper to arrange to advertise the Easter brunch and dinner as well as the upcoming crib tournament for next Saturday. Janice had just walked into the office and overheard Debbie on the phone.

"How does the crib tournament work, anyhow?" Janice asked. "And what do we need to do for it?"

"People come for the day and play crib. They pay twenty dollars per person, which gets them a buffet lunch and an afternoon of playing crib with cash prizes."

"How many people usually come?"

"I just looked that up. Last year we had thirty-five players. The year before that we only had twenty-eight."

"So we need to put together a lunch buffet and set up tables and chairs, I am assuming in the banquet room."

"You got it sis. See, you are getting the hang of how things work around here. I must say I am quite pleased with how you are stepping up and helping out. I want you to know that I appreciate all your help."

"Well I am here, and I want to learn. You are a good teacher. Who knew?" Janice teased Debbie.

On Easter Sunday they offered a brunch buffet that was enjoyed by twenty-five guests. The buffet had the usual assortment of brunch items. This time Chef made them quiche Loraine with ham and cheese filling. He also made pancakes with mini candy-coated chocolate Easter eggs which were shaped like a rabbit's head with the two pointed ears. They were almost too cute to eat. The dessert table included a fresh fruit tray and an assortment of tarts, French pastries, and cupcakes iced in Easter colours. There was also a beautiful flat cake that Janice had decorated as a big Easter basket filled with chocolate bunnies and eggs in the pastel colours.

They served another thirty-eight people with the dinner buffet. Chef had made his famous cream of potato and bacon soup. There was also a breadbasket which included some of his fabulous fresh dinner rolls. As expected, for Easter dinner Chef prepared ham and scalloped potatoes. For dessert, there was another cake decorated similarly to the one they had earlier with the colourful Easter basket. There were also freshly baked pies. Chef had made pumpkin pie and raspberry pie, which he knew was Debbie's absolute favourite dessert.

Brad and Tina Mumford came in for dinner. Debbie walked through the dining room just as they were finishing their cake.

"How was dinner, everything okay?" she asked them.

"Wonderful as usual. That glazed ham and the pineapple sauce was amazing. If I could cook that well, I might try more often," Tina offered.

"I am glad you enjoyed it. So the Ski-Doo season must be almost over, Brad, what are you going to do with all your spare time now?" Debbie asked him.

"This is the time I get busy building cottages and houses. My phone is already starting to ring off the hook." His phone rang in his pocket as if on cue. "I brought those pictures in for you. If you have a minute and we could find an empty table, I can explain them to you if you'd like." Brad handed her an oversized envelope and answered his phone.

Looking around she realized there was no empty tables available in the dining room. "I think we will have to go to the back kitchen table if that is okay."

"Sure. Tina, I'll be right back," he told his wife.

"Go ahead. I will be out here eating some more of that delicious cake."

Once the photos were opened up, Brad explained where her boundary lines were. He even had a red marker in his pocket and marked her copies for easier reference.

"I do so appreciate you giving me these copies. I figured that would be my first cost for this project to get these aerial shots."

"They were already done, so why pay for it again. The club has not had its final spring meeting yet, but I knew I was coming for dinner and figured you might be anxious to see them."

"You know me too well, old friend."

"Hey lady, watch who you're calling old. You are just as old as me."

"I meant old as in long-time friend, not age, you smartass," she told him.

"I know, I was just having fun with you, snookum." He put his arm around her shoulder and gave her a squeeze. "If you have any more questions about the pictures, just give me a call. I can stop by anytime."

"Thanks Brad, I am sure I will have questions when I try to study these." Debbie told him. "You are truly the best."

"Okay, then I better get back out to Tina before she finishes off your cake."

Snookum? Is that what Brad had called her? She didn't like the name but had to admit the little squeeze sure was nice. She had to keep her emotions in check whenever Brad was around. He still made her pulse race.

After all the guests had left, the family and staff all sat down and enjoyed a meal together. Debbie even called and invited Henry to come join them. No sense on him sitting at home eating alone.

They all seemed to be in good spirits. There was a lot of laughing and teasing, mostly directed at Tony and Janice. Tony was quickly becoming a fixture around the lodge. He seemed to be there every weekend, but no one minded. He was always happy and pleasant to be around, and he wasn't afraid to step in and lend a hand when he could be of any use. Everyone liked him, especially Janice. She was head over heels in love with Tony, even if she didn't know it yet.

Chapter 34

On Monday, the three sisters were sitting in the lounge talking about the summer's upcoming bookings. They still had cabins available, and they had a major event booked for almost every weekend from the first of June right through till the end of September. It was shaping up to be a good year.

They had upcoming weddings, anniversary and birthday parties as well as fishing derbies and boat races. That was all above the steady flow of guests that were there for holidays and vacations.

Debbie was explaining how in the past, she went to the sportsman show and the local home and cottage show to promote the resort and hopefully get more room reservations, but both shows cost money to attend. With the entrance fees, cost of labour to staff the booth for the three days per show, and the travel and meals expenses involved she was debating going to the shows and wanted her sisters input.

"The big sportsman show in Toronto is the most expensive show. I guestimate the cost to do that show will be almost four thousand dollars. The local show will only cost half of that, more like two thousand dollars." Debbie explained to them.

Janice asked, "Why such a difference in the price?"

"Well Toronto is bigger, so more exposure, more possible sales and it is farther away so the travel portion will also cost more. And for the show in Toronto, you have to go in and set up your booth on the Thursday which adds another day you have to stay there but with no potential for sales for that day. The local show in Clifford is smaller, so less possibilities, so their entry fee is less and we don't have to stay in a hotel to do the show. Our travel and meal expense is substantially less for the smaller show." Debbie explained.

They talked about the past shows and made the decision to skip the Toronto show and focus on the Clifford show instead. They also discussed giving out a breakfast reward card and reusable bags with the Cedar Grove Resort logo printed on the side.

"It is so nice to have you guys to bounce ideas off. I really appreciate your input on these kinds of things. So, it is settled then. We are going to get one hundred reward cards made for the show, and I will send in the entry fee to reserve us a booth. Janice, you will need to get the design done quite quickly as the show is the second week of June, which only gives us like eight weeks to pull this off. And Susan, can you call to find out the cost and if they can get them done in time? We will need two thousand bags for the show and depending on the price per bag perhaps we could order extra that we could us in the gift shop. I have the logo on the office computer in a file all ready to go."

"I will take care of the bags," Susan offered.

"This is fun!" Janice said. "We are really getting the hang of this resort entrepreneur thing."

"You go, girl." Susan told her, they all laughed.

Chapter 35

The day of the crib tournament was a wet, rainy day. The buffet lunch was scheduled to start at noon, but some of the anxious players arrived earlier than expected. Gail seated them and gave them all tea and coffee.

The lunch buffet was a cold buffet. Chef had made trays of sandwiches and wraps. There were several salads, including tossed and Caesar, potato, macaroni and coleslaw as well as broccoli and carrot salads. There were pickles and a cheese tray. For dessert, Chef made a fresh fruit salad along with an assortment of French pastries filled with chocolate and whipped cream. Janice had decorated a slab cake to look like a crib board.

Once everyone was finished lunch, Debbie invited them all into the banquet room. It was still decorated with the tulle and lights and a couple of the players had commented how pretty it was and that she didn't need to go to all that trouble just for them.

They had an even forty players and they played in teams of two until the winners were declared. Debbie came in and awarded the prizes.

"I would like to thank all you nice folks for coming out for our annual crib tournament. As you know the prizes are calculated from the number of participants. 3rd place will receive seventy-five dollars, 2nd place gets one hundred dollars, and the winning team receives two hundred dollars in cash. Will the winning teams please come forward to collect your loot?"

Once the money was all handed out, Debbie told them, "I hope you all had a fun afternoon and I will see you all again next year."

Later, sitting in the office, Janice told Debbie, "I didn't think of it soon enough but we could make this Mom's memorial tournament. Wasn't this originally her idea? I know she loved crib."

"That is a very good idea. Perhaps we could have a trophy with the yearly winners added like we do for the hockey tournament." Debbie agreed. "Let's look into that for next year."

After the crib players were all gone, Debbie and Janice took a drive to go visit Cousin Agnes. Debbie had called and found out she was indeed home and would love to see them. It would be about a forty-five minute drive out past Clifford. When the girls got there, Agnes made them tea and served them homemade cookies.

"Sorry about your mom's passing. I don't get out much anymore and could not make the trip to go to the memorial service. I sure do miss our phone chats though. So, I assume you girls have some questions you would like to ask me? Go ahead, then." Agnes folded her hands.

Debbie explained about the letters they found and asked Agnes, "Did you know that Susan's biological father is Jefferson Penfold?"

"Yes, I knew. Your mother loved him very much when she was a young woman. She was dating him and your dad at the same time many years ago."

"Do you know where he lives?" Janice asked.

"Last I heard, he was retired and lived down around the Ottawa area somewhere. I haven't seen him in a couple of years though." Agnes told them. "I am sure if you wanted to find him it wouldn't be too hard now with that internet thingy."

"Do you know if our dad knew that he was raising another man's daughter?"

"As far as I know, your mother never told him. But knowing the kind of man he was, I doubt that it would have made no difference to him." Agnes said. "He was a good father to all three of you girls and he loved your mother very much."

"I can't help but wonder why Mom didn't tell us after our dad passed away." Debbie commented.

"I asked her that once and your mom told me that Susan was doing just fine and telling her then would be a big mistake." Agnes admitted. "Your mom felt it was best to just let sleeping dogs lie, so to speak."

"You don't think Susan had a right to know?" Janice asked.

"Not my place to say, really. It was your mother's decision to make, and as her cousin and friend I had to respect her wishes."

They thanked Agnes for the tea, cookies, and answers, and headed home. They discussed it between them and decided to see if they could locate Jefferson Penfold on "that internet thingy," as Agnes had put it.

Chapter 36

Janice and Debbie spent the next couple weeks working in the office. Janice had made some contacts regarding the girls' weekend package.

"I think I have the girls' weekend package figured out," she told Debbie. "I have found a lady who will come here to do manicures and pedicures, a different lady will do facials, and another who will do massages. Here is a list of their contact information and prices."

"This is wonderful," said Debbie. "So let's talk it out. You and a few of your girlfriends come for the weekend. You all arrive Friday night and probably spend the night in the bar. Saturday, let us say after lunch, you are scheduled to get your nails done. The six of you can't all get done at the same time, so while some are doing that, others are getting a message or a facial. You should find out if the lady doing the facials could also apply makeup. So by Saturday night you are all pampered up and no place to go. So, what then, perhaps there is a band in the bar you might as well go listen to. Sunday you would enjoy a late farewell brunch, check out and on your way home all pampered and relaxed."

"Sounds good to me," Janice said. "Sign me up."

"I wouldn't expect the girls to spend two nights in the bar unless there was some attraction like a band. What about Friday night, maybe something like doing a wine tasting party? Ted is very knowledgeable bartender and I am sure he could handle a wine tasting."

"Good idea. I like that. Yes, I definitely think that would be a nice bonus." Janice agreed. "You told me that you usually have a mini vacation this time of year. What do you think about having a staycation here and we test drive this girls weekend package? We could invite Susan and her friend Beverly I will invite my friend Sherry and you could invite Valerie. Just a thought."

"Geez I have never been a guest here before, but I do like that idea. Let's call Susan and see what she thinks. First, we need to pick a date and see if everyone is available. It would have to be soon. Next Saturday is Chef's seventieth birthday so it would have to be the weekend after that." Debbie told her.

"What are we doing for Chef's birthday?"

"I thought we could throw him a little surprise party. I have already spoken with his two kids. His daughter Kathy and his son Ben are both coming home for the weekend, but don't mention it to Chef. We are hoping to keep it a surprise."

"Oh, what fun? Who is going to make the food?"

"Chef is. I am going to tell him it is a cold buffet for a retirement party. Then the day of the party, he will be surprised when his kids show up and realize the party is actually for his birthday that he thinks we have forgotten about."

"And I can decorate the cake, but he will have to bake it first," Janice offered. "I will have to be sneaky about it though."

"I am sure we can pull it off if we all work together on it," Debbie assured her. "Now, let's call Susan."

Susan told them yes, to count her in. Janice went ahead and booked all the necessary ladies to do the girls' weekend. The original lady to do the nails was not available that weekend so she had to find a different lady for that. While Janice worked on that, Debbie worked out the details for the birthday party.

By Friday night, Chef's kids had arrived. Kathy lived just outside Toronto and had brought her husband and three kids with her. Her brother Ben had come from Arizona, so he flew into Toronto and Kathy picked him up at the airport. They arrived at the resort late on Friday night. Debbie put them all in the closest chalet. After they were settled in, they all came over to the lounge and had a visit. Tomorrow morning, they were going to Clifford and would not return until after lunch. The party would start at two o'clock and hopefully they would surprise their dad. Chef George didn't know anything about the party yet.

Saturday morning Chef arrived with his usual cheerful greeting.

"Morning, Chef" Debbie responded. "Looks like it is going to be a nice sunny day today for a change. Glad to see the sunshine. Getting a little tired of all the rain we have had over the past couple weeks."

Chef went ahead and started the breakfast prep. Debbie was sure that he was probably disappointed that she hadn't told him happy birthday. He likely figured that she had forgotten, and he would not bring it up.

The morning went by, business as usual. They had a few guests who stopped in for breakfast. Chef was busy getting prepared for the retirement party. He had made a nice cold buffet. There were trays of sandwiches and wraps, veggies and dip, pickles, and cheese trays. For dessert, he had made an assortment of pastries, tarts and cupcakes. He had baked a cake yesterday, but Janice had decorated it and had taped the box shut so he knew the cake was ready, but just hadn't seen it yet.

There were two tables that had come in for lunch, and when Chef had finished making their food Debbie asked him to join her at a table in the dining room for a quick meeting.

Why are we not meeting at the back kitchen table?" he asked Debbie.

"Well I was already sitting here working and I just wanted to discuss the upcoming girls' weekend with you." Debbie told him. "And by the way, happy birthday Chef."

Chef's kids were just walking through the front door. The look on Chef's face was worth all their efforts to keep the secret. When he saw his kids and grandkids, he was overwhelmed. Debbie excused herself while they got the hugs and greetings out of the way.

By one thirty, there were fifty people there to celebrate Chef George's seventieth birthday. All the staff had come, as well as many friends and neighbours. Brad and Tina Mumford were there as well as Nancy and Robert Martin from the ski lodge. Thomas Townsend from the golf course came, as did Sanford and Mary Bradley, their syrup suppliers. Jake and Sally Nicholson had come just for the day. They could not get across Muskogie Lake to their cottage until the ice finished going out, probably another couple of weeks before that could happen.

Everyone helped themselves to the buffet, and at about three o'clock, Janice brought the cake out. She had decorated it like a chef's hat. Written across the cake were the words "happy seventieth birthday" and "Chef George" was written across the band. It had a dozen candles stuck into it.

"Make a wish," Janice told him.

"My wish has already come true. My kids are here. What more could I possible need to wish for?" Chef blew out his candles and cut the cake. He then opened all his gifts. He received a lot of cookbooks, which he enjoyed. The staff had gone together and bought him a bottle of twelve-year-old scotch. Debbie had bought him a beautiful leather notebook and had his initials embossed on the front. His son gave him an airline ticket for a trip to Arizona attached to a box of cigars. His daughter gave him a new beautiful housecoat and slippers.

When all the gifts were opened, Chef stood up. "Thank you all so much for all these beautiful gifts. I would have to admit that I thought everyone had forgotten that today was my birthday. I am so thankful for all the friends I have here and my lovely family. Thank you all for coming and celebrating this old man's birthday."

They had three tables come in for dinner and Debbie did the cooking. She had kicked Chef out of the kitchen. He was over at the chalet enjoying time with his family. She was very pleased at how the party had gone. They actually managed to surprise Chef George. That in itself was amazing. Generally speaking, you could not keep a secret in the resort but they had managed to keep this one from him at least.

Chapter 37

Spring was always messy usually because of all the rain, but it was also a time of rebirth. The sunrises and sunsets were breathtakingly beautiful. The flowers were bravely poking their heads up through the ground. The birds were happily singing and even the air smelt new. Everyone seemed to be in high spirits. Sunshine can do that to people.

Debbie and Janice spent a couple days outside playing in the flower beds. Debbie discovered that Janice was quite the gardener. Janice had gone into Clifford and had bought some new plants. The flower beds were mostly full of perennials which came back each year and Janice had added a few annuals in the front of the beds just for a splash of colour. Henry had finished all the scheduled cabin renovations and was now starting to clean up outside. He had raked all the front yard in front of the lodge. The resort was starting to look real nice. Debbie was pleased to see all their hard work paying off.

Henry walked by on his way in for lunch. "Those petunias make me think of your mom. I can almost hear her saying, *'you're as welcome as the flowers in May.'*"

"I was just having the exact same thought." Janice chuckled.

By the time Friday rolled around, they were all tired but pleased with their efforts. The resort looked good and Debbie felt good leaving it in the capable hands of Gail and Chef while she was going to enjoy having the weekend off. At their Friday morning meeting, Gail asked her for her pager. Gail had told her that she was a guest, not a manager this weekend. Chef told her she was not allowed in the kitchen or the office for the entire weekend. It felt very strange to Debbie. She couldn't help but think that the staff was having way too much fun with the boss being a guest.

Gail told Debbie to go upstairs and pack her bags. She was moving over to the chalet for the weekend and they would see her and Janice for lunch in the dining room. When they arrived at the chalet there was a big bottle of wine already chilling in the wine bucket on the living room table with six glasses and the bottle opener waiting for them.

"That is a nice touch. Wonder who thought of that?" Janice asked her sister.

"I don't know, it is only ten a.m. It's not too early to open it, is it?"

"It's five o'clock somewhere." Janice popped the cork and poured them both a glass. "Well, here's to a wonderful weekend sis. When are the rest of the ladies arriving, I wonder?"

"Valerie won't get here till this afternoon. She said she had a meeting this morning and would be leaving after that. Susan and Beverly will be here by dinnertime. Have you heard from Sherry?"

"She is already on her way. She might even make it in time for lunch." Janice told her. "I haven't seen Sherry since my breakup. We talk on the phone all the time, but I haven't been able to hug her in a long time. I am excited to see her."

"So, should we go ahead and pick rooms or wait to decide until everyone arrives?" Debbie asked.

"Well I know you and Valerie had shared a bed before so I think you should get the king size bed in the master bedroom."

"I don't know that I should necessarily get the best bed, but I am smart enough to agree with you when you have a good idea."

"It is all yours, sis. God knows you deserve it."

"All right then, I am going to finish this glass of wine and then take my stuff upstairs."

"Sounds like a plan, but I am in no hurry." Janice said as she refilled their wine glasses.

The door opened. "Is this the blue jay chalet?" Sherry asked.

"Come on in here girl." Janice got up to help her friend. "Here, let me get that for you." Janice took her luggage and added it to the growing pile. Sherry removed her coat and boots then got hugs from both the sisters.

"Oh, it is so nice to be here. The place looks good, and this chalet is beautiful," Sherry told them. "Thanks so much for the invite. This is just what I needed, a little rest and relaxation to get rejuvenated."

"Cheers to that." Janice handed her friend a glass of wine and they all clinked glasses.

Eventually the girls did manage to get their luggage hauled up to the rooms. Janice filled the hot tub with water and bubbles in case anyone wanted to use it later. Then they all congregated back in the living room and the three ladies had another glass of wine.

They eventually made it to the lodge to have lunch. Gail greeted them and wanted to take their drink orders. The all ordered pop since they had already gotten into the wine and were to do a wine tasting later that evening. The girls all ordered the soup and sandwich special, cream of broccoli soup with a grilled ham and cheese sandwich.

Debbie asked Gail if she would jot down some notes for her over the weekend, otherwise she was going to have to go into the office to do it herself. Gail agreed to keep notes for her.

"For starters, the bottle of wine was a very nice touch. Whose idea was that anyways?"

"Ted's idea. He actually bought that for you gals to enjoy." Gail told them.

"Well I think that should be included in the package. It is a nice touch. We would not advertise it, but just add it into the cost and it will be a nice surprise when the ladies arrive." Debbie said. When the ladies finished their lunch, they headed back to the chalet.

Janice and Sherry had another glass of wine, but Debbie opted for a bottle of water from the fridge. They were sitting in the comfy couches in the living room.

"I noticed that beautiful picture of the blue jay earlier but just now made the connection that this is the blue jay chalet." Sherry commented. "So does the cardinal chalet have a picture of a cardinal, and the robin chalet a picture of a robin?"

"Good guess. Yes, that would be exactly right." Janice told her. "Kind of corny but cute at the same time, and the pictures are all quite beautiful in their own right."

When Valerie arrived, she knocked but no one answered. The door wasn't locked so she stuck her head in. "Hello, anybody here? Where are you guys?"

"Hi Val, we are all in the hot tub. Grab a glass of wine and your swimsuit and come join us." Debbie told her while she stood there dripping on the floor. Valerie got a glass of wine and joined the ladies in the oversized bathroom where she sat on the edge of the tub.

"Looks like you have started the party without me." Valerie commented.

"Come here and give me a hug," Debbie offered, standing up out of the water.

"That's okay. I will hug you later, when you're not quite so wet if it's all the same to you. Hi Janice, nice to see you again." Val said.

"Hi Val. This is my best friend Sherry. Sherry this is Debbie's BFF Valerie." Janice was kind enough to make the introductions. "I guess I will have to wait for my hug, too."

"Yep, I think that would be best. So what room am I in? I will go unpack some stuff and see if I can find my suit. That hot tub does look very inviting. Are you gals planning on being in here much longer?" Val said.

"We just got in the tub. You're bunking with me again, but at least we get the king size bed this weekend. You okay with that?" Debbie asked her.

"Not a problem. I can live with that. Thank God at least you don't snore."

"Last door on the right." Debbie told the back of her head as she walked out of the bathroom.

When they were all getting out of the hot tub Debbie started handing out towels and robes from the warmer. "Holy crap, warm robes, I absolutely love this place," Valerie told them. "Don't get me wrong, the cabins are nice, but this is so much nicer."

"I sure hope so. These luxury chalets are twice the price of our regular cabins, so they need to be twice as nice to stay in." Debbie explained.

"They definitely are. Rich people just get to live so much nicer than us regular folks, don't they?" Sherry commented. "I guess what they say is true. Money does afford privilege."

After they finished their time in the hot tub, they hung out around the big kitchen table and shared some funny memories. Susan had called Janice's cell phone. Janice put her on speaker phone. Susan said they were in Clifford at the grocery store. She wanted to know what everyone wanted for snacks for later. Sherry and Valerie volunteered that they had both brought chips and dips. Debbie suggested perhaps some kielbasa and cheese, and maybe some fresh bagels and cream cheese for breakfast, and some coffee cream as well.

Susan and Beverly arrived just before dinner. There was still chilled wine left in the ice bucket, and they emptied the bottle. Susan went to her luggage still sitting at the door and produced another bottle to replace it with. After all the introductions were made and everyone got their hugs, they settled in. Susan and Beverly took their luggage into their room and when they came back out, they both had very colourful Hawaiian shirts on.

"Oh cool, what a good idea. Wish we had of thought of that." Janice said.

"It's okay, we got you covered." Susan produced four more Hawaiian shirts for her friends. "Just in case any of you ladies wants to join us. We are on vacation, after all."

"At least we won't lose anyone in the bar later," Janice joked.

Debbie smiled. "We will have to wear them for dinner because we are going directly to the bar from the dining room. We might get some strange looks, but that's okay. If anyone complains, we will tell them to take it up with the manger. Gail won't know what to say about that." They spent the next half hour laughing at what poor Gail would do in that silly situation.

When the six ladies walked into the dining room, the three tables already eating dinner couldn't help but notice. Debbie knew the guests at two of the tables, so she went over just to say hi and explained loud enough for everyone to hear that her sisters and friends were having a girls' weekend holiday and were just out for some fun.

Gail commented, "It is nice to see you ladies this evening. You all look so festive in your pretty shirts. May I suggest cocktails, perhaps something with an umbrella in it."

That was all it took, and the silly laughter started all over again. Even the other tables were laughing along with them. Chef George poked his head into the dining room to see what was so funny. He came over to their table just to say hello.

"Chef, we have another shirt in the cabin if you're interested," Susan offered.

"Thanks, but no thanks. I think I will just make do with the one I already have on."

Their drinks arrived and every one of them had an umbrella in it, even Sherry's beer. And the laughter started all over again.

Gail offered them menus and they settled down and got dinners ordered. Debbie ordered a garlic bread with cheese to start them off. Perhaps it would absorb some of the wine they had already consumed.

For dinner, Janice and Susan both had the baked salmon with hollandaise sauce. Sherry had a charbroiled steak, Beverly had the maple glazed chicken, and Debbie was the only one to order the Chef's special. She had pork medallions in a raspberry wine sauce. Over the course of the meal, they all tried each other's entrees. Debbie had, of course, tried all the dinner entrees, but the other five ladies were curious to try everything. While they were eating, two more tables came in for dinner. One of the couples was Brad and Tina.

He just nodded and smiled as they passed bye on the way to their table. Valarie gave Debbie a nudge, raised her eyebrows and quietly said, "Hubba Hubba."

"Down girl, can't you see he is with his wife?" Debbie quietly questioned her friend. "Besides I heard you had a new man in your life."

"I absolutely do, but I still have eyes. It is a sin not to appreciate eye candy like that," Val told her.

"I agree with Val. Hubba Hubba," Sherry said.

"Sherry. Aren't you a happily married woman?" Susan asked her.

"Sure am, but like Val, I still have an appreciation for the finer things in life." Sherry grinned.

As Gail picked up their empty plates, she offered them desserts. "Tonight for dessert, we have a decadent chocolate cake, fresh baked apple pie Or Chef's famous Crème Brule. What can I get you ladies?" Debbie took note that Gail had not just asked it they wanted dessert. It is a proven fact that if the waitress asks if you want dessert the instant response is no. But, if you tell them the selections and ask which one they would like, they at least think about what they were asked before they respond. Even though Gail had done a good job of offering, no one could be tempted with dessert. They all knew they needed room for the wine they were all about to taste. Although the dinner would be included in the package, Debbie still left Gail a fifty dollar tip. She slid it under Valarie's glass so that Gail wouldn't know it came from Debbie, or she probably wouldn't have accepted it.

Once the ladies moved on into the bar and got seated, Ted came over to say hi. "Ladies, don't you all look beautiful tonight. I understand you want to do some wine tasting."

"We would love to taste whatever you are offering," Beverly told him in a sultry voice. Debbie couldn't help but think to herself that this was going to be a long night.

Ted blushed. "Oh, it's gonna be like that is it?"

They all laughed at his response.

When they were quiet, he continued. "Okay then, shall we get started? First of all, what kind of wine do you each prefer, white or red?"

The general consensus was five to one in favor of the white.

"Okay then, we will focus on the white wines. Anyone who drinks red wine can also drink white, but not many people who prefer white will drink red. I have chosen three different wines for you to try. I will be right back with the first samples."

Ted came back with a wine bottle and six glasses, each with an inch of wine in it. He passed the glasses around, showed them the label on the bottle and explained the name of the wine and where it was from. The first taste was good but a little on the dry side.

"Tell me what you taste. What flavours do you feel on your tongues?" While they were discussing that, Ted gave them a basket of tiny bread pieces to clean their pallets, took the bottle back, and set it on the bar with the label facing out.

He then came back with a different bottle and six new glasses, again with an inch of wine in each glass. He explained the name of this wine and its origins. "Can you taste the difference? You may notice this one is not as dry." He explained about the different sugar contents in each wine and that this particular wine would be a medium wine. Again, he put the second bottle on the bar beside the first one and returned with the third and final bottle and six new glasses.

"Tell me what you taste. Can you taste the difference? This would be considered a sweeter wine." He took the third bottle to the bar and set it with the other two. Just as he was explaining the differences, Brad and Tina came in from the dining room and two guys Debbie recognized from Clifford came in the front door.

"Wow, you ladies drink much?" Brad asked referring to all the empty wine glasses currently sitting on the table in front of them.

"We were thirsty," Janice offered. And they started into the laughing again.

Ted got the other guests their drinks and then came back to his ladies. "So, now you can each have a glass of wine compliments of the house. You need to tell me which bottle you liked the best, which of the wines would you like to have a glass of, and I will even get a red wine if you prefer."

Susan picked the first bottle, Valerie and Sherry picked the third bottle, Beverly asked for the red and Debbie and Janice chose the number two bottle which was the medium dryness. Ted grabbed a handful of empty glasses from their table and went back to the bar to pour the wine. He brought the first three glasses and took away some more of the empty glasses on his way back to the bar. By the time he delivered the last glasses of wine they were left with only their full six glasses of wine on the table.

"Thank you, Ted, that was interesting and well presented. And also thank you for the bottle of wine in our chalet as well. It was a very welcome surprise." Debbie told him.

"You are most welcome. Glad you enjoyed it." Ted retreated back behind the bar. He had some wine glasses to wash and put away.

When they finished their wine, they graduated to cocktails. The ladies all ordered a different drink and then spent the next half hour trying each other's drinks. Brad put some quarters in the old jukebox just as more people came in. The bar was really starting to rock. It was close to midnight before Janice said she was hungry. They decided to call it a night and head back to the chalet. They had margaritas and Pina coladas ready to go in the blender waiting for them. Debbie gave Val a fifty dollar bill and asked her to slip it into Ted's tip jar on the bar. They left the bar arm in arm, singing to the song that was currently playing on the jukebox.

Back at the chalet, Valerie was put in charge of the blender and Susan volunteered to provide the snacks. They all sat around the big kitchen table, mostly because it was closest to the blender and the snacks. From there, it was drinks in the hot tub. It was past two a.m. before they pulled the plug on the tub and all settled in bed for the night.

Chapter 38

When the next morning dawned, it was going on ten a.m. before everyone was up and had a coffee. They went over to the lodge for lunch. Debbie asked Gail to make a note that each chalet should have a blender and some coffee mate, the artificial powdered creamer to go with the complimentary coffee and sugar.

After lunch, the ladies all got back into their bathing suits. They were expecting their pampering to start at one thirty. Julie was the first lady to arrive. She was there to give the pedicures and manicures. Next came Sally, the lady who was going to be giving them all half hour massages. Marge was there to do haircuts and styles. And finally, Crystal arrived a few minutes later to do facials and makeup.

Janice had already filled the hot tub and three of the ladies were already in the tub when their beauty team arrived.

Debbie made sure the ladies were all set up where they needed to be and had everything they needed. Then she delivered the ladies each a glass of wine. "Let the pampering begin!"

First Debbie had the message. It was amazing. Sally found sore spots on her body that she didn't even know were there. When Debbie finished her message, Crystal was free, so she went and had her facial. Next, she went for a soak in the hot tub before she went to Julie for a pedicure and manicure. Debbie was allergic to the artificial nails so Julie just buffed and polished Debbie's own nails in a bright red colour. Some of the girls had artificial nails put on. Then she went to see Marge for a haircut and style. Marge talked her into getting some highlights. The only thing left for Debbie to do was to see Crystal again for her to put her makeup on. By five thirty, the ladies were all gathered back in the living room, all pampered and beautiful.

"We still clean up good for a bunch of old ladies, don't you think?" Janice asked the group.

"Yes you do, and as for me, I am absolutely gorgeous. I just love my new hair style. I feel pretty, oh so pretty," Sherry said as she twirled around the living room.

"Yes you are gorgeous. I think we all look beautiful." Susan said. "I am glad we all agreed to bring dresses for dinner and dancing."

"When everyone is finished their wine, we will head over to the lodge for dinner. There's no hurry, but I am starting to get hungry." Debbie's stomach rumbled.

"Let's all have one more glass," Janice said as she refilled everyone's glasses.

"I think Ted would tell us this chardonnay is a medium, wouldn't you agree?" Sherry asked. "See, we did learn something this weekend."

"Ted the bartender is kind of cute didn't you think?" Beverly asked them.

"You ladies have a one-track mind. Do your husbands and boyfriends know you talk like this when they are not around?" Debbie asked.

"Don't you think they do the same thing when we are not there?" Susan pointed out. "You can bet your sweet behind they do the exact same thing. Besides we are just looking, not touching. It is all harmless fun."

"Well if I may, I would like to make a toast." Beverly raised her glass. "To Debbie, Susan and Janice, congrats on being resort owners. The resort looks like it is thriving, and this chalet is gorgeous. Thanks so much for inviting me this weekend. I think your girls' weekend package is amazing. I can't remember the last time I felt this spoiled and pampered. Here's to good food, good friends and good times." Beverly told them. "Cheers."

They all clinked glasses.

"Here, here. I couldn't have said it better myself," Sherry added. Thanks so much for including me. Having friends in high places definitely has its advantages."

"Me three," Valerie added. "This has been amazing. I didn't realize how badly I needed a little R&R from my life. A weekend away with some good friends is just what I needed. Thanks for inviting me. Cheers."

They clinked glasses again.

"Well, you are all welcome. Thanks for coming and helping us try out this girls' weekend package. This is the first time I have ever been a guest at my resort and it has been very enjoyable, thanks to you lovely ladies." Debbie told them. "Now, can we go eat? I have worked up an appetite."

When the ladies arrived at the dining room there were two other tables already eating and another table had just sat down.

"Wow, you ladies all look so pretty tonight. How did you all enjoy your afternoon of pampering?" Gail asked them.

"It was truly amazing. Although I may need some time to get used to these bright red fingernails." Debbie told her.

"I like the highlights in your hair," Gail commented. "Okay, so let's start you off with some beverages. What are you ladies drinking tonight?" Again, they all ordered a different cocktail and then each tried the others' drinks. Debbie had ordered a strawberry daiquiri which was one her favourite drinks.

For dinner, Debbie ordered the nacho platter as a starter they could share while Chef prepared their dinners. The special tonight was beef stroganoff, which Susan, Beverly, and Debbie ordered. Valerie ordered garlic shrimp on wild rice, Sherry chose the glazed ham and Janice ordered chicken parmesan. And then they all had to taste each other's dinners. While they were eating their meal, another table of two came in. The ladies were actually being quiet tonight.

Debbie always contributed it to good food when the guests were quiet because they were too busy enjoying their meals to be talking.

When they finished, Gail came over to pick up their empty plates. "For dessert tonight we have a selection of pies. There is cherry, raspberry or pumpkin. And we also have the Chef's famous crème brûlée. What can I bring you ladies for dessert?"

"I would have a piece of raspberry pie with ice cream please," Debbie said.

"Well it would just be rude to let you eat dessert by yourself so I think I will try the crème brûlée, please." Sherry said.

"I would try the pumpkin pie with whipped cream," Beverly said.

"You better make that two pumpkin pies," Susan added.

Janice and Valerie declined. "But," said Valerie, "you should bring us both forks just in case anyone needs help finishing their desserts."

"Gail, could you ask Ted to make us six Cedar Grove toddies please?" Debbie asked her.

They enjoyed their drinks and desserts and were just content to sit there enjoying each other's company. They were all so relaxed from the afternoon of pampering and now they were all full from the wonderful dinner they had just eaten. No one seemed to be in a hurry to get up from the table.

Finally, Janice suggested "We better get moved into the bar. I can hear the band warming up and we want to get a good table." Janice chose a table in the middle of the room, one that was not too close to the band and not too close to the bar. Once they were seated, Ted came over.

"Good evening to all you beautiful ladies. What is everyone drinking tonight?" Ted asked. "If you like rum, our rum sunrise is very popular."

Debbie chose to have one of those, and the other ladies all picked a different cocktail.

"I would like to order a margarita and six shots of tequila." Susan said. "Maybe I will share with my friends."

"Sounds good, I'll be right back," Ted said as he headed to another table.

The band started playing. Debbie had heard them play before and knew they played old country and soft rock. It wasn't long until the bar started filling up. Debbie wasn't surprised to see Tony walk in. She saw him before Janice did. "Wouldn't it be nice if there was someone to dance with?" Debbie asked her sister.

"Yes, I am missing not seeing Tony this weekend. Kind of getting used to having him around." Janice said.

Tony came up behind her, "Well, pretty lady, your wish is my command."

Janice let out a little shriek. "Oh wow, I didn't know you were coming over tonight." She stood up and gave him a big kiss and a hug. "Ladies, this is my friend Tony." She introduced him to the girls he didn't know. "You better pull up another table and join us."

Ted arrived with the drinks, and Tony ordered a beer. It wasn't long until Charles, the hockey coach, with his wife Hillary, and Thomas from the golf course stopped in. They joined Tony at his end of their table. Shortly after that, Brad Mumford arrived with his friend James. The table was growing in leaps and bounds. Spring was in the air and everyone was in a festive mood. They danced the night away.

At one point, Brad asked Debbie, "Would you like to dance?" It was a fast song, so she agreed. But the next song was a slow song and he pulled her close and kept her there on the dance floor. "You look absolutely beautiful tonight. I am glad I decided to come just to see you all dressed up. You are always pretty but tonight you're absolutely glowing."

"Why thank you sir. So, kind of you to say." Debbie thanked him. She didn't like to slow dance with Brad, this was dangerous because she couldn't help but feel attracted to him, and he was a married man. As soon as the song was over, she said, "Thank you for the dance," and headed back to the table.

Susan quietly said, "You two looked cozy up there. I think he likes you."

"Brad is married Sue, it was just a dance." Debbie assured her sister.

"If he wasn't married, would you be interested in him?" Susan asked.

"But he is married, so what is the point of even thinking about it?" Debbie ended the conversation. "Ted, could I get a glass of white wine please?" Thomas asked her to dance and she was relieved to get away from Susan's inquisition.

The band played three sets, and everyone was enjoying the music. Before they knew it, Ted was announcing last call. Debbie suggested, "We should probably head back to the chalet. I could go for a hot tub. What do you ladies think?"

"Let's do last call and then we can go see what's in the blender." Valerie said. They were all having so much fun that no one was in a hurry to leave. Debbie did not want to be one of the lingering drunks that Ted had to escort out at closing time, but she could see that she was outnumbered. They all ordered another drink for last call.

Janice asked Tony, "You are going to walk me home, aren't you?"

"You got any beer over there?" he asked.

"I've got a case in the back of my truck," Thomas offered.

You could always count on the local boys to have a case of beer in their truck, Debbie thought to herself.

The entire table of fourteen people and a few others all ended up at the chalet. When Ted finished his shift, he joined them as well.

At one point, Debbie had a chance to speak with Ted. They were sitting on a couch in the living room. "You did a good job tonight keeping up with that crowd. I was so tempted to help bus tables, but I refrained."

"Yes I noticed you looking around. I was busy but I managed. On the nights that you do come in and bus tables it helps me get the bar cleaned up that much quicker." He told her. Ted got up to go get another beer and Brad sat down.

"Did you enjoy your weekend off?" Brad asked her. "I really like your hair. It looks good like that."

"Thanks, yes it was a great weekend." Debbie told him. "But being a guest, I would have to admit, has been a little strange."

"Well you sure deserve it." Brad told her. "Maybe you girls will make this an annual event."

"No, I don't think so. When I do take a weekend off, I prefer to go someplace different. I am here twenty-four seven and I do enjoy getting out of here once in a while."

"I know what you mean" Brad took a long sip of his beer. "Are you going to put a booth in the home and cottage show coming up?"

"Yes, I think we will. Are you?"

"Yes, I do every year. I make a lot of new contacts and get a lot of work from the show so it is definite must for me to do it. Besides it gives me a chance to see what the other contractors are doing. It's a good chance for me to check out my completion."

"Where is Tina tonight?' Debbie enquired.

"She went to spend the week with her mother. Thank God I am too busy to go with her. I am not very fond of my in-laws. Have you had a chance to look at the area maps yet?" He asked her.

"Yes I did, and as soon as the bush dries up I will take the four wheeler and go see if I can find the boundary lines. "Debbie sighed. "I will be looking for a company to do the tree removal and brushing. If you know of anyone, could you let me know?"

"Sure, I know a few guys that could help you with that. If you want, I can go with you when you want to take a look at the property lines," Brad offered.

"That would be helpful, if you don't mind" Debbie told him. "I wouldn't have asked because I know you're getting busy with your own business, but if you are offering, I would gladly take you up on it."

"No problem. Just give me a call the day you want to go" Brad told her. "My guys can work without me for a couple of hours. Maybe one afternoon next week."

"Thanks Brad, you are truly the best."

"Well I am also doing it for selfish reasons. If you get trails made, I am sure the Ski-Doo club will be glad to use it. And besides, it will give me a chance to spend time with you."

"Brad, why would you say that? "Debbie frowned at him. "Last time I checked, you are still a happily married man."

"Still married but not happily. "Brad Shrugged. "Tina and I just don't seem to fit anymore. It is like we are growing in different directions. I love living here and she hates it. I love the simple life and she prefers the fast lane. Seems the longer we are together, the further apart we are. I can't say that either one of us is happy. Kind of glad now that we didn't have any kids."

"Oh Brad, I am so sorry. I didn't realize you were having problems." Debbie placed a hand on his arm.

"I didn't mean to tell you all that, but you are so easy to talk to. We have been friends for such a long time, and I am very comfortable around you. I have more in common with you than I do with my own wife. Crazy, isn't it?"

"Well it makes sense" Debbie took a sip of her wine.. "We have been friends since public school. I have always enjoyed your company, old friend."

"I can't remember why we even broke up in high school. I remember we dated for a couple months, but I can't recall why we ended our relationship. Do you?"

"Kathy Miller. That's why. You dumped me for her. I remember it quite well." Debbie gave him a punch on his arm.

"Oh yeah, I had forgotten about her. She was so pretty, but way too wild for this cowboy to handle." Brad rubbed his arm. "I got tired of her rather quickly. What a dope I was back in those days."

"Yep, you won't get any arguments from me." Debbie agreed with him.

"Well, James is looking like he is ready to leave, and I am his ride, so I will bid you a goodnight. Thanks for having us over. By the way, the chalet is beautiful. I haven't been in one since I finished building them. I hope you don't mind, but I took a quick look around. The furniture makes it all so homey. Deb, you are doing a good job here and I am so proud of you."

"Thanks Brad. I will give you a call as soon it dries up, so we can go take a look at that bush."

"Okay. Goodnight, my dear."

It was going on four a.m. before Tony, the last guest left. Debbie, Susan, and Valerie were already in the hot tub.

"This has been a great weekend," Val said. "I hate to see it end."

"Me too. But I have a husband and two kids who will be glad to see me when I get home tomorrow." Susan offered.

"And I guess I will have to get back to work. But I am not ready to start thinking about that just yet," Val said.

"I saw you talking with Brad earlier. I still think he has a crush on you, sis." Susan told Debbie.

"We are friends, so yes I do talk to my friends. We were discussing the trail system that I am thinking of putting in. He is a contractor and I was asking him for a list of excavators that he could recommend."

"All work and no play makes Debbie a dull lady," Val told her.

"Well, Brad is a married man so all we ever talk about is business." Debbie assured them both. "If you ladies will excuse me, I am ready for PJ's and a big nap."

Chapter 39

It was after eleven on Sunday morning before everyone was up and dressed. They all sat around the kitchen table having coffee and talking about what a good time they all had. It was decided that they should all get together for a girls' weekend once a year. Next year it would be Valerie's turn to pick the location. They went to the lodge for brunch and then everyone got packed up and headed home.

Debbie and Janice were still at the chalet. "So, what should we do now?" Janice asked. "Are we staying here tonight or going back to the lodge?"

"I'm thinking I might stay here. I will have another hot tub before bed and go over fresh in the morning," Debbie told her. "The chalet won't be cleaned till tomorrow anyways, and it is already dirty, so why not enjoy it for one last night?"

"I was hoping you would say that. It is such a nice day out, do you want to go for a walk or perhaps go out on the four wheelers?"

"It is still too wet and muddy for the four wheelers just yet. We would most likely get stuck. But a walk sounds good. I would like to go down by the campground and the trailer park and have a look around." Debbie asked her, "Do you have any rubber boots?"

"Just a short pair of duckies." Janice told her. "But they are in my room. I would have to go over and get them.

"I'll go with you. If we are staying tonight, I will shower here in the morning so I will need some clothes for work as well. Give me ten minutes to pack up some things we can take back over, since we're going anyways."

They took some stuff back to their rooms upstairs in the lodge and brought back clothes for work tomorrow and their rubber boots for playing in mud puddles with. They walked down past the cabins into the campground and trailer park area.

"I did not know there were so many trailers down here. How many are there?" Janice asked.

"Last count . . . thirty-two, I think. They pay to use the park here from May to September long weekend. Most of them come back year after year. Some trailers on the back are the newbies."

"I see empty spots back there. How many trailers can you actually fit in here?"

"Right now there are sites for forty trailers. There are two on the front that are double spots. They have been here since before we bought the place."

"That pipe that goes to each site there, is that for water?"

"Yes, each site has a hydro and a water hook up. The water is pumped right out of the lake. See that big water tower way up on the top of that hill. We pump water up there and it is then gravity fed back down for the cabins and the campers."

"And that building over there, I am guessing it is the central washroom?" Janice asked.

"Yes. There are four toilets and sinks and two showers on each side for both the men and women. This one here is for the trailer park, and the campground has a smaller one with only two toilets and one shower per side."

"I never realized there was this much of a business going on down here. You don't see it from the cabins. I see the back sides of the cabins and there are no windows looking this way. Only small bathroom windows and they are all frosted."

"If you were renting a cabin would you want to be looking out at all these trailers? Of course not. That is why all the windows in the cabins face the lake."

They walked around the rows of trailers. Debbie pointed out a few small flower gardens that the guests had planted in front of their trailers. Some had small storage sheds, and some had lattice wood skirted around the bottoms of their trailers. Debbie noticed a wasp hive hanging in a tree close to a trailer. She would have to mention to Henry to get the wasp nest knocked down before the campers started coming back.

"I see the fire pit here in the centre of the park looks a little neglected." Janice pointed out. "That is a bit of an eyesore. I guess with all the fire bans, no one uses it much anymore."

"I have been thinking about that. I am thinking perhaps we could get one of those propane fire pits. I have seen people use them right on their decks, so they must be safe. I must remember to talk to Henry about that. If we do it, the propane tank would have to be locked in an enclosure likely. I don't know what all the legalities concerning it are, but I will ask the propane guy. I think he is delivering one day this week," Debbie explained.

"That would be nice. I am sure the campers would use it if they could. Perhaps you could put a timer on it. It could come on at, say, eight o'clock in the evening and go out at eleven o'clock when everyone needs to quiet down."

From there they walked on farther into the campground. This was basically just a big flat empty space with a dirt road running down the middle of it. In the middle of it all was another neglected fire pit, and off at the far side was the smaller washroom the same as was in the trailer park. There was a fallen tree that would have to be taken care of. Henry's to-do list was growing steadily.

"And these trails you've been talking about would start from down here somewhere?" Janice asked her.

"Yes, I think just past the campground. Probably in that back corner over there. The property is kind of a pie shape with the narrow side running parallel with the road above us. If we had a trail straight through there, you could walk to the golf course club house in about fifteen minutes. Five minutes if you were riding a golf cart."

"Why haven't you done it already?"

"Mom and I talked about it last year, but we decided to winterize the three big cabins instead. So the trails got put on hold. We have had an exceptional winter so I am thinking this could be the year to at least investigate it and see if it is feasible. It is going to be a huge expense and it may take ten years to recoup our money." Debbie continued, "We may not be able to afford it this year, what with everyone moving back home. We will just have to see how it all plays out. I will have a better idea after we meet with the accountant. He is doing our year end stuff and should be getting in touch soon, I hope."

"Moving parts . . . wow, sis, you sure weren't kidding about that. It is truly amazing what you have accomplished her in the last fifteen years." Janice complimented her sister. "I can't wait to see what you do with the next fifteen years."

"The way I see it, you always need to be renovating things to keep them fresh and current. People like the Swanson's have been coming here at least once a year, sometimes more often than that, for the past thirty years. They always comment on how nice the resort always looks. Anyone can give you a bed to sleep in, but we try to give them a little bit more than the average."

"What other big ideas do you have up your sleeve?"

"None at the moment, but who knows? Maybe you or Susan will have a big idea of your own? Your sugar shack idea sure panned out well. Nothing gets done in the summertime because we are way too busy taking care of guests. But come September, when things slow down again, that is when we strategize and make the major decisions of things we want to accomplish."

By the time they got back from their walk it was dinnertime. They stopped into the lodge and had a nice quiet, leisurely dinner.

"Evening, ladies, just the two of you for dinner tonight? Chef has made chicken and dumplings for the special tonight. Can I get you ladies a drink?"

"Perhaps a white wine for me. That will go well with the chicken I am going to have for dinner." Janice said.

"Sound good, Gail, two wines and two chicken and dumplings, please." Debbie agreed.

When Gail brought their wine she asked, "So did you enjoy your weekend staycation? I expect you're staying at the chalet tonight. I imagine it would be hard to give up that hot tub."

"You are very right about that. Gail, too bad we didn't think to invite you earlier, you could have come over and joined us after your shift. I don't suppose you want to run home and grab your swimsuit. You are welcome to come join us if you like." Debbie told her.

"Are you serious? I will call Peter and get him to drop it off. I would love a hot tub."

"If we had been thinking ahead, we could have also invited Chef and Ted." Janice suggested.

"Why don't I go ask them and see if either of them are interested? I know I am." Gail admitted.

"Go ask them and let me know what they say," Debbie told her.

When Gail brought their dinners, she said Chef has declined. "He already has plans for later. Ted said he would love to, but doesn't have any shorts. My hubby Peter is about the same size as Ted, so we've got him covered. So, I guess Ted and I will see you both for a hot tub as soon as we close up here. Been quiet here tonight. I have only had ten people so far tonight."

"Okay, sounds like a plan." Debbie told her. "These dumplings are incredible. They are like light fluffy clouds. Tell Chef I send my compliments, please."

When Gail picked up their dirty plates, she said, "For dessert, can I get you chocolate cake or pumpkin pie?"

"Isn't there any raspberry pie left?" Debbie asked.

"Sorry boss, we sold that out last night."

"Probably for the best anyways. I think I will pass on dessert tonight." Debbie told her.

"What about you Janice? What can I bring you for dessert?"

"Nothing thanks. I am full. That dinner was very good."

Just then, a table of four came in so Debbie told her, "Come over when you're finished work. I will leave the door unlocked if we go into the tub before you and Ted arrive. See you later."

"Looking forward to it," Gail said as she headed to her next table.

Back at the chalet, Janice asked Debbie, "What would you like to drink, sis? We still have some piña coladas and some margarita fixings here."

"Oh goodness, I have consumed more alcohol this weekend than I did in the whole past year," Debbie told her sister.

"That does not answer my question, now does it?"

"Oh, I guess a margarita sounds good. Are you buying?"

"I think I could manage that." Debbie followed Janice up to the kitchen.

"This has been the best weekend since . . . I don't remember when." Janice told her. "Susan said when we get all the bar tab figured out, we can just split it three ways."

"I plan to write the whole thing off as a business expense. We can't do that very often, but this was all research. We could not have experienced it any better if we had tried."

"When you do get it all figured out, we will need to decide what is included in the girls' weekend package. So I will need what, the cost of the meals if we are still going to include them as part of the weekend package. I already know the cost of all the pampering. I will need your help with costing out the wine tasting. That sort of thing."

"No problem. We will break it all down to a cost per person. I don't expect to have it up and going before fall anyways. Next weekend is the Victoria Day long weekend, and we will be too busy to do much of anything extra for the whole summer.

"The dining room closes at eight on Sunday nights, right?" Janice asked. "It is almost eight now. Should we wait for Gail and Ted or go get in the hot tub now?"

"Well, I still have to get changed so I think I will do that, freshen up my drink and head on in." Debbie told her.

It was close to nine p.m. before Gail and Ted showed up.

"Hello, we are here." Gail hollered up to the girls.

"Come on in, we are upstairs in the hot tub." Debbie hollered back.

Gail and Ted were standing in the bathroom doorway.

"What are you two doing standing there? You can change in any bedroom you like, and there is margarita mix and crushed ice in the blender. Please help yourselves because I just got wet here and I am still on holidays or I would go get it for you." Janice said with her best smile.

"Got any beer?" Ted asked.

"I'm not sure, check the cooler on the floor. There may be some left over from the party last night." Janice told him.

Gail got a margarita and joined the ladies. Ted found a beer and climbed in. "This chalet is nice. I can see why people like them better than the cabins." Ted commented.

"I have been inside, but this is my first dip in the hot tub. Love all the bubbles. Nice touch" Gail said.

"I must remember I want to add a nice bubble bath to the gift baskets. Fortunately, we brought our own," Debbie commented.

"I'll write that down for you when I come in on Wednesday," Gail offered with a chuckle.

"So what else did I ask you to write down?" Debbie asked her.

"Oh gosh, something about the complimentary bottle of wine waiting for them and I forget what else, but there is a list on your desk with your pager. I must admit, I didn't think you could pull it off, being a guest here and not checking in on all the little details for the whole weekend," Gail admitted. "I owe Chef five bucks."

"What, you two had a bet that I couldn't behave, and you bet against me? Wow, thanks a lot." Debbie laughed at the look on Gail's face. "Full disclosure, I got up to help Ted bus tables in the bar last night, but then someone took my hand and led me to the dance floor, otherwise I was probably going to pick up a handful of empty glasses."

"Well you ladies were all having so much fun that the other customers were asking what was going on with your table." Ted said. "I told them you were celebrating losing your virginity." They all had a good laugh over that. Janice almost choked on her drink.

They stayed in the hot tub for over an hour. Debbie got out first and started passing out warm housecoats and towels.

"Thanks for inviting us over, boss. Any time you need some hot tub company, I am your guy." Ted told her.

"I will keep that in mind," Debbie said. "See you both on Wednesday."

"That was a nice idea, inviting Ted and Gail for a hot tub. They both do a really good job. It is nice to reward them occasionally," Debbie commented.

"Well I am pooped. I am going to get my PJ's on. Then I am going to see what is left for a snack," Janice told her sister.

"Meet you in the kitchen in ten minutes then." Debbie told her. "I am going to make a tea, would you like one?"

"No thanks." Janice finished off what was left in the blender, Debbie had her tea and they finished off the kielbasa and cheese and crackers before they called it a night and headed off to bed.

Chapter 40

Back to the real world. Debbie carried all her luggage back to her room at the lodge. When she came downstairs, Janice had already started the coffee.

"Morning, sis. Back to the old grind today. I see a stack of messages on my desk so I think I will start with that this morning. What are you planning on doing?" Debbie asked Janice.

"Whatever you need me to do. I expect I will be making a trip into town this afternoon to do bank deposits for you, right?"

"Yes, but I probably won't be ready for a while." Debbie and Janice joined Henry at the waitress station where he was standing cup in hand ready for the coffee to finish brewing.

"Morning ladies, how was your vacation weekend?" Henry asked them.

"Morning. It was fantastic," Janice said as she poured his coffee.

"Henry, what are you planning on doing today?" Debbie asked him.

"Thought I would do some more raking and clean up around the boat house. Is there something else you need me to do?"

"Well I walked down around the trailer park and the campground yesterday and there are a few things that need your attention." Debbie told him.

"Yes, I noticed there is a tree down that I need to clean up. And I was going to ask you about putting a fresh coat of paint on the washrooms down there."

"That would be a good idea. Also, I noticed a hornets' nest hanging in the tree by the exit sign on this side of the trailer park. Can you knock that down before the campers arrive, please?" Debbie asked him.

"Yep, I will take care of that. Hard to believe this is the May long weekend already. Things are about to get busy so if there are any little jobs still needing doing, I only have this week to get to them," he told her.

"Henry, I don't know what we would do without you around here. You know you are a valued asset to the team, right?" Debbie gave him a light punch in the arm.

"Oh shucks, I enjoy working here. If I wasn't working, I would get old and wither up and die. Besides, I have never eaten better in my whole life as I do nowadays," he assured her. "I should probably tell you that the Martins have asked me to keep an eye on their place while they do some traveling. They want me to cut the grass, water the flower beds, that kind of thing."

"That's good. I am sure you will do a good job for them."

"Thanks. And it won't interfere with anything I am doing here," Henry told her.

"If either of you see Carol the housekeeper this morning, please tell her I would like to speak with her. Well, if you two will excuse me, I have work to do in the office," Debbie told them as she walked away.

Debbie had lots to do this morning. She had taken the weekend off, but the resort sure had not. It was ten o'clock when Carol stuck her head in the office door.

"Morning, boss, heard you wanted to speak to me," Carol said.

"Yes, I do Carol, let me grab a coffee and I will meet you at the kitchen table." Debbie told her.

"Should I join you or leave you to it?" Janice asked as she entered the office from the front door.

"Don't matter, I just need to discuss so cleaning issues with her. "Debbie explained. "You might as well join us. This is all part of running the operation."

When they were all seated at the back kitchen table, Debbie started. "How's things going, are we ready for the upcoming busy season?"

"I think so, you may want to look into buying more towels for the cabins. Some of them are getting quite used up." Carol told them.

"How many do you need?"

"I would say two dozen at least and perhaps two dozen new face-cloths as well."

"Okay, done. Anything else?" Debbie asked as she made herself a reminder note.

"No, I think we are in good shape otherwise," Carol assured them.

"Have you been over the blue jay chalet yet this morning?"

"Yes, I just finished over there. Looks like there was some major partying going on over there this weekend."

"Yes, there was. We were the party. We spend the weekend in the chalet and there are a couple of things that I would like to point out that I noticed. First, I noticed the books in the library room were quite dusty. I literally could make tracks in the dust with my finger. And secondly, there are cobwebs in the corner in the laundry room."

"I just knocked the cobwebs down this morning, and I will go back and do a more thorough dusting." Carol offered.

"I am not knit-picking, please understand that. I just happened to be there and noticed. But the point is, if I hadn't noticed, I wonder how long the dust would have stayed there. It looks like is has been accumulating for a while," Debbie told her. "Those chalets cost twice the price of the cabins and they need to be spotless all the time.

"Yes, you're right. I am sorry that got overlooked. I will take care of it," Carol assured her.

"We have every cabin and two chalets booked for this upcoming weekend. I would like you to go into each cabin and make sure that everything is dusted, swept, scrubbed and basically ship shape for the weekend. Some of the cabins haven't been used in a while. It is time to freshen them up for the upcoming busy season."

"Yes, I planned to start that on Wednesday. I have scheduled an extra girl just for that reason."

"Good, I think that is wise," Debbie agreed. "You know my philosophy. Anyone can give people a bed to sleep in, but we try to go above and beyond and give them the little things they don't think of. And just so you know, we will be adding bubble bath to the bathroom gift baskets for the three chalets, as well as powdered coffee creamer for the kitchen baskets as soon as they come in."

"We will also be putting a blender in each chalet. They should be here this week as well," Janice added.

"That is a good idea. A lot of folks like blender drinks." Carol agreed. "Have we turned on the ice maker in the boat house yet? We're probably going to need it this weekend."

"It is on my summer start-up checklist. Carol, can you specifically make a check on the three big cabins that have been renovated. They will probably be extra dusty. And can you check the water, hot and cold, in all the cabins? We don't want any surprises this weekend. We had to replace the hot water tank in a cabin three just last month."

"Yes, I also have a starter check list that we will start in on Wednesday."

"I would like to see your list someday, when you have time to show me" Debbie told her.

"No problem. It is checking things like dusting, cobwebs, sweeping, checking the beds, freshening towels, checking light bulbs, checking on the gift baskets in case the mice have gotten in, that kind of thing," Carol told her. "Just basically making a visual inspection of each cabin before you do your annual inspection."

"Yes, I will be doing that on Thursday. Do you think you will be ready by then?"

"Yes, I think so. We have been so busy this winter that most of the cabins have been used anyways, so that means they have be cleaned regularly all winter."

"And how are you looking for staff this year. Is everyone coming back to work this summer?" Debbie asked her.

"As far as I know, they are. I have three girls who will work full time starting Sunday for the changeover and another three that I can call in part time. That worked out fine last summer."

"Good to know. Is there anything else then?" Debbie asked her.

"No, I think we are good," Carol assured her.

"Okay then, just so you know, Carol I think you are doing a bang-up job. It is a lot of responsibility managing your department. I see how well you handle everything, and I just want you to know it is noticed and I definitely appreciate all your hard work and effort you put into your job."

"Thanks Debbie, I enjoy it. I will give you my list when we meet on Thursday after your inspection, okay?"

"Sound good, now let's get back to work then." Debbie got up to freshen up her coffee.

Back in the office, Janice commented, "I never noticed the dust or the cobwebs in the chalet. Did you go looking for things to complain about or what?"

"No, I just notice things like that. It is just another part of my job. You should be noticing things like that as well, now that you are the owner. If you see something that needs to be repaired or replaced leave me a note or at least point it out."

"You mean like the flagpole that desperately needs a coat of paint?"

"Yes exactly. I have already mentioned that to Henry. He is quite busy this week and may not get to it, but it is on his to-do list."

"I could paint the flagpole if you like, and I will try to be more observant in the future. I was impressed at your meeting with Carol. You told her the problems you noticed and also told her she was doing a good job. And what is this inspection that Carol was talking about?" Janice asked.

"Each spring before the May long weekend, I do a walk through on all the cabins to make sure they are ready. It encourages the staff to do their best job."

"Smart. Good idea. What about the other areas, do they get annual inspections as well?"

"Yes. On Thursday, I also inspect the bar, the service station, dining room, kitchen cold room, fridges, and storage areas. Basically, any place that a guest can look and beyond. All the staff will be ready for the annual inspection on Thursday. I expect that everyone will be doing some major house cleaning on Wednesday."

"I notice Chef was washing off shelves in the cold room last week and I also saw Ted had taken all the bottles of liquor down and cleaned all the glass shelves behind the bar. Now I know why. They are all getting ready for your inspection. At the time I didn't think much about it. Makes sense now," Janice said.

"You need to remember that all my key staff have all worked here for at least the past five years and they all know their jobs and what is expected of them. If you pay attention, you will notice that they are good at helping each other as well."

"Yes, I have seen that already. I have noticed Ted bussing tables for Gail, and I have noticed Gail helping Chef on more than one occasion. You have them all well-trained, that's for sure."

"And your job is to step in and help out whenever you see a staff member that is swamped. An extra pair of hands for a few minutes makes all the difference. Usually the staff will ask me to help if they need it. I am not sure if they will be comfortable asking you yet so if you see something that you can do, just step in and do it. Trust me, they will be glad for the help."

"I will. There is still a lot of things I don't know yet, but I am learning every day. And if you think there is something that I should be doing, please tell me. I am glad to help but still am not able to read your mind," Janice told her.

"I still have to finish the bank deposits so let me go finish that. Perhaps you could come up with something for lunch. Henry will be in usually by noon."

Debbie went back to the office. It was nice having Janice there, but sometimes they got chatting about different things and Debbie got distracted from the job that she should be working on. She could hear her mom's voice in her head telling her to, *'stay focused, or you're gonna miss the point.'*

Henry, Janice and Debbie were at the back kitchen table having lunch when Josh the boat boy came in the back door. "Hello boss, how's things going?"

"Well hello, stranger." Debbie got up and gave Josh a big hug. She hadn't seen him since the day of her mom's service. "I don't know if you have been introduced to my sister, Janice? Janice this is Josh, our boat boy."

"Nice to meet you." Josh said. "I see I am interrupting your lunch, should I come back?"

"No, pull up a chair. Are you hungry?" Debbie asked him.

"No thanks, I had a late breakfast. Just thought I would come in and see what's going on. Gotta get things ready for the inspection. What day are you doing that on?" Josh asked.

"Thursday, does that work for you?" Debbie asked him.

"Yep, sounds good. I see the gift shop needs a good dusting. Looks like there was people in there over the winter."

"Yes, we used it for Ski-Doo races. The store was not open, they just used the washrooms. I think Carol cleaned them, but perhaps you should check on that."

"Will do, and I will probably have a few things to add to the supply order" Josh told her. "I see I am out of maple syrup."

"There is syrup downstairs, take what you need. I am hoping that Chef is going to make maple fudge to sell this year as well. Janice, don't let me forget to ask him about that, would you?"

"Okay then, I will go get my syrup and then I am going to be down at the boat house doing some house cleaning." Josh stood up to leave. "Enjoy your lunch."

"Did you know Josh was coming in today?" Henry asked her after he left.

"No, not really but I expected I would see him one day this week." Debbie told him.

"I am so glad that I don't have to do anything for the annual inspection." Henry commented.

"Well I could inspect the back of your truck, but I am afraid I would get lost in there." Debbie offered.

"You surely would." Henry laughed at her.

Chapter 41

Wednesday, just as Debbie had predicted, the resort was buzzing with activity. Everyone was cleaning. Janice even pitched in and helped. First, she helped Chef clean out the dry storage pantry. He explained to her all about the inventory rotation and how things had to be used according to the first in had to be the first out. He had a big food order that had come in that morning and had to restock his shelves with the old inventory at the front so that it would be used first.

Next, Janice helped Gail clean up the service areas and wash down tables and chairs, including the legs. Gail assured her that Debbie would be checking that tomorrow. Janice could not help but admire how well the staff worked independently with no need for directions. They all knew what needed to be done. When she was finished with Gail, she offered Ted a hand. He was also wiping off table and chair legs. He had just cleaned out the fireplace and wiped it all down. Janice had to admit, the place was sparkling. When she finished helping Ted, Gail was cleaning windows. There were a lot of windows; the whole entire front wall on the lake side was solid windows. Janice grabbed a rag and joined Gail. Everyone spent the day cleaning in preparation for the annual inspection.

Thursday was the day. Everyone waited with bated breath to see what they had missed. You could feel their anticipation in the air. It was almost tangible. Debbie had her morning coffee and muffin as usual. She seemed oblivious to the tension around her.

Debbie handed Janice a note pad and a checklist. Here it was, the famous checklist. It was quite long. She read it over while they had their coffee.

"Wow that is quite a list. Where do you start?" Janice asked.

"Where do you think we should start?" Debbie asked her.

"We, does that mean you want me to do the inspection with you?"

"Yes ma'am, you are an owner now. Don't you want to see that everything is ready for our guests arriving tomorrow?"

"Sure, I just wasn't sure if I was expected to participate."

"You might as well. This is just another job we have to do," Debbie told her sister. "Let's start at the campground and trailer park, and then do the cabins, boat house, and chalets. You may want to wear shoes you can slip in and out of, as we will be removing our shoes in all the cabins."

"Okay, give me a minute to run upstairs. Then I'll be ready."

At the campground, Debbie told Janice, "How about you check off the list, and I will make notes of any other things we notice, okay?"

"Okay, grass is cut, check. Fire pit has been cleaned up, check. Washroom exterior looks good, check. Interior is clean, check, toilet papers all full, check, paper towels are full, check."

"You don't need to tell me, just make sure everything on that list is checked," Debbie told her sister.

They carried on back into the trailer park and checked in on the washrooms there. Everything was clean. Next, they inspected the cabins. Janice noticed Debbie making a note and asked her, "What are you writing down? What are you seeing that I am not seeing?"

"Just making a note that the screen here is dirty. The windows have been cleaned, but the screen needs some attention."

"Oh, I see it now that you point it out. Good eye, sis."

"I expect that the cabins will be cleaned, I am looking for the little things that get overlooked. Today I am knit-picking, as you call it. That's my job."

Debbie and Janice inspected every area of the resort. They inspected all the cabins, the boat house, the chalets. Then they inspected the lodge including the kitchen, the waitress station, the dining room, the banquet rooms, the washrooms and the bar as well as the office and the gift shop. The only place not inspected was the house. No need to look there as there would be no guests staying there.

"I think we are done, sis, have we checked off everything on the list?" Debbie asked.

"Yes, we have. Wow that was quite the inspection I must say." Janice told her.

"Okay let's grab a coffee and go talk about all our notes before the staff meeting at four o'clock."

When all the staff were gathered together, Debbie began, "Inspection is done. And before I start, I want to say a big thanks for all your hard work. Overall, the resort looks good. But as you all know, the whole point of the annual inspection is to catch things that have been missed or overlooked. This is not a criticism of your work by any means, I am not out to get anybody. That being said, there were a few things that I would like to discuss. I have a list, so let me get through it and then we can discuss it."

She continued, "Let's start with Carol, our head housekeeper. I would like you to take notice of the screens in the windows. I noticed in cabin three that the screen there was so dirty you could hardly see out of it. Perhaps, Henry, you could put a big bucket water on the trailer and pull it with the four-wheeler around to each cabin so Carol could wash the screens." Henry and Carol both nodded in agreement. "Not a big thing, but it should be done occasionally, I would think"

Debbie continued. "I also noticed in cabin five, the fridge had a lot of ice build in the freezer area and needs to be defrosted. I would like you to keep a note of when the fridges are defrosted so we can tell if maybe there is a problem with the fridge, and it may need to be repaired or replaced."

Debbie turned her attention to Josh. "Down at the boathouse I would like you to stand on the other side of the counter as if you were the paying customer and look behind the cash register. It is full of dust and bits of paper back there." Josh nodded.

Debbie continued, "Ted, the same goes for you in the bar. Behind your cash register is a bit of a mess. All of you should stand in your areas, in the spot where your customers will stand and try to see your stations from your customer's point of view. Ted, I think the mantle above the fireplace is starting to look cluttered. There is too much stuff up there. Can we get rid of some of it, please? I was thinking the new open-air hockey trophy could possibly go up there. Just an idea, I will leave it up to you." Ted gave her a shrug.

Debbie turned to Chef. "Can you see to it that the glass on the dining room doors gets cleaned? It is covered in fingerprints. Henry, can you take the kitchen light covers down to be washed and get the dead flies out of them, please? Chef, I also have on my list to ask you could you please make a batch of your maple fudge. Gail, when he does, could you get them bagged and delivered to the two gift shops? I think it will be a nice addition."

Next Debbie addressed Gail. "The coffee machine needs to be periodically pulled out and cleaned in behind it. I know this is a hard job to do alone so please ask Henry or someone to help you. Just so you know, I will be ordering a case of new ketchup bottles. The ones we are currently using are starting to look overused. You can replace them as they become empty." Gail smiled in acknowledgement.

Debbie continued. "Henry, this fall we will be repainting the interior of the boat house as well as staining the decks on the three chalets. That will have to wait till the fall, but let's get the paint and stain and other supplies ready before September" Henry gave her a sloppy salute.

Debbie raised her coffee cup. "And that is it. Nothing major. Just a few little things I noticed. Janice, do you have anything to add?"

"No, I think that covers everything. I will however say that I am impressed with all the staff here. You guys are amazing. The resort is fresh and clean and from a customer's point of view, I would be happy to come spend my money here. Good job, everyone." Janice told them all.

"So basically, I would like everyone to look at your stations from your customer's point of view. We only get one chance to make a good first impression. Good job guys. Thanks for all your hard work," Debbie told them. "Does anyone have any questions or concerns while we are all here together?"

Ted asked, "What do you want me to do with all that crap on the fireplace? Most of it is stuff customers have given me."

"I would say just throw it out. If anyone asks, tell them you tried to clean it but it was no longer cleanable and so you had no choice but to get rid of it. There is just too much clutter up there." Debbie looked around the room. "Well then, if there is nothing else, I would like to take this opportunity to again say thank you to you all for all your hard work." Debbie told her staff. "I would also like to wish you all an enjoyable, prosperous summer. Let's have fun and make some money while we do."

Back in the office, Janice told her sister, "That all went well. I would have to say I was impressed both with the inspection and the meeting. Deb, you have a good staff here, and they all like and respect you. I am so proud of all you. You work hard, and it shows."

"Thanks sis. That is kind of you to say. I am just doing my job the best way I know how." Debbie told her. "Now, I need to go through the inventories in both the gift shops and see what we need to order. Do you want to help with that?"

"Absolutely, I assume you have a list?" Janice asked.

"Of course. The checklist is under each cash register."

Chapter 42

On Friday they were busy. They had a steady flow of people in and out of the office all day. The guests were anxious to get their vacations started.

Susan came in through the back door. "Hi guys. How's everything going?"

"Busy. Holy crap, it is busy here today," Janice told her sister while getting a hug.

"Nice to see you. Where's Keith and the kids?" Debbie asked her during her hug.

"They are up at the house unloading the car. I just wanted to slip down and say hi." A couple had just come in the office door to get checked in. Debbie went to help them.

"Can we get together later for dinner?" Susan asked.

"I don't know if we will be able to. It is quite busy. Let's just wait and see how it goes." Janice told her.

"Okay, I won't keep you, but if you get a chance, stop up to the house later," Susan told her.

"I can't make any promises. We are a little swamped here right now. Still expecting six more cabins that need to be checked in," Janice told her.

"Great to see everyone busy. See you later." Susan told her as she headed out the back door.

By the time they headed up to bed that night, Janice was exhausted. "Wow that was an incredibly busy crazy day."

"Get used to it, it will be steady busy like that every day until the end of September." Debbie told her. "As Mom used to say, *'buckle up, buttercup, it's gonna be a bumpy ride.'*"

As Debbie was trying to fall asleep, she couldn't help but think about things. She had done everything she could in preparation for the upcoming busy season. They were ready for whatever was about to happen. She felt like she was riding a tidal wave. Now all she could do was ride the wave, try to stay on top and enjoy the ride.

Janice had searched and found Mr. Penfold on the internet.. Agnes was right, he lived just this side of Ottawa. Debbie and Janice had discussed what to do with this new found information. They talked about contacting him and decided against it. They thought that decision should be left up to Susan and they also agreed that they would tell Susan. Now they just had to find the right time to do so. This was going to be a shock, no matter how or when then told her. Life sure had a way of complicating things.

By the time Tuesday rolled around there was a big list of things to do. One of the outboard motors for one of the boats was shot and needed to be replaced. One of the kitchen fridges had quit working, so a repair man needed to be called. And the food orders, and liquor orders were double and triple what they were just a week ago. Day to day operations was just a way of life for Debbie, but Janice was still amazed by it all.

They didn't get much of a visit with Susan and her family. They were just too busy. But that was the nature of the beast. As Mom used to say, *"You gotta make hay while the sun is shining."* Susan would be back up in a couple of weeks. They were moving home permanently as soon as school was out. Susan had told them that their house was already sold, and the closing date was the end of June. This was really happening. Both sisters were moving home to help run their resort. Debbie thought, *good, bad or otherwise, it is actually happening.* Mom got her final wish: all three sisters were home running the resort together.

Chapter 43

This upcoming weekend, they had a booth in the Home and Cottage Show in Clifford. They had their brochures and complimentary breakfast gift cards ready. The reusable bags had arrived. Susan had ordered three thousand bags to get the best price. They were all going to take turns manning the booth and seeing the rest of the show.

On Friday, Henry and Debbie had taken all their products, a set of patio lights, and a small bistro set to go set up their booth at the show. They also took the staple gun, a hammer and nails and each took a coffee in their takeaway cups. Henry put up a string of lights with those little patio lanterns around their booth. By the time he was finished, it looked like you were sitting on a patio. Henry and Debbie sat in their booth watching the other participants setting up their booths.

Brad Mumford walked by and laughed at them. "Looking good guys, makes you think about grabbing a beer and pulling up a chair."

"Thanks Brad that was what we were hoping for. Is your booth set up yet?" Debbie asked him.

"Not yet, I just arrived," he told her.

"Well we are done, so we are out of here. Good luck on your booth," Debbie told him as she started packing up things to go. She couldn't help but think how handsome he was dressed up in jeans and a nice shirt. She usually saw him in work clothes. Why did she always feel butterflies in the pit of her stomach every time she saw him?

They would be back by nine a.m. tomorrow morning and wouldn't be done until Sunday at five p.m. Debbie was to work the booth tomorrow from nine until noon, and then Janice was taking the noon to four shift. Susan was from four till eight, when the show closed. They were each taking turns, which would be a huge help to Debbie. Last year it was just her and her mom. She had to hire staff to man the booth.

On Saturday morning, Debbie was at the show, wearing her Hawaiian shirt, by nine a.m. The sisters had all agreed they would wear their festive shirts to the show, along with their new nametags. There was a steady stream of people wandering through. Debbie had a copy of the reservation book to refer to when a few guests stopped to chat, and she got two bookings that morning. Janice and Tony arrived just before noon to relieve her. Debbie showed her sister the two reservations and wished her luck.

Debbie walked around to see the rest of the show. She saw Brad's booth. It looked like the front of a small cottage. He smiled at her, but he was busy with a customer, so she just nodded and walked on by. She said a quick hello to John Grant, who had his real estate booth set up to look like his storefront. She saw Ann's Flower booth—actually, she smelt it before she saw it. The show provided a great opportunity to see what other resorts, hotels, and campgrounds were doing. She picked up some of the competitions' brochures and pamphlets. Her closest major competitor had added a new indoor swimming pool to their resort.

Back at the lodge, Susan seemed a little frazzled. "Glad you're back. It has been busy in here. How is the show going?" she asked.

"Good, I think. I got two reservations booked this morning so far. The bags are a hit. People are coming to our booth just for that reason alone. And the gift cards seem to be appreciated. I gave out about twenty so far. I only gave them to people who seemed sincere in asking about the resort."

"Sounds good. Keith and I will go over for four o'clock. Right now, he is out with Mr. Nicholson going for a boat ride. You would have laughed at him, he was actually nervous about it."

"Yes, as soon as we get this show over with, we need to get focused on Shelby's wedding. They were in for lunch the other day and she is getting excited about it."

When Janice got back, she told Debbie, "I only got one more reservation for a one weeks' vacation in August. There sure were a lot of people there. Where do they all come from?"

"All over. Most of them have cottages in the area. Our population triples here in the summertime. Did you get a chance to walk around and see the other booths?"

"Yes, I did. I learned there are a lot of different businesses that all depend on tourism for their livelihood. I even got a key chain. See? A really cute guy from the Head Lake Cottage Association. That is actually a good idea for us next time, don't you think?"

"Something to look into for sure. I think our bags are a hit." Debbie said.

"Yes, people were coming up asking for them. I gave out about fifteen gift cards. I think I might have given one to a competitor, but I didn't realize it until I was walking around the show later and saw the guy behind his booth."

"That happens. I picked up brochures from our competitors. That is kind of the point of the show, to check out your competition."

Susan and Keith came early, and they had already walked through the show. Keith was bragging about driving the Nicholson yacht. "We should get him a captain's hat as a joke," Janice murmured quietly. "I bet he would wear it."

Josh was calling on the intercom, so Debbie went to answer him. "Hi Josh, what's up?"

"I have a guy here with a fish hook stuck in his ear. It is a mess and I don't think I can take it out. Can someone take him to the hospital?" Josh asked her.

"Yes, I will send someone right down." Debbie assured him. "Janice could you take this guy into the Clifford hospital?"

"Sure, I can do that," she said as she headed out the door. Debbie couldn't help but think how useful Janet had become to her and the resort.

They had a full dining room for dinner and the bar had a small band, so it was also busy. It was going on three o'clock before they got things locked up for the night.

Chapter 44

Sunday morning, Janice took the first shift at the show and Susan relieved her at noon. Debbie didn't have to go over to the show until three. The resort was busy but under control, so Debbie left for the show a little early. She did another walk around the show. There was a new print shop that had opened in Clifford and she wanted to speak to them about printing brochures for the resort. The place she was currently using had put their prices up again for the third time in three years so Debbie wanted to check out the new place to see what their prices were like. The sales associate was talking to someone else, so Debbie went to her own booth first.

Susan looked glad to see her. "You are early," Keith said.

"Actually, I am not here yet. I need a copy of our brochure, a bag and a gift card. I want to show them to the guy at the new print shop. I'll be back shortly."

"Take your time, we got this" Susan said.

Debbie went back and got talking to the man about printing. He could do her brochures and menus no problem, but he did not do bags or gift cards yet. She got all his pricing and information. Debbie thanked him for his time and went to relieve Susan and Keith

"So, how is it going?" Debbie asked them.

"Good, we only have ten gift cards left. I got three more reservations," Susan told her.

"Wow, good job. We got what, six yesterday? Janice got two this morning, you got three more, that's eleven bookings so far from the show. That has to be a record for us," Debbie commented.

"All right you guys, get out of here. Check in on Janice when you get back to the lodge. I will take over here and Henry is coming at five to help me take down the booth."

Debbie did not get any more bookings, but she did give out the rest of the gift cards. One couple assured her they would use it over the summer as they would be coming back to the area to look at cottages for sale, but they just weren't sure on the date yet. Debbie suggested they should talk to her sister and gave them her Cedar Grove Resort business card.

When Henry arrived, there were still people coming through the show. All the attendees were dismantling their booths, but Debbie wasn't in any big hurry, so Henry just sat at the table and waited. It was almost six before Debbie told him, "I think we can take the lights down now. It is finally slowing down."

Between the two of them, they had everything loaded and were headed home within a half an hour. On the way home, Debbie thought about how the show had gone. They had eleven bookings and had given out one hundred gift cards and over two thousand bags with the resort logo on them. Only time would tell if they worked. The show was a lot of work, but eleven bookings made it all worthwhile. She couldn't help but feel optimistic. Janice was fitting into the routine of things relatively easily and Susan was moving home to stay in a couple weeks.

She would have to be mindful not to let Susan take over, as was her tendency to do, but with Janice already on board, hopefully Susan would follow Janice's lead.

Later that night they were all sitting around the back kitchen table. "I can't believe how well we did at the show," Janice said. "I saw that one of the other resorts had jet skis for rent. Do we have any jet skis at Cedar Grove?"

"No, not yet. I think they cost a fortune to buy and another fortune in the increase to your insurance, but you could look into that if you think it could make us money," Debbie told her.

"I noticed one of the resorts had a pontoon boat. Do we have one of those?" Susan asked. "You could use it for tours and even moving people to and from their cottages from the back side of the lake."

"No, we don't. Those pontoon boats are not cheap, either, but if you want to investigate the idea, feel free to do so," Debbie told her.

"Maybe we better figure out the vehicle situation first," Janice suggested.

"You girls are making me tired just thinking about it all," Debbie told them.

Keith laughed at them. "I think you have created two monsters, Deb. Good luck holding them back."

"Although I do appreciate your enthusiasm, let's not do everything all in one day. Right now, we need to get focused on this wedding coming up."

"I would love to help out, but I will be busy driving the yacht." Keith beamed with pride. Everyone laughed at him.

Chapter 45

It was summer, and therefore it was busy. There was a constant flow of traffic in and out of the office. Debbie removed the bells from the office door. Now that Janice and Susan were pitching in, there was always someone in the office. Susan had decided to work her real estate business from the resort office. She claimed Mom's old desk and brought in a large filing cabinet. They installed another phone line just for her, and it seemed to be working out just fine.

It was weighing heavily on Debbie's mind that she still needed to talk to Susan about her father. She was not looking forward to that conversation but the decision had been made and it was nagging at her to get it done and off her to do list.

With Susan always being in the office, it freed up Debbie's time to be in other places she was needed. Today she was confirming arrangements for the upcoming wedding. Shelby Nicholson, the soon to be bride of John Wannamaker, was now Debbie's top focus for this week.

She confirmed the menus with Chef for the Friday night BBQ, and the Saturday night dinner. He assured her all was well.

"How is the new cook working out?"

"Good, so far. He has a short attention span, but works well under pressure. He needs to learn the way I cook each meal so he can cook it exactly the same way that I do, and that will just take time."

"If you let Gail know what dish you want him to learn, she could suggest it to the customers. They always ask for her recommendations. She could be of some help to you if you just let her know."

"Yeah, that's actually not a bad idea. You are more than just a pretty face, you know."

When Debbie got back to the office, she asked Janice, "Do you have all the stuff to decorate the wedding cake, and are all the flowers ordered for this wedding?"

"Yes, and yes. I am on it," Janice told her sister. "Shelby has chosen a flat cake, so I think I will decorate it with the two entwined wedding rings. And the flowers will be gorgeous. She has chosen all roses. Red, white and pink roses. Add to that some ivy and baby's breath, and they should be quite exquisite."

"Have you figured out how you are going to get the flowers to them?" Debbie asked.

"I am not sure who exactly will be where. Could be a scramble at the last minute." Janice told her.

"Believe me, I have learned from past experience that you do not under any circumstances want to leave anything to chance or the last minute. There are already so many things that can go wrong. If you can confirm with them beforehand, you will be glad you did."

"Okay, I will confirm where all the important people will be," Janice assured her.

Debbie made herself a note to check Friday night about the flower delivery. She decided to take a walk down to the boat house.

"How is everything going down here?" Debbie asked Josh. "I just wanted to touch base and remind you that from Friday night till Sunday morning we need to keep that outside slip open for the Nicholson yacht."

"Yep I know, Keith has reminded me three times so far, this week." Josh chuckled. "We even carpeted that wooden ramp we have, so when they arrive, they can use the ramp from the boat down to the dock instead of climbing down the ladder. It's over there if you want to see it. He did a really good job."

"I see, that was a good idea, thank you, Josh." She was always pleased to see staff take initiative. She would make a note of that in her secret staff book where she kept notes on all her staff.

Next, Debbie went to check in with Gail. She expected Gail would have everything under control, but she still liked to touch base with her.

"Are we ready for this wedding? A table for fourteen in the dining room for BBQ chicken and ribs on Friday night and then the buffet for 112 people in the banquet room for Saturday?"

"Yes, I've got it all figured out," Gail assured her.

"Do we have enough of the pink cloth napkins?" Janice just told me the flowers are red, white and pink roses."

"I know we have enough red for sure, but I will have to check on the pink. You know what would look nice? If we used all three colours of napkins. What do you think about that?"

"Sounds good to me, and Janice is going to use the new flower bowls for the tables. After the wedding, I would like to replace the vases on the dining room tables with the bowls."

"Thank you. I was going to ask if I could use them out here. The vases are so tall they sometimes get knocked over. I think the bowls would work better and they look just as nice."

"After the wedding, they are all yours. At least until the next wedding." Debbie gave her a quick smile on her way out. Gail groaned.

Late Thursday afternoon, Keith had taken the kids out fishing which meant that Susan was up at the house all alone. Janice and Debbie decided that this would be a good time to talk to Susan in private. They were about to shatter her world but it needed to be done. Debbie retrieved the letters from her drawer, Janice grabbed a bottle of wine, and they walked up to the house to visit Susan.

"Well, now, this is a nice surprise when your sisters can just pop in. I think I am going to like living here," Susan said.

"I hope so, because we sure like having you living close enough that we can pop in when we get a break," Debbie commented.

"Who's watching the office?" Susan wanted to know.

"One of the waitresses," Janice answered. "You got any glasses?"

Once they were all settled around the kitchen table and had the pleasantries out of the way Debbie pulled out the letters, still tied with the red ribbon. She thought to herself, *here goes nothing.*

"Susan, I found these letters among Mom's things. There is information in them that you will want to know. But before you read them, Janice and I both want you to know that we love you unconditionally and love that you are our sister."

"What the hell are you talking about?" Susan asked. "You're starting to scare me."

"Just read these letters and you will understand." Janice handed her the letters.

Debbie and Janice sat quietly while Susan read the letters. When she was finished, she just sat there in a silent stupor. Debbie got up and went around the table to put her arm around Susan.

"You okay?" Debbie asked her.

"I don't know. I guess so." Susan buried her face in her hands. "How long have you two known about this?"

"I found the letters when I cleaned out Mom's old room and didn't get around to reading them till about three weeks ago "Debbie explained. "I then showed them to Janice. We went and had a visit with Cousin Agnes, but she really wasn't much help."

"I looked up this Jefferson Penfold on the internet. Your father is living down by Ottawa." Janice offered.

"He's still living? Do you think I should look him up?" Susan wanted to know. "Why did mom not tell me about hem?"

"Sue, that is totally up to you. Give yourself time to process it all. Whatever you decide, we will support you one hundred percent," Debbie offered. "I don't know why mom didn't tell you. She kept the letters all these years so I can only conclude that she was planning to tell you eventually but just never got up the nerve or something like that"

Susan went to hand the letters back to Janice, but Janice told her to keep them.

"You may want to read them again, or show them to Keith." Janice told her.

"I guess you are right. Thanks for deciding to tell me." Susan said. "I am going to need some time to figure out what to do about this Mr. Penfold, my father."

"Take all the time you need." Janice patted Susan's arm. "We are both so glad that you are our sister and that will never change."

"Well thanks for that." Susan gave them a weak smile. "Half-sister at least"

"It doesn't matter half or whole you are still my sister and I still love you." Debbie tried to reassure her.

"I agree with Debbie" Janice took Susan's hand. "It is totally up to you if you want to find Mr. Penfold. Either way, we are still all in this together."

Chapter 46

By Friday, the banquet room was all set up and looking very pretty. Gail had used all three coloured napkins when she set the tables. Friday night, there were fourteen people from the Nicholson wedding that had come in for the rehearsal dinner. Since they planned to hold the wedding outside on the front lawn, they did the walk through before they came in for dinner.

Chef had chicken and ribs on as the dinner special, at Jake's request. The dining room overflowed for dinner, and some guests had to wait in the lounge just to get a table. Although it was busy, Gail and her wait staff had everything under control.

At the Nicholson table, Jake told her, "Thanks for doing the BBQ chicken and ribs. They were excellent. I must get Chef's recipe for the sauce."

"You can ask, but he is quite secretive about his sauces," Debbie had to tell him. "So, are you all excited about the big day tomorrow?"

"Yes, I just hope it is nice weather. Shelby so wants to get married outside," Sally told her. "My little girl is going to be an old married woman by this time tomorrow."

"I checked the weather. It is supposed to be a beautiful sunny day, but if not, we can still do the ceremony inside. It is always good to have a plan B. Enjoy your dinner."

When Debbie got back into the office, she asked Janice. "So, did you get the flowers all figured out for tomorrow?"

"Yes, sis. I am taking the wedding party's flowers over to the chalet before the wedding." Janice assured her. "I will need some help, since there will be a lot of flowers to transport."

Saturday morning Debbie was relieved to see the sun shining. This would be a beautiful day for a wedding. Janice was already working on the flowers. They were stunning. She had the wedding party's bouquets, corsages and boutonnieres all done in boxes in the cold room and was now working on the swags for the archway, which Henry was currently setting up out on the front lawn.

"I just saw the bouquets in the cold room, Jan, they are beautiful. And the cake turned out real nice too." Debbie told her sister. "You are the most talented person I know. Glad you're on my team."

"The wedding ceremony is scheduled for four o'clock, so could you come about three and we will take the flowers over to the chalets?" Janice asked her.

"Yes, of course." Debbie assured her. "I will leave you to it."

Just before lunch, Sally, the bride's mother, came into the office. "We have a problem." She said. "The hairdresser we had hired just called and cancelled. What are we going to do now?"

"Let's not panic," Debbie told her. "I know a lady that might be able to help. Leave it with me for a minute. Why don't you go have a coffee and let me make some phone calls?"

Debbie called Marge. She was the hairdresser who had come for her girls' weekend. Marge agreed to come and help out. She could be there for two o'clock. They agreed on her fee and Debbie told her to come ahead. She found Sally in the dining room talking to Gail.

"Good news. I have a hairdresser who will be here at two o'clock. She's not cheap but she is good, and she is available. Is that okay?" Debbie asked her.

"Yes, thank you so much. Just add it to the bill," Sally told her.

"How is everything else going?" Debbie asked.

"Good so far. Shelby is getting excited. Right now she is getting her makeup done, I hope. We had quite a time getting the bridesmaids convinced to get out of the hot tub. I think Jake is going to want a hot tub at the cottage after this."

"Yes, those tubs are hard to leave. Which chalet is Shelby in?"

"The girls are in the blue jay chalet and the guys are in the Cardinal chalet." Sally said.

"All right, then we will be over about three o'clock to deliver the flowers. Don't worry, it is going to be a beautiful wedding. Everything is going to be fine, you'll see." Debbie reassured her.

When Debbie and Janice carried the flowers over, Marge was just finishing braiding the bride's hair. Janice had saved a few rose buds in case Shelby wanted them for her hair. She did and Marge quickly pinned them in. She was a beautiful bride.

"The flowers are beautiful. Thank you so much. I see the archway is decorated and have noticed other guests from the resort have been over there checking it out and taking pictures," Sally commented.

"Thank you. It was my pleasure," Janice told her. "We better go get the boutonnieres delivered to the guys."

"The next time I see you, you will be the new Mrs. Wannamaker. Shelby, I hope you enjoy your special day and I wish you and John all the best." Debbie told Shelby.

"Thanks Debbie. I am sure I will."

From there Debbie and Janice went to the Cardinal chalet where the guys were getting ready.

John opened the door. "Come on in. Do either one of you know how to tie a tie?" he asked them.

"Sure, let me help you," Debbie offered. "There, perfect. If you put your jacket on, Janice will attach your boutonniere." Kirk, Shelby's brother, the best man also needed help with his tie. Jake declined the offer of help. He was an old pro at ties, he assured her. Once they had all the men's flowers attached Debbie said, "You gentlemen all look nice, all spit and polished, ready for a wedding. John, I just saw Shelby. You have a very beautiful bride. Next time I see you, you'll be a married man. All the best to both of you."

On the way back to the lodge Debbie noticed more guests taking pictures in front of the decorated archway.

"I wonder if we should have put up some barriers around the area and the archway." Janice asked.

"I imagine it will be fine once the wedding guests start arriving. I am just not sure about not having any chairs. I know Jake said the ceremony would be short and sweet, so he didn't think chairs were needed, but I wonder about the guests wandering around until the ceremony starts." Debbie said. "I am concerned about the grandparents. I think I will ask Henry to put a dozen chairs on the edge in case they are needed. I also think we should be out here at show time to make sure the resort guests are not going to interfere with the wedding."

By four o'clock everyone was in place. Jake went into the chalet to accompany his daughter. The bridesmaids started proceeding down the steps and up through the middle of the crowd towards the archway. It was perfect. The ceremony only took about ten minutes, followed immediately by pictures. The guests wandered into the banquet room, and by six o'clock, everyone was seated and ready for dinner.

The wedding had gone off without much fuss. That was exactly how Debbie liked it. She would send a thank you note with the cheque to Marge, the hairdresser who had saved the day. It was those little details that could make or break the success of an event and Debbie did everything she could to make sure all the little details were taken care of.

Chapter 47

It was hard to believe they were already at the end of June. The summers were so busy that time just seemed to fly by. This upcoming weekend, Valerie would be here for a week's holidays with her new boyfriend, Brian. Debbie was looking forward to meeting him. Now that Susan and Janice were getting the hang of things, Debbie might actually get to spend some time with her best friend.

Susan had started working with John Grant at the Grant real estate agency in Clifford. She worked on straight commission and worked mostly from home, or in this case, the office in the lodge, but she had to commit to spending one day a week in the Clifford office. She chose Wednesdays. Janice preferred to be out helping in the dining room, or in the kitchen helping Chef.

By now the staff were getting used to seeing them around and were starting to ask Janice when they needed help. It was actually working out better than Debbie expected it would. Debbie still was anticipating the other shoe to drop, but for now it was working. Debbie had even gotten around to getting out the newspaper clippings that she had found in Mom's closet.

"Look what I found when I was cleaning out Mom's room," she told Janice and Susan one morning when they were both sitting at the back kitchen table. "These are newspaper clippings from twenty-five years ago when our family first bought the resort."

"Oh my goodness, would you look at that. Look how young we all were. Janice, you had the goofiest haircut in this picture." Susan commented.

"I was thinking maybe we could get these framed and hang them in the dining room. What do you guys think?" Debbie asked them.

"I like it, good idea. Let me take care of that," Susan volunteered. "These are wrinkled and folded. I bet I can get the original copies from the newspaper archives. Let me see what I can do."

"Okay, it is all yours, sis." Debbie told her. "I will leave it in your capable hands."

"Debbie, I have been meaning to tell you that this Saturday I am having an open house at a big cottage I am selling. I will need the day off on Saturday, but will be back for the dinner rush." Susan told her.

"That's fine. Just make a note on the calendar, would you please?" Debbie told her. "Don't forget, Val is coming for the week. She should be here sometime Friday afternoon and I am hoping to be able to spend some time with her and her new boyfriend."

Just then Brad came into the kitchen from the dining room. He said, "so this is where all the pretty ladies are hiding. Afternoon, ladies."

"Hey Brad, nice to see you," Janice told him. "What are you up to these days?"

"Staying busy. I just got a contract to build a cottage across the lake and would like to talk about renting some dock space for a couple months."

"I will have to go take a look at the book. It is down at the boat house. Do you want to walk down with me?" Debbie asked him.

"Lead the way," Brad told her.

On the walk down to the boat house Brad asked her, "I have some spare time this afternoon, would you be available to go run the property lines today? It is a nice day, what do you say, want to have a little fun?"

"Yes, I think I could do that. Let's get your docking needs looked at and I will see if Henry can spare me a couple of four wheelers." She paged Henry. They reserved a slip on the cottager's dock for

Brad. He had a barge-type boat that would be tied there for moving material across the lake.

On the way back to the lodge Debbie asked Brad, "I would like you to give me a quote on building an arch for the front lawn. We are doing more and more weddings and in the nice weather, brides like to get married outside. I am thinking a permanent archway, or a gazebo type thing. It should be set with the trees as the background and we will plant rose bushes around it."

"Let me think about it, and I will get back to you with some options," Brad told her.

"There's Henry. Let's go see if he has any four wheelers we can use," Debbie said.

"I have mine in the back of my truck, so you only need one for you unless you want to ride behind me" Brad suggested. Don't forget to grab the maps"

Debbie headed back into the lodge and Brad headed to the parking lot where his truck was parked. He pulled the ramps out and then backed the four wheeler off the truck.

He drove up to where Debbie was just getting on to her machine.

"Here, wear this helmet. It has headphones in it, so we can talk to each other as we ride." Brad offered. "We will go in from the campground and see how far we can get."

They spent the whole afternoon driving around in the bush. There were lots of little hills and a few low spots. In some places, the trees were too thick to get through, but they had fun. Debbie could imagine trails all through the area. She was thinking there would be a four-wheeler, Ski-Doo trail, as well as smaller hiking trails. There was a spot she particularly liked at the top of a small hill where they could make a clearing and have a sitting area. From the elevated vantage point, the end of the lake was visible. It would be about a mile from the resort and would make a nice hike. People could stop there for a picnic if they wanted to. The possibilities were endless.

At the far end of the property, they came out of the bush on farmer John's property. He was out in his field, so they had stopped and had a chat with him. He told them where his trails were for the horses and gave them permission to take a look at his trails. They proceeded back through the bush and at one point they had crossed the road. They ended up at the Ski-Doo club's clubhouse.

"Do you want to go in and see the clubhouse, since we are here?" Brad asked her.

"If it has a washroom, yes, I would love to see your clubhouse," Debbie said.

"There is pop and water in the little fridge, would you like something to drink?" Brad asked.

"A water would be nice. Thank you." Debbie walked around the clubhouse looking at all the pictures on the walls. There was quite a few, including the picture she had given them this past winter of the poker run.

Brad came up behind her. "That was so thoughtful of you to give us that picture."

"No problem. Do you think you will do the poker run from the lodge again this winter?" she asked.

"Yes definitely. Everyone was so pleased with the location."

Debbie turned away from the picture and right into his arms. Before she could have time to react, Brad kissed her. Every sense in her body went into overdrive. Before she knew it, she was returning his kiss. When she finally came to her senses, she stepped back and pushed him away.

"What the hell was that?" Debbie asked him. "Brad, what are you doing?"

"Kissing you breathless."

"That can never happen again." Debbie backed away from him.

"I didn't mean for that to happen. It just did. I should be sorry, but I am not sorry. Debbie, you know how I feel about you."

"No, I don't know, and I don't want to know. Last time I checked, you are still married."

"But you kissed me back. I know you feel the same way as I do."

"Yes, I did kiss you back, I was swept up in the moment, but unlike you, I am sorry. And it can never happen again. Are we clear on that?" A tear escaped and ran down her cheek.

Brad reached out to brush away her tear, but she pulled away from him.

"Please don't. Just leave me alone."

"I am sorry I hurt you. That is the last thing I want to do," he told her.

"Let's just go. I need to be getting back to the lodge." She grabbed her helmet and headed for the door.

Brad followed her out. "Deb, please don't be angry with me. I didn't mean for that to happen. I promise I will keep my distance. Please tell me we are still friends?"

"Yes, Brad we are okay, we have been friends forever and that will not change, but this can never happen again."

They maintained radio silence on the short trip back to the lodge. When they got home, Debbie handed him his helmet.

"Thanks for the tour of the bush. I learned a lot today. I really appreciated your help with that. The maps make more sense now at least."

"If you have any more questions, don't hesitate to call me, all right."

Debbie went inside. Everything seemed to be going fine in the lodge, so she went up to her room for a cold shower and some solitude. What was he thinking? How could he have thought that she would be okay with kissing him? He was still a married man. Happily or not, he was still married. And she liked his wife, Tina. How dare he assume that she would be okay with him kissing her? He probably though she would be a convenient fling he could have on the side. Perhaps he thought they could have secret rendezvous up at his clubhouse. Is that why he had taken her there? Was that his plan all along? No, she didn't think so, he seemed as surprised as she was with the kiss, and oh, what a kiss it was. She had enjoyed the kiss, there was no denying that. Hell, she had even kissed him back. But she did not have the right to be kissing him. He was still a married man, and she would not be responsible for breaking up a marriage. Not Brad's, or anyone else's. How dare he do that to her. She was a great big emotional mess.

And then her pager went off. Duty calls.

Chapter 48

On Friday afternoon, Val came bouncing in through the office door. Susan was in the office.

"Hi Sue, just wanting to get checked in and pick up my key. Is Deb around?" Val asked.

"I believe she is in the kitchen having a meeting with a couple guys about the upcoming bass fishing derby." Susan told her.

"Alright, I won't disturb her, but could you tell her we are here?" Val signed the register and took her key. "Tell her to slip down for a drink when she has time, if you don't mind."

It was an hour later when Susan got around to telling her. Debbie went down to cabin three to see her best friend.

"Knock, knock, anybody home?" Debbie asked.

"Come on in here, girlfriend of mine." Val met her at the door with open arms. "It is so good to see you. Deb, this is my boyfriend Brian. Brian, this is Debbie, my best friend in the whole world." She made the introductions.

"Pleased to meet you," Brian said. "I have heard a lot about you."

"All good, I bet," Debbie said. "If not, don't believe anything she told you."

"No, it was all good. Sounds like you two have been getting in trouble together for a very long time," he said.

"Only the past thirty years or so," Valerie offered.

"Oh gosh, have I really known you that long?" Debbie asked. "Seems like forever. I think we met in grade one."

"A few moons ago, any way you want to count it. Want a beer?" Val asked her.

"Sure, I have time for a quick beer," Debbie told her friend.

"I figured now that Janice and Susan were here, you would get a bit more free time. How is that all working out?" Val asked her.

"Good, actually. We haven't even had an argument yet. Probably because we are so busy, we just haven't had the time."

"Well that will happen soon enough." Val assured her.

"You are probably right."

Debbie, Valerie, and Brian sat and chatted over the cold beer and then Debbie excused herself to get back up to the lodge. She had promised to join them for dinner in the dining room that evening.

Saturday morning was busy as usual, but Debbie had recruited Janice to help her decorate the float for the afternoon parade in Clifford. This year's parade theme was fun on the water. Debbie had planned on putting banners down both sides of the trailer, with Cedar Grove Resort written down each one. On the trailer they had a canoe and a rowboat which would be full of kids for the parade. Gail's husband Peter had volunteered to drive the van and her three kids, and a few neighbourhood kids volunteered to be in the boats. They would be wearing bathing suits and life jackets.

Janice suggested they put blue tarps on before the boats so that is would look like they were in the water. Henry suggested putting sand on top, so the canoe and rowboat could be on the shore, getting ready to go into the water. Debbie let them have a free hand. She felt that it really didn't matter much about the float, as long as they were in the local parade. By noon they had the float ready for when Peter and the six kids arrived. Debbie gave them bags of candy to pass out to the spectators and sent them on their way.

Valerie and Brian were both avid golfers and spent most of their time over at the golf course. Debbie had never gotten into the sport. Golf required patience, and Debbie had never been a patient person. The game was just too slow for her liking. She did see how people liked it, but it just wasn't for her. Debbie tried to spend some time with the couple in the evenings and before she knew it, their holiday was just about over.

On Friday afternoon, Debbie had taken the afternoon off, and Valerie joined her for a shopping trip into Clifford. They went to a new café in town for lunch.

"Debbie," said Val, "I have known you all your life and I can't help but feel that there is something weighing on your mind. Do you want to talk about it?"

"Everything is fine," Debbie assured her best friend. "Why do you think anything is wrong?"

"Well, I can't put my finger on it, but you seem quieter than usual and not as content as you usually are. What is it that is weighing so heavily on your mind? I know you girl, so spill."

"Brad kissed me," Debbie blurted out.

"When did that happen? I knew it would happen eventually, you two have been circling around each other for years," Val said.

"Last week. We had spent the afternoon four-wheeling. I am thinking about putting some trails through the bush and he was helping me find the boundary lines. He wanted to show me the club house they use for his Ski-Doo club. I was looking at some pictures around the clubhouse, and he just kissed me. And what is worse, I enjoyed it. Hell, I even kissed him back."

"That is wonderful," Val said. "I always knew he was sweet on you."

"It is not wonderful, Val, more like horrible. He is a married man and you know I won't go there," Debbie told her friend. "Don't say anything to anyone about this. I am a little embarrassed about it all."

"Why? You are attracted to him. God knows you have always carried a torch for him. Why should you be embarrassed?"

"Because he is married. Isn't that reason enough?" Debbie gave her a frowned look.

"You know, that would not stop most people."

"Well I am not most people, and it goes against all my principals" Debbie told her. "My momma raised me better than that. I can't be the reason he ends his marriage. Besides, I like Tina, his wife."

"Well his marriage can't be that strong if he goes around kissing other women," she said.

"His marriage is none of my business. I wish the kiss had never happened" Debbie shrugged. ."It is going to be weird between us now. I have to make sure we are never alone with each other again. I don't know how strong my resolve is."

"Have you not seen him since the kiss happened?" Val asked.

"No, but I just know it is going to be weird."

"I think you are being too hard on yourself. It was inevitable that something like this was bound to happen between the two of you. Even Susan commented on it on our girls' weekend." Val told her. "It is obvious to everyone but you apparently."

"What am I supposed to do now? How do I carry on a friendship now that I have been reminded of what it feels like to be held in his arms and kissed senseless?"

"Can you just treat him like any other business associate? Unless you change your mind and decide to have a sultry affair."

"Not likely. I just can't do that to Tina. I would feel so cheap and dirty. I am already feeling guilty about kissing her husband."

"Well if you're resigned to secretly loving him from afar, then you will just have to give him the cold shoulder," Val told her.

"Who said anything about loving him?"

"You don't need to say it. I know you have loved him since high school. Remember I have known you forever and I remember how heartbroken you were when he broke up with you all those years ago."

"I can't love him. That is just not in the cards for us. This is just an impossible situation. Now let's change the subject, please."

"Well if it was me, I would go for it, consequences be dammed."

"I know you would, but I just can't. Now I need to figure out how to live with it," Debbie told her friend. "What about you and Brian? He seems nice. Are you happy?"

"We get along well enough but I don't love him. We are compatible, but he is ready for marriage and I don't see me spending the rest of my life with him."

"So, why are you with him, then?"

"We have a lot of the same interests and enjoy each other's company well enough, but he just doesn't light my fire, if you know what I mean. He is comfortable and stable, but I don't think I can settle for that. I need some excitement to go with stable, and I just can't seem to get there with Brian."

"That's a shame. He seems like such a nice man. I think he would give you the moon."

"Yes, I am sure he would, but what he can't give me is passion. We are quite a pair, aren't we? I have a guy that is perfect in most every way but just doesn't excite me enough, and you won't let yourself have the guy that would excite you beyond your wildest dreams."

"Love sure is complicated. It makes me tired just thinking about it."

"That right there is your problem, my friend. You spend too much time thinking about it instead of just doing it."

"Oh, shut up and eat your damn lunch." Debbie told her friend.

They had a band in the bar on Saturday night, and Valerie and Brian invited Debbie to join them. They had a few drinks and a few laughs. When Brad and Tina came in, they joined Valerie's table. Debbie was very uncomfortable. She felt guilty for feeling jealous. She had no right to be feeling any of these feelings. She just wasn't ready to sit there and watch Brad and Tina dancing and having fun. Debbie was polite and said hello, and shortly thereafter made an excuse and left.

On Sunday, Valerie stopped into the office to say her goodbyes. Debbie walked her to her car.

As they were sharing a goodbye hug, Val quietly told her, "Brad and I danced last night, and he asked me if you were okay."

"I'm almost afraid to ask. What did you tell him?" Debbie asked her.

"I told him to just give you some time and space to figure it out. He said that he could do that. I'm gonna miss you, girl. Now that you have all this extra help around here, why don't you come to the city for a weekend? I am sure we could find some trouble to get into." Val hugged her friend goodbye.

Chapter 49

The next week went by in a blur. Debbie was glad they were so busy, but with all the extra help around, she had too much free time on her hands. Susan was looking after the office and Janice was managing the dining room and kitchen quite well. Debbie found herself at loose ends. Everything at the resort was running smoothly, busy as usual with no major problems.

Because she had spare time on her hands, she was able to focus on some issues that usually would not get her attention until the fall. It felt good to be ahead of the game for once. Previously she would not be able to even think about extra things until past the September long weekend. But here she was, in the middle of July, with spare time to deal with extra things.

Debbie had spent some time and put the girls' weekend package together. She even designed the brochure for it. She included pictures of the chalet interior, pictures of people enjoying the hot tub, and some spa pictures. She showed it to Janice and Susan, and they both liked it. Susan had suggested that they didn't put the prices on it, but Janice and Debbie thought they should, so the prices were included in smaller print.

When the brochure was designed to their satisfaction, Debbie took it to the new print shop in Clifford. They did a really good job, and Debbie would use them again in the future. She even had Susan add the brochure to their website. It was only on the site about two weeks when they got their first booking for a girls' weekend in September.

Debbie also had time to look into the fire pit situation. Because there was always a fire ban on in the summer, no one was allowed to have a wood fire. She contacted the propane supplier and they were going to install two propane fire pits, one in the campground and the other in the trailer park. The propane lines would be buried and run to a big tank off to the side which would be fenced in for security and hidden from sight. The three sisters had discussed and agreed to go ahead with the installation for next spring. They did not want to be tearing anything up while there were guests there enjoying their holidays, but next spring before they arrived, the work would all be done. Next summer the campers were going to have a fire pit again.

Debbie even had time to work on the trail system she wanted to design. She had it mapped out where they would put the combined four-wheeler and Ski-Doo trails, as well as interior hiking trails. She even allowed for a part of the hiking trail to go directly onto the golf course so that if guests wanted to walk, they could walk through the woods instead of on the roadway. At some point, they may even purchase some golf carts for their guests to use.

She had made a few calls to find out about getting the trees cut and removed. Also, the cost of putting gravel down on the trail bed and when it was all totaled up, the three sisters decided to wait one more year before they started that project. But this winter, they could start removing trees as they needed for firewood for the lodge.

Debbie met with Bob Bowman of Bowman Excavating and he agreed to go ahead and mark the trees that would be cut for the trails. Bob told her when he had the trees marked, she could remove any of them she wanted for firewood. The more she cut down, the cheaper it would be in the end.

It took him almost two weeks to get the trails all marked out. Now that the tree marking was done, Debbie rode the four-wheeler up to see Sanford Bradley. Sanford and Mary were sitting out in their sunroom, enjoying the breeze off the Muskogie Lake.

"Afternoon, you two. Look at you, enjoying this beautiful day," Debbie greeted them.

"How are you, girl? Come on in here and have an iced tea," Sanford said.

"Thank you. It is a perfect day for some iced tea."

"I imagine you are here to talk about honey. Are you wanting the same as last year?"

"Yes, that would be fine. Here before I forget I brought you a little treat." Debbie handed him a bag of maple fudge. "We are selling it now in our gift shops."

"Oh child, bless your heart" Sanford immediately opened the bag and sampled a piece. "You are just the sweetest girl. Thank you so much."

"Sanford Bradley, I hope you intend to share with your loving wife," Mary said as she returned with Debbie's iced tea.

"I guess, if I have to," he said as he handed the bag to her.

"There is also another reason I stopped in. I wanted to let you know that we have the bush marked for the trails we are going to put in."

"You are really going to do that then. Well good for you. I imagine it will cost a small fortune, but once you get over the initial investment, you can use the trails for years to come." Sanford said.

"Yes, that is the plan. We are not sure of our start date yet. We have to be careful not to take on too much expense all at one time."

"I can understand that. I put in my own trails through my sugar bush, but I just worked away at it over the years. It is still a work in progress," he told her.

"You had expressed an interest in cutting some trees for your firewood. We only use firewood in the lodge for the fireplace in the lounge. I am actually thinking about converting it to propane. The wood is messy and quite frankly a nuisance. Henry keeps us supplied from dead or fallen trees around the property, but I am sure he would not miss that task if he didn't have to do it anymore."

"Yes, it is a lot of work. I split and pile wood for myself. I have even sold some, but it is time-consuming and hard, messy work," Sanford assured her.

"Would you be interested in cutting wood from my bush?"

"Yes, I would. If the price is right, that is," he told her.

"Well the bush is all marked. All the trees that are going to be removed are marked with a big red X, and you can take as many as you like keeping in mind that I don't want to hear any chain saws in the campground until past the September long weekend. As long as you can agree to that, you can take as many marked trees as you like between now and when we start working on the trails."

"You have what, nine acres down there? I am sure I could cut far enough away that the campers won't be disturbed. What is it going to cost me?"

"I don't know, what would you think a fair price would be?" Debbie asked him. When he didn't offer an answer, she asked, "When you sell a cord of wood, what do you charge?"

"Eighty dollars a bush cord," he told her.

"Tell you what, whatever wood you sell I get ten dollars of your hundred," Debbie told him.

Sanford just smiled at her. He knew that she knew that he really sold it for a hundred. "You drive a hard bargain, missy. That is ten percent of my profit."

"Yes, but you are getting the raw material for free, so you are still making ninety bucks a cord," Debbie pointed out. "And just so you know, I will be making the same offer to farmer John and a few others. He can start cutting out at his end of my property if he wants to."

"And how long does this offer stand?" he asked her.

"Until we start brushing. We still haven't decided if it will be next spring or the spring of the following year."

"All right then. I accept your offer. I will cut some trees out. I will start out past the first corner on the road there. That will be far enough away that it shouldn't bother any campers and in September, when camping season is over then I can cut closer to home."

Debbie shook his hand, thanked Mary for the tea and headed off to see farmer John, who also agreed to her terms. She didn't expect any great return, but every tree they cut off her property, was one less tree she would have to pay to have removed when the project started full swing. She was doing them a favor and if she got a few bucks back on top of the money she would be saving that would just be a bonus..

Chapter 50

On Tuesday morning, Janice and Debbie were sitting at the back kitchen table, talking, when Brad came in through the back door. After the pleasantries were over, he told them he had some drawings for archways and gazebos for them to look at. He explained to them the different options.

"A permanent archway started about five hundred dollars and I could build it in my shop. Basically, all I would have to do here is dig four anchor holes to cement it into the ground. If you like, I could build matching raised flowerbeds for either side for another hundred apiece," Brad told them. "Or, if you want to go all out, a ten-sided wooden gazebo with a shingled room would set you back about eight grand. A smaller eight-sided gazebo would be about six grand.

"Wow, that is a lot to think about," Janice told him. "How long would it take to build a gazebo?"

"Probably a week. I would most likely do all the precutting in my shop. That would take a couple days, I would have to come here to pour the cement anchors and then another two days here to put it together," he told her.

"Thanks Brad, we will discuss this with Susan and get back to you shortly." Debbie told him as she picked up the drawings and headed into the office.

After the three sisters discussed it, they decided on a small gazebo that they would have installed next spring. They all agreed that they would need a hydro cable buried from the lodge out to the gazebo, so they could hang lights in it or plug in an amplifier if they needed a microphone for any events. In the meantime, if they had any more outdoor weddings this summer, they would use the archway they used from the banquet room like they did before. Debbie asked Susan if she would call Brad and let him know their decision.

"Why don't you call him yourself?" Susan asked her.

"Because I am going down to the boat house to talk to Josh about the fish derby and you're sitting right there in front of the phone." Debbie told her as she walked out of the office. She wasn't necessarily avoiding Brad, but she certainly wasn't going out of her was to be in contact with him either. She was keeping a cool distance trying to protect what shred of dignity she still had left.

She walked down to the boathouse and talked with Josh. He was in the gift shop putting together his next order for some more supplies. They talked about the derby and he assured her that everything was all set. The organizer of the derby, had already stopped in and talked with him about how they would get the boats unloaded and launched, the vehicles parked, how they would weigh the fish caught and all the other details. It was a catch and release derby, so the fish had to be weighed quickly and then released back into the lake. They had hosted this derby in past years and by now the staff all knew what to expect. Some of the fishermen would come into the lodge for a fish fry dinner after the derby.

Mr. Whitfield arrived Friday night with a couple of his buddies. They had booked the robin chalet. Debbie happened to be in the office with Susan when he arrived.

"Hello Mr. Whitfield. Nice to see you. How are the newlyweds doing? How did Sam and Jennifer enjoy their honeymoon?" Debbie asked him.

"Please, call me Jerry. Jen and Sam are both doing fine. They totally enjoyed the honeymoon. She told me to say hi. We were all so happy with the wedding. You sure do have a great staff here."

"Thank you. That is kind of you to say Jerry. I don't know if you have met my sister Susan?"

"Yes, we met at the wedding," he assured her.

"I believe he is reserved in the robin chalet with some of his buddies for the fishing derby tomorrow. "Debbie told her sister.

"I can help you with that." Susan told him. "I will just need you to sign the register book if you would."

"Well in case I don't see you beforehand, good luck fishing tomorrow. And if there is anything you need in the chalet, don't hesitate to ask." Debbie told him as he was leaving with his key in hand.

The fishing derby ended up with forty-four entries. When the day was over, all the fish were weighted and released, and the boats were all loaded back onto trailers, about thirty of the fishermen came in for dinner. One of Jerry Whitfield's buddies had won the top prize of five hundred dollars for the biggest bass. Jerry had won a new rod and reel for the most fish caught. When Debbie saw them in the dining room having dinner, she congratulated them all. They told her after dinner they were all going to soak in the hot tub.

"The beer was cold, the tub was hot, and both were ready just waiting for them," Jerry told her.

Susan and Janice had started joining Debbie, Chef and Gail for their morning meetings. They were discussing the upcoming month. August this year had five Saturdays, and they had events planned for every Saturday for the entire month. This Saturday was the Freemont anniversary party for sixty people. Then there was the Henry's Jack and Jill party, followed by a sixty-fifth birthday bash for Jake Nicholson, then the Henry Miller wedding reception for a hundred people, and finally, the last Saturday was the banquet for the baseball team the resort sponsored.

They discussed all of the events, but mostly focused on the upcoming anniversary party. The Freemont couple were celebrating fifty years married. They had booked the banquet room for the dance only. They did not want dinner, but did order a cold buffet for eleven pm. Chef had the menu all planned out, and Janice was planning on decorating a flat cake for them. They also ordered the portable bar. The band was arranged to start at eight p.m., and the only decorations they had agreed to were streamers and the anniversary banner. It was a very simple party. It would be a walk in the park for the staff.

The Henry party, a Jack and Jill, was going to be much the same. They would provide the cold buffet, but no cake, they would provide the portable bar, and no extra decorations. The guests were bringing their own decorations.

Jake Nicholson's sixty-fifth birthday party was going to be a surprise for him. His best friend Joel had arranged everything. They also wanted a cold buffet, the bar, lots of decorations, and a cake. Joel had reserved one chalet and one large cabin for the weekend. The chalet would be for the adults and the cabin would be for the teenagers.

The Henry Miller wedding was going to be a lot of work. They had booked all three chalets and were having the full-service dinner. Chef told them the menu that night would be a choice of the maple glazed chicken or baked salmon. Janice was commissioned to do the flowers as well as a three-tier wedding cake. They were having the wedding ceremony outside and requested a tent and chairs for one hundred guests. Debbie had quite a hard time but eventually found a company that would come and set up and then come back the next day and take down the tent. It was going to cost the Millers a small fortune. She called and got their approval for the tent before she confirmed with the tent company. Perhaps someday the resort might look into purchasing a tent for events like this, but it was not going to happen anytime soon.

The baseball banquet was for the home team and the families of the players. Chef did a buffet which included hamburgers, hot dogs and BBQ chicken. This was done in the banquet room, as the kids tended to be a bit noisy. In past years, they had waited till after the long weekend to hold the banquet, but the kids all wanted to go swimming. Now they held the banquet at the end of August and the team came and spent the afternoon at the beach before they came in for dinner. She had asked Keith to stick around the boat house to help Josh, since two of her staff, a boat boy and a maintenance guy, would need the day off as they were part of the ball team.

Yes, August was going to be a busy month. Excluding the rooms upstairs, which they didn't really use in the summer, they were going to be at one hundred percent occupancy for three weekends in a row.

The month just flew by. Debbie so enjoyed it when they were busy like this. The staff were always happy when they were busy, the busier they were the better the tips were as well.

Janice had even spent one whole day cleaning cabins with Carol. One of her girls had to take the day off unexpectedly for her grandfather's funeral so Carol was short-staffed. Janice volunteered to help out. By the end of the day, Janice admitted to Debbie that cleaning cabins all day long was harder than she expected it would be.

Chapter 51

The first weekend in September, there was a big golf tournament and the resort had six cabins booked with golfers. Chef did a buffet for dinner on the Saturday night. According to all reports, the tournament went well. Between the golfers and the spectators, Thomas had told her that there were over one hundred people at the golf course on Saturday. The bar and the dining room were extra busy, but Gail had everything under control. Sometimes Debbie just stood and watched her staff at work. They were all professional, and she couldn't ask for a better group of people to work with.

Two weeks later, they had another wedding in the banquet room. The family wanted the full service dinner. The ceremony was to be outside, so the pictures would have the fall foliage in the background. The rolling hill behind the lodge was gorgeous this time of year. With rolling hills full of maple trees, the scenery in the background would show beautifully in the wedding pictures. The actual day of the wedding, it was sunny but extremely windy. At the last minute, they moved the ceremony into the banquet room, even though the tables were already set for dinner. Janice had already decorated the archway outside, so Keith and Henry carried it in and set it in front of the head table. Once the ceremony and pictures were done, the arch was removed. The wedding party did some outdoor shots, some on the chalet steps and some at the water's edge with the maple tree reflecting in the water behind them.

The following Saturday, they hosted an eightieth birthday luncheon. Chef had provided a cold buffet of sandwiches and wraps, and Janice had decorated the cake to look like a gift all wrapped up.

One of the guests fell coming in the front entrance and they had to call the ambulance to come get the lady. It did put a damper on the festivities, but the party carried on after the ambulance left. They found out later that she had tripped on her dress and had broken her hip. Janice suggested they send flowers to her at home.

Not surprisingly the resort was starting to slow down now. Fall was in the air and the staff quickly dwindled down to just the department heads Janice suggested they should have a party or something for the staff. Debbie explained, "We have a big Christmas party and invite all the staff back for a banquet."

The dining room was still quite busy. Now with the trees changing colour, they were busy with tourists out for a drive to see the leaves. They even had chartered bus tours that stopped in for lunch. On the days that they knew they were having a bus in, Chef did a lunch buffet.

Fall was still Debbie's favourite time of year. With all the trees changing colour, it was like each day was a new picture. The bush was alive with colour, and the air was starting to cool off at night. They could finally shut the air conditioners off and open the windows to enjoy the breeze coming off the lake. It was perfect weather for sleeping. Bright warm and sunny in the daytime and cool at night.

Although the cabin occupancy dropped, the lodge was still busy enough. The banquet room was booked for several parties, as well as two upcoming company retreats. They would use the banquet room for seminars and team building exercises during the week and then party for the weekend. Because the banquet room was full of screens, projectors and binders full of their company's newest ideas, the guests ate their meals in the dining room.

It was towards the end of October that Debbie decided to take a few days and go visit Valerie in the city. They had tickets to go see the play, Far and Away, at the theatre and Debbie would enjoy the break. Now that Janice and Susan were "broken in," as she called it, she felt confident in being away for a few days.

When she arrived at Val's apartment, Val was still at work, so she let herself in and had a long nap. Val woke her up when she came in.

"I can't believe you are actually here," Val told her friend. "I am so glad to see you." Valerie did not have much food in the apartment as she ate out in restaurants mostly. They went out to a nice upscale restaurant and enjoyed a leisurely dinner, then went back to Val's place and shared a bottle of wine and got caught up.

"So, what happened with you and Brian?" Debbie asked her.

"I had to break it off with him. He was talking about the future. He wanted to get married and have kids and basically, I didn't. I had to let him go."

"Val, I am so sorry it didn't work out. I really liked Brian," Debbie told her.

"I did too, but more like a good friend. I would have been happy to stay friends with benefits, but he wanted more. He said he loved me, but honestly, I think he loved the idea of us settling down and having the two point five kids and the white picket fence scenario. I don't know that he loved me for me personally, but rather the idea of it all."

"Well it is too bad, but better to cut your losses and try to find your Mr. Right. I know he is out there somewhere waiting for you."

"And what about you, how are things going? Is Brad behaving himself?"

"Yes, I am keeping a cool distance whenever I can. I make sure we are not alone when I do have to see him. It is a bit weird between us, but we are managing it for now. I wish our kiss had never happened. It has just complicated things between us."

"If he was single, would you be dating him?"

"I don't know. Maybe, but he is still married, and I am not going to interfere with that. I know they are not happy, but I am not going to be the reason they call it quits."

"Well if you wait another ten years, he will be single again and then finally all your dreams can come true." Val was teasing her. "What about that golf course owner? He seems like a good catch."

"Thomas? No, I don't think so. We are just friends. Besides, I think he might be gay. I have never seen him with a woman ever. But he does come for dinner sometimes with his friend Sam."

"Well I am sure if you turned on the charm, you could convert him." Val suggested.

"Nah, I think I will take a hard pass on that."

Debbie and Valerie spent the rest of the weekend shopping and going to the theatre. When Debbie headed for home Sunday night she was totally relaxed and rested. On the way home she couldn't help but think of how much she valued her friend Val. They had remained best friends for over thirty years.

When Debbie arrived home, she instantly felt tension in the air. Janice and Susan seemed to be hardly speaking to each other. *Here we go,* Debbie thought, *I go away for a weekend and these two are going to start problems.* When she asked what the problems was, they both replied there was nothing wrong. Debbie didn't believe either one of them.

That night upstairs Debbie went over to Janice's room to try to find out what had happened.

"Susan told Keith, who told Tony, that my marriage blew up because Fred was tired of always fighting to get my affection or my attention."

"I am sure she didn't say it that harshly," Debbie offered. "And why would Keith tell that to Tony anyways?"

"Keith was trying to warn his newest drinking buddy Tony that I might not be such a good catch after all. I am too hard on my exes. And of course, you know it came directly from my own dear sister."

"Did you ask Susan about it?"

"No, I am too dammed upset to even speak to her."

"Well obviously she knows you're mad at her. Why wouldn't you just confront her about it? We all have to live and work together and there are going to be times when we don't all agree and even hurt each other's feelings, but we must get it out in the open and deal with it head on as quickly as possible," Debbie told her. "Get some sleep, and we will get this straightened out first think in the morning."

Debbie went to bed and lay there for a long time, aching from missing her mom so much. What would Mom do in this situation? Mom would probably tell them, "You're all full-grown intelligent women, so figure it out."

Debbie did not sign on to be the mediator between her sisters, and had no desire to be in the middle of their issuers, but here she was. She actually felt tears on her cheeks. She didn't realize how much it could hurt your heart when you lose someone close to you.

The next morning when Susan came in, Debbie asked to see her and Janice in the office.

"I understand that you two have a problem that we need to deal with." Debbie started.

"I think Janice is mad at me, but I have no idea why." Susan told her.

"Well, let me tell you why." Janice said. "You think my marriage ended because Fred was always fighting to get my attention. Well let me tell you dear sister, Fred is a cheater and now I know that he was going to cheat regardless of how much attention he got from me. And besides, it is none of your dam business anyways."

"Whoever told you I said that?" Susan wanted to know.

"Your loving husband Keith told that to Tony," Janice informed her. "Apparently, he was warning Tony that I might not be such a good girlfriend."

"Then perhaps you should be mad at Keith, not at me," Susan said.

"I am mad at both of you. I am sure Keith got that opinion from you," Janice told her.

"Well for whatever part I unwillingly had in this, I am sorry. And as for Keith, I don't believe he would have said that, definitely not in a mean way." Susan tried to reassure her sister.

"Well from here forward, you stay out of my love life and I will stay out of yours," Janice told her.

"Fine with me," Susan said. "Now can we get back to work?"

"I just want to inject that we all three need to work together. If any one of us is mad at the other, we need to address it straight away, and head on. It is hard when you live and work with the same people all the time and we all need to be very conscious of that fact," Debbie told them both. "Now, how about a group hug?"

Chapter 52

By November, they already had a foot of snow. Winter was always a bit depressing to Debbie. All the leaves were off the trees, and the days got shorter and shorter, making it darker all that much sooner. It was time to pull out the winter coats and boots. Bah, humbug.

Janice was all excited about decorating for Christmas. Debbie just wasn't ready for that quite yet, so she let Janice take the lead on the decorations. The Christmas parties would start about the middle of November, and they would be busy again right through the New Year.

Debbie was sitting at the bar talking with Ted on a Friday night when Brad and three of his buddies came in. Brad, a bit on the tipsy side, sauntered up to the bar. He told Ted and Debbie, "I am celebrating tonight. For my birthday my wife gave me the best present of all. She has left me for good. Gone back home to her mother. She quit her job, packed her crap and left. Happy birthday to me."

"Oh Brad, I am so sorry for your troubles," Debbie offered.

"Don't be sorry sweetheart, I'm sure not." Brad said. "Ted, we need a round of tequila shooters and some beers if you don't mind."

"Who's driving you guys home?" Ted asked.

"Billy is the designated driver tonight. He only gets one beer but the rest of us need some tequila," Brad told him.

"Well don't celebrate so hard that is hurts tomorrow. You boys take good care of him tonight," Debbie told them on her way into the dining room.

"Won't you stay and celebrate with us?" Brad asked her. "It is my birthday, after all."

"No Brad, it looks like you're doing a fine job of that all by yourself. Besides, your birthday isn't until Tuesday and I have work to get back to. You boys have a good night."

Once back at the office Debbie wrestled with her conscience. She felt sorry for Brad. His life was going down the crapper and there was nothing she could do to help him. She knew he wasn't happy, but hadn't known his problems were that serious. Perhaps Tuesday she would call him to see how he was doing. Just some friendly concern and a birthday greeting.

Chapter 53

The first Christmas party was held on the second Saturday in November. Most of the parties were all the same. Chef did a cold buffet including a flat cake which Janice decorated with the company's logo or their company name on it. Most of the companies around were small family-based businesses, and the biggest staff party they would do would be for eighty-five people.

Previously they had done the parties in the dining room, but as business was changing, so must the resort. The Christmas parties were now all being done in the banquet room. Janice had it decorated to the nines. There was a tree in the dining room, another in the banquet room, and another in the lounge. There were also three smaller trees decorated in the chalets.

The tree in the banquet room was red and gold, and the decorations were coordinated with the tree. There was red and gold everywhere. The lights and tulle were still draped from the ceiling but now there was red balls and gold bows hanging from it.

Debbie had convinced Keith that since he was there, and such a jolly sort of fellow that he could play Santa Claus and make an appearance at the upcoming parties. Some companies did gift exchanges and some did not. For the parties that did not, Santa handed out bags of candy. Each little bag included chocolates, assorted candy and a candy cane that Janice had put together. She had put them in a white silk bag tied with a red velvet ribbon. People seemed to enjoy the surprise.

Keith was a bit shy for the first party, but when he realized what a hit he was, he started to get into the role of Santa. Before long he was a pro at it. Debbie bought him a new Santa suit and Susan made him an attachable pillow for his belly to fill the suit out. A few people knew it was Keith playing Santa, but a lot of folks didn't know him and those that did, didn't recognize him. Santa usually made his appearance after the buffet was finished. One company already had their own Santa, but the other companies seemed to enjoy the surprise visit from the big man himself. It was those little extras that kept people coming back for more.

Brad Mumford always had two Christmas parties. One for his contracting company and another for the Ski-Doo club. For the company party, he invited all his workers and sub trade workers, as well as a few of his key clients. This year, he had thirty-five people at his first party and eighty-five people for the club party. At both parties, Santa was the star of the show.

The resort staff party was held on the Sunday before Christmas. They had a turkey dinner buffet with all the trimmings prepared by Chef George. With the owner's family, as well as staff and their families, they had thirty-six people for dinner. Each staff member received a personal Christmas card. The part-time and casual staff all received fifty dollar gift certificates for the main retail store in Clifford. The department heads, including Chef, Gail, Ted, Carol, Josh and even Henry each received a five hundred dollar cheque. When the sisters discussed the bonuses, they agreed that Susan's kids, Katie and Josh, should also get the gift cards, as they had both worked hard all summer. All the staff had worked hard all year and they all earned and deserved their bonus cheques. Everyone was pleased. Keith slipped away after a few minutes, and Santa made his last appearance of the season.

Christmas Day was the only day of the year that the resort was closed. This was the only day that Debbie didn't wake up at seven a.m. to her alarm. She slept in until eight thirty. When she did finally wake up, she woke to the smell of coffee. This was already a great day.

When Janice and Debbie went downstairs, still in their PJ's, Susan, Keith and the kids were just coming through the back door. The kids were old enough to know that Santa was a fairy tale, but Mom and Dad still bought them lots of presents and they were excited to get at it.

They all took their coffees and went to sit in front of the fire in the lounge. Everyone had a stocking hanging from the fireplace and the gifts were all under the tree. While the kids dug into their presents, Debbie got the bottle of Baileys Irish Cream from behind the bar and offered the grownups a shot for their coffees.

It was going on noon before they had all the presents opened and had gotten around to eating. Chef had left them croissants and muffins as well as a turkey and ham already cooked for them for later. All Debbie had to do was warm things up.

In the afternoon, they all got bundled up and went out in the cold to build a snowman on the front lawn. When Frosty was built to their satisfaction, Susan went up to the house to get her camera.

Henry arrived on his snow machine. He told the kids that that was the best snowman he had ever seen. Henry took some pictures of everyone with Frosty. Then they all went inside for hot chocolate and Bailey's. Henry had brought them a bottle of Bailey's as a gift.

The back door banged shut and Brad came into the lounge where they were all sitting. He had also brought them a bottle of Bailey's. Seems Debbie's friends knew her well. He joined them and they visited and enjoyed the afternoon together. When it came time for supper, Henry and Brad were both still there, so they stayed for dinner as well. No sense either one of them eating at home alone.

They spent the rest of the evening in the lounge in front of the fireplace. It was going on ten o'clock when Henry left, followed shortly after by Brad. Susan, Keith, and the kids all went up to the house, and Janice and Debbie sat chatting for another hour.

"Have you heard from Tony today? I was kind of expecting we would be seeing him," Debbie said to her sister.

"No, not today. He spent the day with his family," Janice told her. "We have talked on the phone, but today he had other obligations. I expect to see him tomorrow, though."

"You two seem to be quite an item. How is everything going with you two, anyways?"

"Good, I don't know what it is about him, but it is like he knows me, the real me, and I feel like I have known him all my life."

"You sure do make a cute couple. Janice, I am so happy that you have found someone to share your life with."

"If you had told me even a year ago that I would meet this tall, gorgeous hunk of a man that liked me back as much as I liked him, I would have told you that you must be dreaming. But just look at me now. I find myself counting the days and even the hours until I will see him again. I wasn't even this twitter pated with my ex-husband."

"Well, a lot can change in your life in a very short period of time. I can't help but remember last Christmas when Mom was so happy when we were all home to visit at the same time. She was so proud of us all. Christmas Day last year, it was just Mom and me. God, I sure miss that woman."

"Yes, me too. I was thinking about that earlier. I wonder what she would think now that her dream has finally come true, and we are all home for good."

Trying to go to sleep that night seemed to be a challenge. Debbie was thinking about how much she missed her mom. And what would Mom think about Brad spending Christmas with them this year? He had tried to get Debbie alone all day, but she kept making sure that didn't happen. What was a girl to do? She knew she loved him, and he was officially single, and she didn't want to wait too long and take a chance on losing him again. He was a handsome man and Debbie saw women flirting with him all the time. She wondered how long he should wait to start dating now that his marriage had just ended.

Chapter 54

Janice was getting all geared up for the big New Year's Eve party. She decided to take the Christmas trees down, but leave up some of the decorations for a few more weeks. She decorated the lounge with New Year's decorations. Debbie was never big on decorating and because Janice enjoyed it and was very good at it, Debbie let her have free rein.

The night of the party, Chef prepared a cold buffet that would be brought out at eleven. There was about fifty people at the party, and they were all in a very festive mood. The band was keeping the dance floor full and Janice and Tony were busy dancing the night away. Jake and Sally Nicholson were there, as were Sanford and Mary Bradley. Susan and Keith were at the party, but the kids were up at the house. Keith went up and checked on them periodically.

Just before eleven, Debbie excused herself and went to put out the buffet. She was almost finished when Janice came to help her. Once the buffet was ready, Debbie had the band leader make the announcement. She took a plate of food into the lounge to get people interested. It wasn't long before most of the guests made their way out to the buffet set up in the dining room. When people were finished eating, Debbie picked up empty plates and bussed some tables. About eleven thirty, she picked up empty beer bottles and glasses. Ted was so busy behind the bar he hardly noticed her helping. When she was finished with that, she covered the food but left the buffet out in case anyone still wanted anything. Then she disappeared into the office. Admittedly she was avoiding the whole

New Year's Eve kissing part of the evening. She had never enjoyed that whole concept of kissing a lot of strangers just because it was New Year's Eve. And yes, she was avoiding Brad specifically. She was a coward. She could admit that to herself.

She pulled out the reservation book and pretended to be busy with that. Brad came into the office from the kitchen. She didn't even hear him until he was right behind her. "I get the feeling you are trying to avoid me," he told her.

"You would be right, but I am not just avoiding you, I am avoiding everyone. I am not into kissing a bunch of strangers, thank you very much," Debbie told him.

"What about me, can't I at least get a New Year's kiss?" he asked while he pulled her to her feet and into his arms. "I might be strange, but I am certainly no stranger." With that he kissed her deeply and passionately.

Debbie felt herself melting like a pad of butter in a hot frying pan. She offered no resistance.

"Happy New Year, lovely lady," Brad told her.

"Yes, same to you," Debbie said as he kissed her again.

"Come back in and dance with me. I promise to behave myself," Brad assured her.

Debbie's cell phone was ringing. Debbie was glad for the interruption, as she needed to let her heartbeat settle down and she wasn't sure her legs would carry her at the moment. Brad's kisses had left her a little flustered.

"Don't be too long," Brad said on his way out.

Wow, that was mind blowing. Debbie had never let herself go with him before. It was a nice feeling. One she was not used to. She wondered what people would think if they were to start dating.

"Happy New Year, my friend." Debbie answered the phone.

"Same to you, darling. What are you doing?" Valarie asked her.

"I am sitting in the office. Brad has just come in and kissed me senseless," Debbie told her.

"Oh sweetie, that is wonderful. I am rooting for you two," Valerie told her.

"What about you, did you go to your friend's party?"

"Yep I am here, I kissed every man in the room. What fun?"

"Val, you are too much. I miss you."

"Miss you too, gotta go. Just wanted to say happy New Year."

After Valerie hung up, Debbie just sat there. If she had any previous doubts about her feelings for Brad, she was no longer going to deny them. She still loved him, just like she had all those years ago in high school. Perhaps now was their time. She was done being the nice girl. Now that he was single, she decided she was going to stop resisting him. She owed it to him and to herself to see where this could go. She was going to go for it, as Val would say, consequences be damned.

She wandered back to the lounge. Janice and Susan both gave her hugs and wished her a happy New Year. It was three a.m. before everyone was gone home and Debbie got to bed.

Chapter 55

Trying to go to sleep, Debbie couldn't help but think about Christmas and New Year's last year when it was just her and her mom. She wondered if she would ever stop missing her mom so much. She doubted it. It was hard to believe, but it was almost a year since Mom had passed away and it still felt like it was just yesterday.

Even though she had lost her mom, Deb couldn't help but feel good about the rest of the changes in her life in the past year. The future was not as scary now as it was a year ago. At least now the major immediate decisions had all been made, the changes were implemented, and things were moving in a forward direction. Her skepticism was slowly being replaced with hope and optimism.

Susan had told both her sisters that she had decided to try to contact Jefferson Penfold in the New Year. She now had his address and phone number and was planning on contacting him. She wanted to meet him in person and perhaps would be taking a short trip to Ottawa in the near future. Susan was spending most of her time in the office and seemed to be managing quite well. She had told Debbie that she would only have to sell about a dozen properties over the course of a year to make what she was making previously and felt quite confident that she could do that easily. She had already sold one cottage.

Keith was so much happier now that he had a good job that he enjoyed. It was working out perfectly. He would have the summers off, and he worked at the resort when he was not planning lessons, grading test papers or at school teaching.

Janice was proving to be very useful. She was full of wonderful new ideas and new energy which would only help the resort thrive. She had already worked a couple days with Ann, the lady that owned the flower shop in town, and planned to work with her off and on as needed. This would provide her with some extra income; "pin money," as Mom used to call it. And, now she had Tony. They had been inseparable since they started dating. He was at the resort most every weekend and never minded pitching in when he could be of help. He was fitting in quite nicely, and Debbie and Susan both really liked him. They were both happy that Janice found such a nice guy that she wasn't even looking for.

Debbie had to admit that even though she definitely had doubts, it did seem to be coming together. All of them working together to make Cedar Grove Resort the best they could make it and of course at the same time, make a nice tidy profit.

The next morning, Janice and Debbie were chatting over their morning coffee at the back kitchen table.

"You are a really good coffee buddy, but I still miss my morning coffee with Mom." Debbie told her sister. "I was thinking about her last night. I can hardly believe she's been gone almost a year already. To me it still feels like yesterday. We still need to scatter her ashes."

"Would it be too weird to do that on the thirtieth?" Janice asked. "That would be the one-year mark of when we lost her. I think that would be fitting, in a corny sort of way."

"Let's run it by Susan and see what she thinks. I think it would be the perfect day. She wants to be scattered in Muskogie Lake. She didn't specify if she wanted to be scattered on the water or on the ice. Same difference either way, right?" Debbie asked.

"Right, same end result," Janice agreed.

"We would not be able to do it privately in the summer. It is just too busy then. At least if we do it now, we could have some privacy. The more I think about it, the more I personally think it is a good idea."

When they broached the subject with Susan, she agreed it was a good idea. The ice was already starting to freeze and by the thirtieth of January it would be frozen a foot thick.

On January the thirtieth, one year to the day since they had lost their mom, they all got bundled up and Keith carried Mom's urn out onto the frozen lake in front of the lodge. They walked halfway across the lake so that the ashes would not likely be disturbed.

They all took turns saying a final goodbye to their mom and grandma. There were tears, but together they got through it. When they all had their turn at saying something for their mom and grandma, Keith sprinkled the ashes from the urn into a small pile on the ice. They stood around it in a circle holding hands and sang Amazing Grace. Being out in the open in the middle of frozen Muskogie Lake, their voices echoed back from the trees. When they were finished, they walked back to the lodge in total silence, each lost in their own thoughts.

"Oh look." Debbie broke the silence. "Over to the right on that little knoll, there is a deer standing there. Do you guys see it? That doe is watching us. I can't help but think Mom is smiling down on us right now."

About the Author

Deloris Packard grew up in Harcourt Ontario, a small town based at the bottom tip of Algonquin Provincial Park. She is the youngest of eight children raised on a small hobby farm.

As a teenager she spent her summers working in various lodges in and around the Haliburton Highlands. She graduated from Canadore College in North Bay with a diploma in Hotel, Resort and Restaurant Management.

Deloris worked many years in the hospitality industry in various positions. She has worked in Alberta, Manitoba and the North West Territories but spent most of her career working in Ontario. Along with her husband she was the owner operator of The Corner Café, a restaurant in the heart of cottage country, five miles from her family home. Having many siblings and varied experience in the hospitality industry, has given her the capability to tell this story from an inside perspective.

Bring your coffee and come meet the author on her website at delorispackard.com

CPSIA information can be obtained
at www.ICGtesting.com
Printed in the USA
BVHW030526090821
613136BV00009B/10

9 781525 597091